K. SEAN HARRIS

The STUD

Cover Design: Sanya Dockery
Typeset & Book layout: Sanya Dockery

Published by: Book Fetish

www.kseanharris.com

Printed in the U.S.A   ISBN: 978-976-95303-3-1

But *whoso committeth adultery with a woman lacketh understanding: he that doeth destroyeth his own soul.*

PROVERBS 6:32

Now *the works of the flesh are manifest, which are these: Adultery, fornication, uncleanness, lasciviousness.*

GALATIONS 5:19

Jerome James' handsome face was a study of concentration as he prepared to take the penalty kick. He had been brought down by the hard-tackling US central defender after making a brilliant run towards goal, skillfully leaving several defenders in his wake. The referee had pointed to the penalty spot without hesitation, despite vigorous protests from the US players that it was a clean tackle.

The sea of spectators, most of whom were decked out in the Jamaican team colours of black, green and gold; held their collective breath as the star forward looked at the goal and calmly picked his spot. Jamaica's hope of qualifying for the World Cup finals to be held in South Africa, hung delicately in the balance.

The noise from the crowd was deafening as they watched Jerome put the ball into the back of the net with a well-placed kick that sailed pass the outstretched arms of the opposing goalkeeper. The Reggae Boyz, as the team was affectionately known worldwide, were five minutes away from making history. No Caribbean country had ever qualified for the World Cup finals.

Everyone was on their feet as they loudly chanted 'Go Reggae Boyz!' anxiously awaiting the final whistle. The team withstood a furious rally from the Americans in the waning minutes and when the referee blew his whistle signaling the end of the match, the team hoisted a beaming Jerome atop their shoulders as balloons and confetti rained down from the stands. The wonderkid had just secured Jamaica's place in South Africa.

Later that evening, the team was feted at a dinner hosted by the Prime Minister. Man of the moment, Jerome, looking resplendent in a powder blue blazer and white shirt, sipped champagne and looked around at the women in the room as the Prime Minister toasted the team and coaching staff, and pontificated on how much of a huge achievement qualifying for the World Cup was for Jamaica. Tara Reid, the daughter of a high profile government minister, caught his eye. She was extremely pretty but was said to be very snobbish. She briefly held his gaze, her large brown eyes giving away nothing. Jerome made a mental note to meet her after dinner. He felt eyes on him and casually glanced to his right. A very attractive lady who seemed to be in her mid-forties was staring at him openly. She looks familiar, Jerome thought, wondering where he had seen the woman before. She averted her eyes as the man next to her started a conversation.

Jerome sighed. He wished the Prime Minister would hurry up. He had been a criminal lawyer before his foray into politics and he still loved the sound of his own voice. Jerome was feeling horny. As usual. He planned to hit up all the clubs in New Kingston later that night with his entourage but right now he wanted some sex – with somebody new. He was given VIP treatment most places he went as football was a big deal in Jamaica and he was the biggest star of them all. Now that Jamaica had qualified for the World Cup due to his game winning goal, he would be treated like a god. Two top-flight premier league clubs from England had taken note of his prodigious talents, and had recently extended contract offers. He was to fly to London next week to meet with both of them. Jerome smiled to himself; life was good and was about to get even better.

Dinner, which had consisted of smoked marlin filled with cream cheese, baked chicken with honey mustard sauce, pumpkin rice, chateau potatoes and buttered stringbeans, was over twenty minutes later and the guests milled about sipping cocktails and networking. There were a lot of politicians and prominent businessmen present at the dinner. Jerome saw Tara excuse herself from the two men with whom she had been conversing and their eyes met as she casually made her way out to the balcony.

"I'll soon be back," Jerome told Paul and Gary, his two good friends and fellow teammates. He was stopped by a soft touch to his arm as he neared the large poinsettia plant that was close to the entrance of the balcony. It was the older woman who had been watching him earlier.

"Congratulations on that magnificent play," she purred, extending a soft, manicured hand. "I'm Elizabeth Rhoden."

"Nice to meet you and thanks," Jerome replied. Now he knew why she had looked so familiar. The Rhoden family owned the Caribbean's largest sports apparel company and they were one of the sponsors of the national football team. He had glimpsed her beside Karl Rhoden in the VIP box at the game. She was obviously his wife. Jerome looked at the understated but obviously expensive wedding band on her finger.

"I wonder if you are that talented in other areas," she said softly, arching her elegant eyebrows.

Jerome grinned. She was talking his kind of language. Finding willing bed partners to satisfy his voracious sexual appetite had always been easy, but his success on the football field had opened new doors for him. The quality and pedigree of his conquests would now increase tenfold.

"Want to find out?" he asked boldly.

She slipped him a small business card. "Call me tomorrow evening. I don't want to keep you any longer." She looked at him knowingly, a smile playing at the corner of her thin, glossy lips. Jerome realized that she had noticed the byplay between him and Tara Reid. This woman didn't miss a beat, Jerome mused, as he slipped the card into his pocket and went out to the balcony.

Tara was standing at the far end of the balcony with her back to him. Jerome admired her derriere as he walked over to her. She possessed what he called an 'onion booty', the kind of ass that was so round and perfect it could bring tears of appreciation to one's eyes. The black dress she was wearing clung to her shapely body and the deep V-cut in the back displayed a generous amount of lightly freckled flesh. Her long jet-black hair cascaded in waves down her shoulders.

"What took you so long," she said to him as she turned around, her eyes filled with confidence and excitement. "Can't you tell when a woman wants to fuck you?"

Jerome was not surprised at her boldness. He knew how the Jamaican upper class operated. The women were spoiled and rich and didn't play by the rules. They did what they wanted to do when they wanted to do it.

He smiled. "Where...?"

"I maintain an apartment ten minutes from here," she announced airily.

They made their way down the stairs and Jerome made a call as he followed her to the parking lot.

"Paul," he said as his friend answered the phone. "Don't wait on me; I have to make a fast flex so we'll link up back later."

"Alright, cool," Paul replied and hung up. He turned to Gary.

"Jerome seems to have made another conquest," He told him. Gary nodded and gestured to one of the many waiters on hand to refill his glass.

"Pussy ah go kill him," he commented, adding, "So he's not going clubbing again tonight?"

"Yeah, man," Paul replied. "He's going to call us when he gets home later."

Tara deactivated the alarm on her spanking new red Mercedes coupe that her father had given her as a graduation gift, and started the car using the remote. They got in and she dropped the top. Jerome reclined in the plush leather seat as Tara quickly exited the parking lot. They didn't speak for the duration of the ride as Mary J. Blige's latest album pumped from the speakers. They got to the apartment complex in five minutes. Tara had a heavy foot. I guess when your father is the Minister of National Security you don't have to worry about a speeding ticket, Jerome thought as he exited the vehicle. The apartment complex housed six large units and was very exclusive. It was one of the most prominent addresses in Kingston. Tara's neighbours included a retired Ambassador, a wealthy businessman and a successful surgeon. Jerome followed as Tara opened the door to the apartment. He looked around impressed as Tara kicked off her stilettos and went over to a fully-stocked mini-bar. "What's your poison?"

"Hennessy. Straight," Jerome responded as he shrugged off his blazer and placed it on the tan leather couch.

The apartment was decorated in subdued earth tones and boasted very expensive contemporary furnishings. Several captivating works of art, including one by Jamaica's most celebrated artist, along with a seventy-two inch plasma flat screen TV, adorned the walls.

She handed him the drink and pulled his zipper as he took a sip. He liked her assertiveness. It turned him on. They looked steadily at each other as Tara slowly pulled out his semi-erect member. She gently ran her soft hand along its length. It rapidly grew in her grasp.

"Wow...you're huge," she commented, her big brown eyes now glazed with lust. "I trust you know how to use it."

Jerome took another sip of his drink and pulled her to him with his free hand.

"Yuh come here to talk or to fuck," he growled as he crushed his mouth against hers.

Tara wasn't used to men dealing with her so roughly but found it a welcome change.

Men were usually intimidated by her domineering personality.

This should be fun she thought, as Jerome continued to explore her mouth. She loved the way he kissed her: Demanding; probing;

deep; primal. She could only imagine how he would feel inside her. Her knees buckled.

He placed his drink on the cedar coffee table and guided them down to the plush beige carpet.

Tara moaned in his mouth as Jerome caressed her full breasts, gently pinching her prominent nipples. Jerome then rose and quickly retrieved a condom from his pocket. Tara anxiously discarded her black thong and pulled up her Diane Von Furstenberg dress around her waist.

"Give it to me Jerome," she implored as she impatiently ran her fingers through her hair.

Jerome grunted as he entered her with a firm thrust. Tara wrapped her legs around his back and pulled him inside her as deeply as possible. Unlike most women, she loved a really huge dick; the bigger the better and Jerome's definitely fit the bill.

"That's it...just like that," she moaned appreciatively as Jerome moved his waistline in a circular, up and down motion. He was impossibly deep.

Jerome could feel her getting wetter as he continued to hold her close and fuck her deeply. She bit him on his neck and pounded his back with her small fists as she felt her orgasm building up.

She got religious.

"Oh god....sweet jesus...oh lord..."

Then blasphemous.

"Oh... my... fucking... god...it feels so damn good...so fucking good..."

Jerome held her even tighter as he increased the speed of his movements. He could feel that she was on the verge. Her orifice clutched him and pulsed, and she shuddered uncontrollably as she climaxed, screaming out his name.

"Jesus...Jerome...I've never had an orgasm from penetration so quickly," she told him in breathless amazement. "That was just...incredible."

Jerome was still deeply buried inside her. He smiled smugly and rolled them over so that they were on their sides. He held a fistful of her hair and started giving her slow, long strokes.

Tara groaned and placed one hand on her upright ass cheek, spreading it to give him more leverage. The sounds of their coupling filled the otherwise quiet apartment as Jerome's testicles slapped noisily against her thighs.

Jerome gritted his teeth as he increased his tempo. His toes were curling. That meant he was going to have one of those volcano-like eruptions. He groaned loudly in anticipation.

So engrossed were they in their love-making that neither of them heard the front door open.

The figure in the doorway smiled as she watched the erotic show on the carpeted floor. She had come over to see Tara and maybe have a quick session – it had been a few weeks since they had had sex – but the athletically built guy that was presently making Tara groan like a wounded animal was an added bonus. She watched as the man quickly pulled out of Tara and ripped off the condom. He positioned himself over Tara's face and ejaculated as she moaned and stroked his scrotum, enjoying the feel of the warm fluid against her skin.

She started to clap.

Startled by the sound of applause, Jerome and Tara looked up at the doorway.

"Gina!" Tara said, grinning. "How long have you been standing there?"

"Long enough," she replied, taking a cigarette out of her Coach bag and lighting it. "Who's the stud?"

"Have you been under a rock? This is Jerome James, he's the star player for the Reggae Boyz," Tara responded as she got up unsteadily and snatched the cigarette from her good friend. She took a deep drag.

"Jerome, meet Gina, a very close friend of mine."

"Hi Gina," Jerome said, not in the least bothered by his now flaccid penis hanging from his fly. Hard or soft, it was a very impressive sight.

"Nice to meet you, Jerome," she purred, treating his dick to a lustful gaze.

"How long before you'll be able to get that thing back up?" she asked in a strained voice. Walking in on them getting it on had gotten her juices flowing.

Jerome looked at the slender, short haired, brown-skinned beauty. She wasn't a classic beauty like Tara, but she could definitely hold her own in the looks department. Wide, generous mouthfull pouty lips; high cheekbones and alluring eyes made her real easy to look at.

"Why don't you come over here and find out," he suggested, as he gestured for Tara to replenish his drink.

Tara made him another drink and went into the bathroom to wash her face.

Tara and Gina had been good friends for four years. Though they had known each other for over ten years as both of their families moved in the same circles, it wasn't until they were both enrolled at the same university abroad that they had become friends. The university was as renowned for its wild parties as it was for being expensive. One night after a raunchy frat party, Tara, tipsy and feeling adventurous, had kissed Gina in the hallway of the dormitory. The kiss had led to some passionate sex in Tara's room and they had slept with each other intermittently ever since.

Gina approached Jerome, taking off her halter top and freeing her luscious breasts in the process. Jerome whistled appreciatively at the sight of her breasts. They looked perfect. They were very round and firm, and slightly more than a handful. Her erect nipples were large and pointy. *Damn, I could hang a couple of CDs on those nipples*, Jerome mused, licking his lips as he felt his manhood stir. Gina smiled. She knew her breasts were incredible. She reached Jerome and took a sip from his glass. She then planted soft fluttery kisses all over his chest. Jerome groaned when he felt a hot mouth on his back. Tara had returned to the room. Gina removed her jeans and sank to her knees. Jerome reached over to run his hands through Tara's hair as she ran her velvety tongue along his shoulder blade. He shivered when Gina deep-throated his now turgid dick. He marveled at her skill. He couldn't even tell she was wearing braces and swallowing the entire length of his dick was no easy feat. He gently rocked in Gina's benevolent mouth as Tara caressed his chest and whispered nasty nothings in his ear. Jerome sighed contentedly as Gina got up and bent over the arm of the couch, spreading her legs and exposing her slick pinkness. *This is what my life is supposed to be like* he thought, as Tara rolled a condom onto his dick. *I'm a star.*

Three hours later, a few minutes after Gina had left, Jerome hopped in Tara's convertible and she gave him a lift to the apartment in New Kingston where he lived, courtesy of the Jamaica Football Association. Jerome was originally from Tawes Pen, a squalid, violence-prone community located in Spanish Town, but since his emergence as the island's top footballer, the Association housed him rent free in one of their properties.

"I had fun Jerome," Tara said to him when she pulled up in front of the apartment. "We need to hook up again real soon. A girl could get used to sex like this quite easily."

Jerome looked at her and smiled. He knew she was hooked. No one had ever rocked her world quite the way he had. She had practically wept after her fifth orgasm, causing him and Gina to roar with laughter. Definitely one worth holding on to for awhile, he thought. Having a girl like Tara Reid sprung on him could be beneficial in a number of ways.

"Sure," Jerome replied easily. "We can see each other again."

"Call me," she said and gave him a kiss. Jerome tweaked her braless right nipple through her baby-T and exited the car. He gave her a wave and made his way up to the apartment.

Tara sighed as she reversed and turned to exit the property. Jerome had satisfied her in a spine-tingling, mind-boggling way that she hadn't thought possible. He wasn't her usual cup of tea, being from the ghetto and all, but Jerome was definitely not your average ghetto youth. He was very handsome, clean cut, well-dressed and was also the best football player in the country. And last but not least, she thought with a contented sigh, he had an enormous dick that he knew how to use in the most delightful ways. The rumours that had prompted her to seduce him were true. Jerome was a real 'cocksman'. She wanted to have him around for as long as possible. He looked like he liked nice things. She decided to get him a couple of blazers when she went shopping the next day. Her favourite boutique had called her earlier in the day saying that they had just gotten new stock, and they also carried select items of men's clothes. Tara yawned as she sped along Trafalgar Road. She decided to go back home and get some rest instead of meeting the gang up by Village Café, where they usually hung out on a Saturday night. Jerome had completely worn her out.

CHAPTER 2

Jerome checked his appearance in the mirror and was pleased with the image staring back at him. He looked good. Damn good. He had on a black Italian blazer, a white designer V-neck T-shirt, trendy ripped jeans and black loafers. Jerome only wore designer threads, the bulk of which came from Dimples; the higgler turned clothing store-owner that he had been sleeping with for the past eight months. She packed a suitcase just for him whenever she went to shop for clothes abroad, and she went at least once a month. She knew he was wild but as long as he made time for her she didn't fuss. She loved the fact that she, a forty-five year old woman who wasn't much to look at, was fucking a handsome twenty-two year old stud who also happened to be one of the most popular sports figures in the country. Only the sprinter who had recently set a new world record for the 100 meters was more popular. After Tara had dropped him off, he had called the boys and told them to get ready and meet him in front of the Quad Nightclub at twelve-thirty. A horn beeped outside. His friend, Lenky, had arrived to pick him up. Jerome turned off the lights and exited the apartment.

"What's up Lenky," he enthused as he climbed into the front of the large SUV. Lenky was a big time drug dealer who had recently befriended Jerome. It began with Lenky sending Jerome and his friends bottles of champagne whenever he saw them at the club. A waiter would come over with an ice bucket containing a couple bottles of chilled Moet saying 'De big man say fi have a drink' gesturing over at the table where Lenky would always be seated surrounded by an entourage. Jerome would nod his thanks and on one such night, he walked over to verbally thank him and Lenky had given Jerome his number, telling him to call him whenever he needed anything. That had been a month ago, and they had been hanging out regularly ever since. Jerome didn't mind as whenever he went out with Lenky he never had to spend his own money and he got to profile in the hottest rides. Lenky owned several luxury vehicles.

"Mi deh yah 'Rome," Lenky replied in his trademark drawl. "Meet Peaches and Stacey."

Jerome turned around and greeted the two women in the rear of the truck.

"Sup ladies," he said, taking in the curvy, voluptuous bodies spilling provocatively out of the sexy clothing in which they were attired.

"Hi, Jerome," they answered in unison.

Jerome grinned and turned back around. It didn't even matter which was Peaches and which was Stacey. He could have either or both of them if he wanted.

They chatted about Jamaica's chances of advancing past the first round of the World Cup finals and how good it would be for Jerome to showcase his tremendous talent on the world stage as Lenky cruised the short distance to the club.

"Trust mi 'Rome, yuh ah go show dem say ah yuh ah de real big man!" Lenky remarked excitedly, as he waited while the parking attendant removed the barrier and allowed him to park in his reserved spot in front of the club. Like most Jamaicans, Lenky was an ardent football fan and it pleased him to no end to be friends with who many considered to potentially be the best talent to ever emerge from the Caribbean.

Jerome surveyed the scene as Lenky maneuvered the truck into the parking spot. The queue to the door was a long one, and almost everyone's attention was focused on the tricked-out Lincoln Navigator. People stared when Jerome stepped out of the vehicle. He loved being in the spotlight. Who didn't know him had most likely heard of him.

He acknowledged some people at the front of the line who waved to him, and the security guard at the front of the club pushed away an overly exuberant street vendor who had rushed up to shake hands with 'de big balla'. Paul, Gary and two of his other team-mates were waiting for him at the entrance of the club. Paul frowned when he saw Jerome with Lenky. He thought they were getting too tight. The guy was very bad news. Paul had heard some stories about Lenky from a girl who used to work as one of his drug couriers. He had raised his concerns with Jerome but his friend was on a high and was totally dismissive of what he had to say. "Yuh come from uptown man, yuh nuh understand how it go with ghetto youth" he would say with a smirk. Paul thought Jerome went out of his way to show how ghetto or how 'street' he was. They had met while playing for opposing schools in Jamaica's premier school-boy football competition. Their respective schools had met in the finals and Paul's team had been beaten 4-3 courtesy of a hat-trick from Jerome. They had become good friends though they were from different worlds. Paul, the son of a senior business executive at a large manufacturing firm, was from an upscale residential area in upper St. Andrew and was only playing football because of his love for the game and the chance to make history as a member of the team that made it to the World Cup finals. He had known it was possible with Jerome on the squad. Paul, who considered him-self an authority on the sport, had never before seen a local player with such brilliant individual skill. He knew that the sky was the limit for Jerome but he also knew that Jerome would have to change his lifestyle in order for him to reach his full potential. He was too much into the fast lane: Way too much partying, drinking, women and bad company. When the World Cup campaign was over, Paul planned to retire from the sport and start his IT consultancy firm. His father had already set aside the funds that he would need.

Jerome greeted them and Lenky nodded at them absently as he fielded calls on one of his two cell phones. The group of six men and two women then made their way through the VIP entrance as the security let them in free of charge.

It took the group several minutes to make it across the crowded club as Lenky and Jerome stopped frequently to exchange a few words with people they knew. The DJ gave a shout out to Jerome as he took a seat at Lenky's reserved table in the VIP area. Lenky had platinum membership status. The club was jumping and Jerome was in high spirits as he drank champagne and danced with Peaches and Stacey. They were equally voluptuous and both of their tongues were pierced. *Tonight is going to be interesting*, Jerome mused as the girls rubbed their bodies sensuously against him. Lenky smiled as he watched Jerome. He had fucked both women before and knew Jerome would be in for a treat. They were certified freaks.

Tara's cell phone buzzed like an angry bee atop the mahogany bed-side table as she slept soundly on her queen-size bed. She had planned to call her friends to let them know she wouldn't be partying tonight but had fallen asleep. The phone stopped ringing after the sixth missed call. Marianne, the Prime Minister's niece, shrugged to the rest of the gang.

"Guess she must be getting some good dick," she said, smirking. Though they were all promiscuous, Tara was widely acknowledged to be heads and shoulders above the rest of them in that department.

The group consisted of five girls and they all had three things in common. They were young, attractive and came from affluent families. Tara was the prettiest of the bunch but Simone was the wealthiest. Her father was an hotelier and construction magnate who, depending on whom you asked, had received all the major government contracts for the past ten years because of his affiliation with the ruling political party. They loved to gossip about each other. As Tara was the only one absent, she was the main topic of discussion. Gina told them about what had transpired earlier that evening. Marianne was very interested in hearing more about Jerome James. She had seen pictures of him in the media, especially recently, but not being a football fan, she had never seen him play. Hearing Gina go on about the size of his dick and his sexual prowess had aroused her interest. She sipped her 'Village Duppy', the house drink, and resolved to meet this stud who sounded too good to be true.

CHAPTER 3

Angela Charlton sighed as she made herself comfortable on the couch and picked up the remote. She was home alone on yet another Saturday night. In the months following the sudden, dramatic end of her six year relationship with Brian, her ex-boyfriend, she used to treasure these moments of solitude. Now the loneliness was eating at her, gnawing at her soul. She needed someone. It was all she knew. Brian had been her first and only boyfriend and they had been very committed to each other. Or so she had thought. Until she caught him with his genitals inside of her sister's mouth on that fateful Monday afternoon when she had left work early because of a migraine. He had jumped up in shock, stupidly protesting that it wasn't what it seemed. Guess he had fallen asleep and woke up to find Sara sucking his dick, or better yet, maybe he had tripped and broken his fall by skillfully landing his erection inside her mouth.

Angela had not spoken to either of them since that day. She had kicked Brian out of the apartment they shared but for which she paid the rent — Brian was a struggling artist who couldn't let the distraction of a regular 9-5 affect his creativity — and she still couldn't bring herself to be civil to her sister. Not after Sara had admitted that she had been sleeping with Brian for over three months. Three months! The bastards. Brian had hurt her deeply. She had been entirely supportive of his talent and was more than willing to be the primary breadwinner until he got his big break. Even when her dad had told her to stop wasting her life with 'the idle rasta bwoy' and find a nice hardworking young man, she had stood by him. Life felt weird and empty without him but the betrayal was just too much to bear. She couldn't bring herself to give him another chance.

She continued to channel surf until she settled on MTV. She watched as the new Sean Paul video came on. *I really need to start getting out again and stop being in the house so much*, she resolved, though she was not ready to get involved with anyone. After what she went through with Brian the last thing she wanted was to get back into a serious relationship and casual flings were not her thing. But she was lonely. She rubbed her chest absently as she wondered what it would be like to be with another man.

"Woi...lawd...Jerome...it inna mi throat..." Stacey whimpered as she laid face down, ass up. Jerome was sinking his member forcefully inside her. He slapped her huge ass with each stroke. He was in one of the guest rooms at Lenky's home in Cherry Gardens, an affluent residential area in Kingston. They had left the club at 4:45 a.m. and gone straight to Lenky's house. Lenky had told him to go ahead and enjoy himself with the two women as he needed to get some sleep. His wife was coming down from New York in a few hours and she didn't like it when he sent one of his soldiers to pick her up instead of coming himself. She had been gone for five weeks to help her cousin, who was a US citizen, get the restaurant that Lenky had invested in up and running. It was the first twenty-four hour Jamaican restaurant in New York and it was an instant hit. Nice way for Lenky to launder his drug money.

Peaches stroked Stacey's large, juicy breasts as Jerome held on to Stacey's wide hips and pummeled her with long, hard strokes. Stacey's eyes were closed as she moaned loudly. What she had heard about Jerome was true and then some. Sex with him defied description. The man had a magic dick. She gripped the sheet tightly and bucked her ample ass rapidly as an orgasm shook her voluptuous body. Jerome pulled out of her and Peaches slid to her knees, removed the condom and began to fellate him vigorously. Jerome held her head in place and slowly gyrated in her mouth. The sun rose at 6:45. They were still at it.

Angela hummed as she set the table. Her friend Jean was already seated. Jean had been pleasantly surprised to receive a phone call that morning from Angela inviting her to breakfast. She had rarely seen her since the breakup and she had missed her dearly. Angela was the sweetest person that she knew. They had been friends since the ninth grade and she loved Angela like a sister. Brian was a real punk for what he did to her. She had never liked him; always thought that he was a user.

Angela quickly blessed the food and they dug into the fried dumplings, fried plantain, liver and boiled bananas that Angela had prepared. She was a good cook.

"It's good to see you Angie," Jean said sincerely. "I was really worried about you."

"Yeah, I was crushed by the whole thing and really needed to be alone for awhile." She paused, and drank some of the freshly squeezed orange juice. "But I'm ok now; ready to move on with my life."

"Well that's great. Want to go check out a movie tonight?" Jean asked. "That new Tyler Perry comedy is now showing and I hear it's quite good."

"Sure, why not," Angela agreed. She could use a good laugh.

Jerome opened his eyes and yawned hungrily. He was alone on the large bed. He had no idea when the two girls had left the room. He got up and pulled on his boxers. He went into the bathroom to urinate and wash his face. There was a knock on the door.

"Yo!" he shouted from the bathroom.

"Yuh finally wake up," Lenky said, as he opened the door and stepped into the room. "Peaches and Stacey say yuh did ah gwaan like yuh never plan fi stop fuck this morning."

Jerome laughed boisterously. He knew that he had incredible stamina.

"You know how I do," he boasted, "I'm the original marathon man."

"Yuh gwaan talk man, ah mussi stone yuh ah use," Lenky teased, referring to the sexual aid some men used to significantly increase their staying power.

Lenky's cell phone rang.

He barked instructions into the phone and hung up.

"Mi sen' home the girls about half hour ago," he said, as Jerome got dressed. "Mi ah head out to the airport fi pick up Laura yah now."

"Alright, any food out there?" Jerome asked, stifling a yawn. He was famished.

"Yeah man, the chef cook some wicked spicy callaoo and dumpling," Lenky replied, turning to go out the door. "If yuh want fi leave before mi come back just mek Mikey drop yuh home."

"Alright, cool," Jerome replied. Mikey was Lenky's younger brother and his main enforcer. He was rumored to be the trigger man in a recent attempt on the life of one of Lenky's rivals. The man had survived the shooting but was paralyzed from the waist down. The police had detained Mikey but had released him due to a lack of evidence.

They walked out to the kitchen and Jerome nodded to the chef who was seated on a stool eating a sandwich, and grabbed a plate. He filled it with food and poured himself a large glass of chilled orange juice.

Lenky summoned two of his soldiers and left to pick up his wife while Jerome ate and chatted with the chef, who had no formal culinary training but was a good cook who used to operate a road-side restaurant in the inner-city community from which Lenky hailed. When Lenky made it big, he had employed him to be his personal chef and he lived in a small apartment on then expansive property.

After breakfast and a spliff, Jerome felt revived. He checked the time, it was almost noon. Time to go home. He went into the bedroom for his blazer and went in search of Mikey so that he could get a ride home.

He found Mikey and two other men in the living room watching a game of football on the large, flat screen TV. It was an English Premier League match and one of the teams playing were one of the teams interested in acquiring his services. Jerome grinned; he couldn't wait until next week to go to England to meet with the two teams. He favoured Manchester FC but he would play for whoever offered him the most money.

"Wha' gwaan balla?" Mikey greeted. The other two men nodded at him. "Ah soon yuh we ah go watch ah play inna de English league."

"Yeah man," Jerome responded. He wasn't surprised that Mikey had heard about it. It was all over the media that most likely he would be signed to a top English club within two weeks. While there were several Jamaican footballers plying their wares in England, none were playing for any of the top clubs so his signing would be a big deal.

Even though it was only a few minutes past twelve, the three men had already consumed two six packs of beer between them, and were now on their third pack. About an ounce of marijuana was on a cutting board on the coffee-table. One of the men was in the process of rolling a large spliff.

"Yuh want some weed balla?" he asked, exposing teeth that looked like he had eaten coal for breakfast.

Having just smoked a small spliff after he had eaten, Jerome told him no and asked Mikey to give him a ride to his apartment.

Mikey got up and stretched. "Oonu come wid mi," he said to his two henchmen.

The men nodded and rose. Jerome could see that all three of them were armed.

It didn't faze him. Having grown up in a gang-infested, violence-prone inner-city community, Jerome was used to being around guns and the type of men who used them to commit atrocious acts. He might have ended up in the same boat were it not for his incredible talent.

They piled into a new white double cab Honda Ridgeline that Lenky had recently purchased, and Mikey headed out. He drove a little too fast for Jerome's liking, especially since he had been drinking and smoking a lot of weed. Getting injured in an accident now would be a devastating blow to his career.

"Slow down rude boy," he said as casually as possible to Mikey. The diminutive Mikey had a short man's complex and was easily offended.

"Nuh worry yuhself man, everyt'ing criss," was the reply as the large truck careened around the corner, tires squealing in protest.

Jerome held his breath and prayed that he made it home in one piece.

Tara removed her sweaty clothes and stepped into the large shower. She had just gotten home from the Trafalgar Club where she played tennis most Sunday mornings. Alston, one of the instructors at the club had been surprised, and a little pissed –though he knew better than to pout – that she hadn't wanted to have sex with him that morning. They usually had a quickie in his little office after a session but she was no longer interested. It was now all about Jerome. All she had to do was think about him and she would get goose bumps all over. She had it bad. Tara lathered her curvy frame and hummed Beenie Man's new hit tune. She began to masturbate as she reminisced about fucking Jerome. She climaxed in five minutes.

Lenky hissed his teeth in annoyance as he pulled the luxurious vehicle to the side of the road. He was on his way home after picking up his wife who had just arrived from New York. The police were conducting a spot check. There were two guns in the truck but the cops would never find them. The van was custom made and had two secret compartments where he stashed his weapons. However, his men sitting in the back were armed and smoking marijuana. "Bloodclaat Babylon" he muttered as he reached for his license and registration. He knew that he was stopped because of the vehicle he was driving. Obviously none of the officers present were on his payroll.

"Nuh you name Lenky?" the officer, a grizzly, bearded man with squinty suspicious eyes asked as he snatched the documents from Lenky.

Laura, Lenky's wife, watched the proceedings coldly from behind her over-sized Dior sunglasses. Greedy ass cops, she thought disgustedly. They were the same wherever you go.

"Yeah," Lenky responded, lighting a cigarette. He knew what was coming next.

"Yuh was going a little fast just now," the cop informed him. "But we nuh really haffi write nuh ticket for that... plus we supposed to search the vehicle for drugs and guns." He looked pointedly at the two men in the back. "You understand?"

Lenky reached into the glove compartment and extracted a coil of money. He slipped the officer five thousand dollars, telling him to 'buy a drink'. He didn't need the hassle.

The cop grinned and accepted the money. He handed back the documents to Lenky. "Take it easy pon de road," he said and walked off to join his colleagues.

Laura shook her head as her husband drove off. To protect and serve my ass, she mused. Who were they kidding? They were the real criminals.

CHAPTER 4

Jerome sprawled out on the couch in his untidy living room. Pieces of clothing were strewn across the room and the place needed to be dusted and swept. He decided to call one of his girls to come over and clean up. He flipped open his cell phone and scrolled through the phonebook. He decided to call Patricia. He hadn't seen her in awhile. She was a cute bank teller he had met two months ago at a car show. He thought about his drive home as he waited for her to answer the phone. Mikey was a lunatic and he was most fortunate to reach home unharmed. The man was a reckless, stupid driver. They had four near misses and one fender bender. The man who's back Mikey had ran into had been so scared when Mikey and his two cohorts angrily approached him - never mind it was Mikey's fault - that he told them it was ok and hurried back into his vehicle.

"Hi Jerome, long time I haven't heard from you," Patricia said when she answered the phone, her tone mildly accusing.

"Yeah, I've been busy Pat...you know how it goes sometimes," Jerome replied. "I'm making some time for you right now though... can you come over?"

"Yes," she answered quickly, ashamed at her eagerness but powerless to say no to Jerome. "Do you want dinner?"

"I'm not really hungry right now but you can pick up a burger on your way over." He usually had Sunday dinner at Dimples but she was presently shopping in Miami. "Ok, I'll see you in a little while baby." She hurried to go take a shower. It wasn't often she got a chance to spend some time with Jerome. She had only seen him twice since the day they had met at the car show. Patricia sighed as she quickly lathered herself. Jerome was something else. He had taken her to an exclusive party that night after the car show and she had uncharacteristically ended up in his bed mere hours after meeting him. And what an experience that had been. She hadn't thought it possible that she could've accommodated his entire length. But she had. And she had wanted more. Lots more. But Jerome hardly had time for her. She wasn't a promiscuous girl by any stretch of the imagination. Prior to Jerome, she had only been intimate with two men. She just couldn't articulate the effect that Jerome had on her. She dried herself with a large, fluffy pink towel and slipped on a pair of white panties. She sighed when she noticed the big wet spot at her crotch. I'm going to jump his bones as soon as I enter his apartment, she vowed as she quickly applied some make-up.

Lenky, his brother Mikey, and two of his enforcers, were seated at the poolside at Lenky's house having dinner and discussing business. Lenky was in a foul mood. He had just received word that two of the three couriers he had sent up with cocaine to the UK last night had been busted by customs at London's Heathrow Airport.

"Jah know star, it ah get harder and harder fi get the product through customs," Lenky bemoaned, through a mouthful of rice and peas and roast beef. "This mek the fifth time in a month mi lose money. The youth dem in Brixton ah bawl say dem ah go have to start buy from the Nigerians because dem caan depend pon mi."

Lenky hissed his teeth in annoyance and took a sip of the thick sour sop juice that he believed gave him stamina. He looked up at his wife, Laura, who was seated on the balcony upstairs engrossed in a telephone conversation.

"Dem ah target de woman dem, it look like we ah go have to find some man fi start carry up de drugs," Lenky surmised.

"It nah go easy fi find man who willing to swallow drugs like de woman dem," Mikey commented.

"Yah fool man," Lenky retorted, "Nuff youth out de woulda glad fi get a chance fi go England and make some money. Plus, dem nuh have to swallow it, that ah nuh de only way we send up drugs."

The two enforcers, Ping Pong and Blacka, snickered at Mikey as they nodded in agreement with Lenky. It would definitely not be difficult to find some youths to take the risk. The money would be tempting. The two thousand pounds that they would be paid to transport the drugs safely through customs was nothing to scoff at. That was over two hundred thousand Jamaican dollars – a lot of money for someone who doesn't know where their next meal is coming from.

"Matter of fact," Lenky said, stroking his thin goatee, "Jerome ah go England next week...mi ah go ask him if him willing fi bring up a package fi mi."

"Jerome nah go do dat man," Mikey countered. "Him soon sign big contract and ah go make whole heap ah money...plus him just ah get ready fi start him career...why him woulda run the risk of losing that?"

"How you so bloodclaat negative?" Lenky snarled, glaring at his younger brother, though he knew that he was right. It was a stupid idea. Besides, it would be a shame for the most promising footballer from the Caribbean to get nabbed in a drug bust before his career even took off. He just didn't need to hear it from his little brother.

"Roll a spliff gimme," he barked at Mikey. He looked up at Laura who was still on the phone. They had been married for only a year now. Laura was from Jamaica but had been living in the US for the past ten years. Lenky met her at a resort in Negril where she had been staying for a week with two of her close friends. Upon meeting her, Lenky was so smitten that he had sent home the woman he had taken to Negril for the weekend, and pursued Laura relentlessly, showering her with gifts and attention. Laura, the consummate 'hot girl', was used to men fawning over her and had played it cool. Laura, street-smart and savvy, was very attractive and voluptuous. She was fair-complexioned, five feet nine inches tall, extremely curvy with a large, heart-shaped ass, firm C cups, long, slightly bowed legs and she had an impossibly flat stomach which sported a diamond encrusted custom-made platinum navel ring. Lenky had fallen for her like a schoolboy. Laura didn't sleep with him until a month later, when after calling her at least three times a day, every day without fail, Lenky sent a ticket for her to come back to Jamaica to see him.

Laura didn't love Lenky but realized that he had a great deal of money and could afford to keep her living the kind of lifestyle to which she had become accustomed. Her last boyfriend had been a professional basketball player but they had broken up when he had a career ending injury. So when Lenky had proposed two months after they met, she made him sweat for four months before accepting his proposal. They had gotten married in the Bahamas in a small but extravagant wedding. Lenky badly wanted them to have a baby, and was trying really hard but to no avail. Unbeknownst to him, Laura was on the pill. She was not ready to have a child. Lenky would just have to be content with the nine year old son he had with Jada, the woman who had been his main squeeze until Laura came along. Laura knew she was playing a dangerous game. Lenky was a gangster and there was no telling what he would do to her if he found out. He had never been abusive to her but she knew that he was very much capable of extreme violence if someone crossed him. Especially the love of his life.

They were yet to have sex since she got back from New York earlier that day. She had gently spurned his advance telling him that she was a bit tired and he should wait until later. He wondered if she was cheating on him. God help her if that's the case, Lenky mused thoughtfully as he lit the spliff that Mikey handed to him.

The thought of another man touching Laura was too much for him to bear.

Angela gathered her shoulder length reddish tint hair into a loose, stylish ponytail and grabbed her keys. She had a patient coming in for a four p.m. appointment. Angela had been a physiotherapist for the past three years and ran her own business. She absolutely loved her work. It gave her great joy when people came in with excruciating pain and she was able to aid in their recovery. She specialized in general physical therapy, with an emphasis on manual therapy, pelvic pain and management of osteoporosis. She operated out of Eden Haven, a wellness centre located about ten minutes away from her apartment on Lady Musgrave Road. It was very difficult to get space at the soughtafter centre, but her dad, a semi-retired chartered accountant and businessman, knew the developers quite well. Business was good from the get go and she only dealt with clients by appointment. The man who was coming to see her was a business executive who suffered from back spasms.

Angela waved to the security guard and parked in her spot. A horn tooted as she exited her car and started walking towards her office. She turned to see a black Mercedes sedan. Mr. Bradshaw. He was five minutes early. She waved and went inside her office to get ready.

"Oh Jerome, I missed you so much..." Patricia groaned between kisses as she hugged Jerome tightly in his living room. True to her word, she had pounced on him the minute he opened the door. Now feeling pleasantly sore, two intense orgasms and forty minutes later, she was cuddling with Jerome on the couch. Jerome grinned inwardly as he looked at Patricia. Never judge a book by the cover, he mused. Patricia was a very petite, soft-spoken, innocent looking girl. One would never imagine her to be the virago she was in the bedroom.

"Ready for your burger?" she asked as she traced the outline of the tattoo on his chest – a huge black panther that looked ready to pounce.

"Yeah, sure," Jerome responded lazily as his cell phone rang. Patricia handed him the phone and went into the kitchen to put the burger in the microwave.

Jerome checked the caller ID. It was Tara Reid.

"Hello."

"Hi handsome, what's up?"

"Nothing much, at home chilling."

"Ok, I'm on my way to an art exhibition," Tara told him as she sped down Halfway-Tree-Road. Her friend, Mishka, a budding contemporary artist, was showcasing her latest creations. "I've been thinking about you Jerome..."

"Is that right..." Jerome teased as Patricia handed him the burger and a glass of fruit punch on a tray. She then went into the bathroom.

"It certainly is. By the way...a friend of mine, the Prime Minister's niece, is having a party on Tuesday night at Azzuri Pub. I'd like you to come with me."

"Ok, I'll keep that in mind," Jerome responded coolly, taking a bite of the burger.

"Good. Talk to you soon."

Patricia emerged from the bathroom as Jerome put the phone down.

"Babes, be a darling and straighten up the apartment," Jerome said as she bent over to pick her clothes up from off the floor.

"Ok...but no big spring cleaning though you know," she told him, standing naked with her hands on her slender hips. "I'll just sweep and dust, and put away all the clothes you have strewn all over the place."

"Yeah, that's cool," Jerome agreed. He finished eating and placed the tray on the coffee table. He turned to ESPN to watch some sports highlights while Patricia put on one of his t-shirts and started to clean.

His mind drifted to his future as he looked at highlights from the top football leagues around the world. He was only twentytwo years old and with his talent, if he could stay healthy and avoid any major injuries, he had a long and lucrative career ahead of him. At least a twelve year run playing at a high level. He would be able to get his dream car, buy property in Jamaica and England, and basically live out his dream of being a star athlete. He was just sorry that his mother and grandmother would not be around to enjoy his pending success. His mother and grandmother had been poor but fortunately Jerome was an only child and because of his prodigious talents, he had been awarded a full scholarship to the high school he had attended, which had eased he burden on his mother tremendously.

They had perished in a fire set by gangsters who had accused his grandmother of being a police informant. He had been away representing the national under-17 football team when it happened. He remembered it like it was yesterday. The coach, a short, compact man with the bushiest eyebrows Jerome had ever seen, had called him out of the hotel room that he was sharing with three of his teammates – even the coaching staff had to share rooms due to the tight budget – and grimly told him the bad news. He had been utterly devastated. The two people that he loved most were gone just like that. They were his only family. The only ones he knew of anyway. He never knew his father. He had disappeared when his mother became pregnant. Football was his solace – he inexplicably had the best game of his young career the next day, scoring four goals and assisting on a fifth as Jamaica crushed the Canadians 5-1 to move on to the next round. Sex became his therapy. He was always a highly-sexed teenager, and had lost his virginity at age twelve, but after the death of his mother and grandmother, it was like he became addicted to sex. Somehow it helped him to deal with the pain. He craved it constantly and was always on the prowl for fresh meat. The team had stayed in Canada for three days and Jerome slept with two women during their stay – including the mother of one of the girls.

"You ok baby?"

Jerome was startled by the sound of Patricia's voice. She was crouched beside him with a concerned look on her face.

"Yeah, yeah...was just deep in thought," he replied, taking a deep breath.

Patricia touched his face. "You looked so sad just now...anything you want to talk about?"

"No...I'm good." He forced a smile.

Patricia patted his shoulder and went back to her cleaning.

Jerome decided that he needed some cheering up and he knew just what would do the trick. Elizabeth Rhoden had told him to call her today. A tryst with the rich, sophisticated married woman should perk him right up. He got up and went into the bedroom to look for her card.

Jerome sat on the bed and looked around the room as he dialed her number. Everything was neat and in order. Patricia had done a good job.

"Hello, good evening."

"Good evening, Mrs. Rhoden?"

"Yes, this is she."

"Hi, it's Jerome James."

"Well, hello there, how are you?" Mrs. Rhoden asked as she luxuriated in her spacious marble bath tub. She had been soaking her well-preserved body in a bubble bath for the past twenty minutes.

"I'm ok...just here chilling...anticipating seeing you..."

She chuckled. "Good. I've booked a suite at the Prometheus Hotel for us to make splendid use of tonight."

The Prometheus was a small, ultra-exclusive hotel located in a cool, tranquil section of Stony Hill. It was ridiculously expensive and was a popular playground for wealthy Jamaicans. It was very discreet and they catered to one's every need. It was notoriously hard to get a room there.

Jerome was impressed. And excited. The night beckoned with great promise.

"That's great," Jerome said, trying to keep the excitement out of his voice. "What time do we meet?"

"I'll pick you up at your apartment at seven."

"Ok, let me give you directions."

Elizabeth Rhoden laughed. "No need. You'd be surprised at the things I know about you, Jerome."

Jerome was thinking of a suitable response when Patricia called out his name from the living room announcing that she was through cleaning.

"Save your strength, Mr. James," Elizabeth said in a wry tone. "You're going to need it."

She hung up before he could respond.

Patricia came into the room and sat beside Jerome on the bed. "So, what's my reward for cleaning up your filthy apartment?" she asked with a sly grin.

"You want cash or kind?"

"Hmmm," Patricia said, pretending to think about it as she reached into his basketball shorts and pulled out his dick. "I think I'll take kind."

Patricia's breathing got more audible as she felt him twitching in her hand. "I love your dick so much," she whispered.

"Show him just how much you love him," Jerome responded, gently directing her head downwards. Jerome reached for two of his pillows and reclined on the bed while Patricia licked him enthusiastically. He glanced at his watch. It was 5:45. He would get rid of Patricia in another half-hour then relax and get ready for Mrs. Rhoden to pick him at 7 p.m. Something told him that she would be on time.

After her hour long session with Mr. Bradshaw, Angela sorted out her appointments for the coming week. Suzette, her receptionist/assistant, was off for two weeks visiting her relatives in New Jersey. She had offered to let her little sister who was a freshman at college fill in for her but Angela had declined. It was only for two weeks and she didn't mind doing everything herself. James Rhoden was her first appointment on Monday. Angela frowned when she remembered the time his wife had called her at the office to warn her not to get any ideas about seducing her husband. Angela had been bewildered and somewhat embarrassed. She considered herself the consummate professional and would never date one of her patients, let alone a married one, as she had relayed politely but firmly to Mrs. Rhoden, who was suitably unimpressed by Angela's assertion. James Rhoden had in fact made a few passes at her when she had first started treating him, but she had made it clear to him that if he didn't cease coming on to her, he would have to find another physiotherapist. At only twenty-five, Angela was regarded as one of the best in the island so he had heeded her warning. Angela paid the office utility bills online and then left for home. She was to pick up Jean at 7:30 for their movie date.

"Mi say ah one box mi give de gal after she ask me that," Mikey said as he took a drag off his spliff. Mikey, Lenky, Ping Pong and Blacka were now in the living room watching a DVD featuring strippers from New York.

The men laughed.

Mikey continued, "Damn out of order...she can ah ask bad man fi eat her pussy."

"Fi real, she bright," Lenky agreed, reaching over to give Mikey a pound.

They then became engrossed in the action on screen. A very dark girl with a large ass that completely swallowed the bright red thong that she was wearing; was skillfully working the pole. Watching her reminded Lenky of how horny he was. He excused himself and went upstairs to look for Laura.

He was greeted by the sight of her lovely heart-shaped ass positioned in the air as she bent over looking for something in one of her suitcases. Lenky moved behind her and rubbed her ass through the tiny denim shorts she was wearing.

"Ah need some now babes," Lenky murmured huskily as Laura straightened up and turned around.

"Baby, let me finish unpacking please," Laura protested as Lenky swiftly pulled the button and unzipped her shorts. He would not be deterred.

He pushed her onto the bed and deftly removed her shorts and underwear. He groaned when her freshly shaven mound came into view. Lenky sank to his knees and buried his face in his wife's vagina. Laura sighed and spread her legs. She rarely had an orgasm when Lenky performed oral sex on her and never during penetration. You would think he would at least know how to handle his business for someone who loves sex so much, Laura bemoaned inwardly as Lenky munched away hungrily.

She moaned dutifully and rubbed his head occasionally to let him think that she was enjoying it. Lenky, like most men, had a fragile ego and Laura didn't think that he would react positively if she informed him that he wasn't satisfying her in bed. Lenky then rose and dropped his pants. He climbed atop his wife and inserted his stubby dick inside her.

"How yuh a gwaan like yuh never want it ...eh?" he asked smugly as Laura moved her waistline expertly beneath him. She flexed her vaginal muscles intermittently, eliciting loud grunts of approval from Lenky. She knew that he would climax soon; he never lasted longer than five minutes.

"Yes...yes...ohh... Lenky..." Laura moaned as Lenky spilled his seed inside her.

"Ahh...whew," Lenky breathed, adding, "Ah true mi did miss you babes mek mi climax so quick."

Yeah right, Laura thought. Aloud she said, "Its ok baby, you know I like it short and sweet."

Lenky grinned. "So where you want to go tonight?" he asked as he pulled on his pants.

Laura went inside the bathroom and turned on the shower. "I don't know yet, I'll decide later."

"Alright, just mek mi know." Lenky left the room and went back downstairs to finish watching the DVD.

I need to find a nice hot boy to 'sort me out' while I'm in Jamaica, Laura mused as she lathered herself. She had a man on the side in New York but she couldn't go up more than once a month or Lenky would complain. She had gotten away with being in New York for almost five weeks because of all the things that had to be done to open the restaurant. Having a man in Jamaica to satisfy her sexually would definitely help to ease the frustration of having to fake it all the time with Lenky.

CHAPTER 5

Jerome checked the time when he was through getting dressed. It was exactly 7 p.m. *Mrs. Rhoden will be arriving any minute now,* he thought as he went to the bathroom to urinate. After Patricia had reluctantly left at 6:20, Jerome had rolled a fat spliff to go along with his protein shake and was now feeling a nice buzz. His cell phone rang as he peed. He slipped his free hand inside the pocket of his grey corduroy blazer and retrieved the phone.

"Hello."

"I'm outside your apartment. Come in the rear of the vehicle."

Jerome finished up and headed outside. A heavily tinted black Mercedes SUV was idling at the curb. He did as he was told and opened one of the back doors.

"Hi there," Jerome said as he joined Elizabeth Rhoden on the back seat.

"Hey," Elizabeth responded, giving him a warm inviting smile.

Jerome looked at her as the driver pulled off. Her hair was in a chignon, and she was wearing a pretty white summer dress with a matching pearl set that gave her a playful yet sophisticated air. She smelled wonderful. He scooted over closer to her.

"You look ravishing," Jerome murmured close to her ear, turning on the charm.

"Thank you, flattery will get you everywhere young man," she responded.

Jerome smiled and reclined comfortably on the plush leather seat. Soothing jazz filtered lightly through the speakers.

"Oh, I'm counting on it."

Mrs. Rhoden casually rested her left hand on Jerome's lap and they settled into a sexually charged silence as the SUV made its way uptown. Mrs. Rhoden gasped audibly when she felt the movement of Jerome's phallus as he slowly achieved a turgid erection. Her bottom lip quivered and she closed her eyes as she subtly massaged his crotch through his trousers.

"Richard," she said in an unsteady voice.

"Yes, Mrs. Rhoden?" The driver replied, looking in the rearview mirror.

"Step on it. We're not going to a bloody funeral you know."

Angela pulled up in front of the house where Jean had rented the self-contained left side for the past two years. It was a nice enough area in Mona, though flooding was a major problem when it rained heavily. She had called Jean to let her know that she was close by so Jean came out as soon as she pulled up.

"Hey, girl," Jean said, as she climbed into the hatchback Honda Civic and shut the door. "Ready to have some fun?"

"Yep. I'm hungry though Jean...I haven't eaten since breakfast," Angela said as they turned down Hope Road.

"I had two slices of cake a few hours ago but I could definitely eat something," Jean replied.

"Well, we have time to get a bite...the movie doesn't actually start until 8:15."

"Yeah, let's get some Wendy's," Jean suggested. She just loved their chicken salad.

Lenky was in the bathroom taking a shower when his cell phone rang. Laura answered it and the person hung up. *One of his little bitches*, Laura fumed in annoyance. She hated being hung up on. She knew that Lenky was still sleeping with his baby-mother occasionally because of the snide looks Jada threw her way whenever they saw each other; and that he had other women though he was careful not to get caught. Or so he thought. Bigga, Lenky's chef, was her confidante and told her everything that Lenky was up to. Laura couldn't care less. She was the wife and she had unlimited access to Lenky's money. At the end of the day, if push came to shove, she could always move back to the US – she was still a citizen – and she had a substantial amount of money saved up. The restaurant in New York was also in her name along with her cousin as minority owner.

"Tell your hoes to have more respect," Laura said nonchalantly when Lenky came out of the shower.

"Weh yuh ah talk 'bout babes?" Lenky asked puzzled, still drying himself.

"Some bitch just called and hung up when I answered the phone," she informed him.

"Easy nuh babes...why it haffi be a woman?" Lenky asked soothingly as he picked up the cell phone to check the number. It was a private number.

"Whatever," Laura said dismissively. "Just tell them don't do that shit again."

Lenky shook his head and pulled an outfit from out of the closet. He had to go down to the ghetto to take care of some business. Love made men do crazy things, he mused. No other woman would've dared to talk to him in such a manner. He looked at her lying on the bed ignoring him and thumbing through a magazine. She was so sexy. The kind of woman who could turn heads anywhere. *She'd better not get any ideas in her pretty head,* Lenky mused as he got dressed. *I'd kill her before I let her walk out of my life.*

Richard pulled up at the Prometheus and the heavily armed security guard checked the license plate, colour and make of the vehicle. Satisfied that it matched the details provided for the vehicle that was to bring the occupants who booked Suite Twelve, he let them through. Richard, having taken Mrs. Rhoden here on several occasions, knew exactly where to go. Jerome looked around with avid interest. Each suite was nestled in a cluster of large, beautiful trees and surrounded by meticulously manicured hedges. Each was completely private.

"Be back at eleven," Mrs. Rhoden instructed when Richard pulled up in front of the suite.

She then exited the vehicle with Jerome in tow. Elizabeth punched a combination of numbers on the security keypad by the door and they went inside.

Jerome whistled appreciatively as he looked the around. It was like stepping into a rain forest. The suite was large and was decorated in a jungle theme. The sound of African drums filtered through unseen speakers; a 'waterfall' on the right side of the room flowed into a steaming 'grotto'; lights shaped like the moon and stars bathed the suite in a soft glow and a lush green carpet that resembled grass covered the floor. There was no bed. A hammock hung from two 'trees' and a thick, large leopard print rug was to the left of the room by an ice bucket which was shaped like a lion's head and contained a bottle of Cristal and two glasses.

"You like?" Mrs. Rhoden purred as she went over to the rug and reclined comfortably.

"Wow...this is like something out of a dream," Jerome replied in awe.

"The bathroom is behind that cluster of 'rocks'," Mrs. Rhoden told him. "In there you'll find a loin cloth. Put it on."

Jerome grinned. Tonight was going to be a night to remember.

Lenky stopped by Jada's home over in Nannyville on his way to conduct business on Windward Road. A shipment of guns that he had ordered had come in and was at one of his stash houses. Braveheart, who had earned his moniker by single-handedly attacking and killing three of Lenky's rivals at a street-dance in West Kingston, had assured him that all was well but Lenky still wanted to see for himself. He trusted no one. Lenky briefly chatted with several youths from the community who had come over to pay their respects to the 'big man'. He then gave them some money and went inside the house. "Daddy!" Nathaniel, his son shouted, before quickly turning his eyes back to the television screen. He was playing wrestling with one of his friends on the Xbox that Lenky had given him for his birthday.

"Yuh alright Natty?" Lenky asked as he rubbed the boy's head affectionately. "Where is yuh mother?"

"She inna har room," Nathaniel replied, shrieking with joy as he defeated his friend for the third time that evening. Lenky smiled and shook his head as he went into the bedroom. Nathaniel would play video games all day and night if he could. Lenky wished he was more athletic and thought he was getting too chubby, but he spoiled his son and gave him whatever he wanted. He loved kids. Roughly thirty children from the community where he grew up depended on his benevolence to go to school. He couldn't wait to have a baby with Laura. He wanted a pretty little girl. He frowned when he thought of how long it was taking for Laura to get pregnant. Maybe he should take her to the doctor for a check up. He was confident that he wasn't the problem.

Jada was sitting on the bed in her bra and panties filing her nails when Lenky entered the room and closed the door.

He grabbed her blonde weave in a painful grip.

"Ouch! Weh yuh a gwaan so fah Lenky?" Jada asked as she vainly tried to remove his hand.

Lenky slapped her in the face. Twice.

"Don't ever call mi phone and hang up pon mi wife again," Lenky snarled. "Ah try yuh a try fi cause trouble between mi and mi wife? Eh gal?"

"Mi neva..."Jada protested tearfully before Lenky slapped her again, cutting her off in mid-sentence.

"Shut up an' nuh lie to mi," Lenky told her coldly. "Just cut out the foolishness."

He released her hair and sat next to her on the bed.

Sobbing, she moved away from him and curled up at the top of the bed.

Lenky looked at her. Jada was a good woman, fiercely loyal and knew how to take care of a man. And she was the mother of his child. If Laura hadn't come along she would've been the one wearing the ring. Jada knew that, and as long as Laura was his wife she would never get over it. Lenky sighed. He understood how she felt but he still had to maintain discipline. Laura was the wife and that was that. He counted out twenty thousand dollars and placed it on the dresser. He patted her leg and left the room.

Angela laughed so much that she had a slight headache and badly needed to pee. The movie was excruciatingly funny. It was now intermission and she hurried to the restroom while Jean went to get them some bottled water at the concessionary stand. She was having such a good time that she had suggested to Jean that they go to New Kingston to have a couple of drinks after the movie. Jean was on the evening shift tomorrow - she was a nurse at Oxford Memorial Hospital – and Angela's first appointment wasn't until 10 a.m. so neither of them had to worry about getting up early.

Jerome returned from the bathroom wearing the leopard print loin cloth much to the delight of Mrs. Rhoden. She admired his chiseled form as he stood in front of her with his hands on his hips. His body was muscular and hard without being big, and his well defined abs and strong arms made her mouth water. *Quite a specimen*, she mused appreciatively. Her eyes drifted south. The loin cloth wasn't short – about mid-thigh – yet she could see the mushroom head of his dick hanging slightly below the cloth. Her body trembled excitedly in anticipation of what was to come.

"Pour us some champagne," she told him softly.

Jerome did her bidding and poured some of the Cristal.

"To good times," Mrs. Rhoden toasted. Jerome knelt beside her on the rug and they linked arms and sipped from each other's glass. Jerome then reclined and Elizabeth poured some of the champagne from her glass onto his chest.

"Mmmm," she moaned softly as she licked his chest. She nibbled and sucked his nipples, extending her stay there when she realized how much he liked it. His loin cloth was now bundled up at his waist, pushed back by his mammoth erection. Jerome squirmed as she worked her magic, her mouth roaming ever so slowly down to his genitals, leaving intersected trails of wetness all over his torso.

Jerome groaned loudly when he felt her knowledgeable tongue on the inside of his thighs. She licked and nibbled his flesh without urgency and Jerome gripped the rug when she licked behind his knees. He hadn't even known that was an erogenous zone. It felt good. So good.

Elizabeth rose from his quivering body and removed her dress. Jerome stroked himself slowly as he watched her undress. She had a good body for a woman of any age, but for a woman in her late forties, it was incredible. Though she had obviously benefited from cosmetic surgery, it was still impressive. Her stomach was very flat, her relatively large breasts were full and perky like a teenager's, her skin was rich and creamy, her naturally curvy frame was toned and her wide hips tapered down to a cleanly shaven vagina. She was obviously wet.

Elizabeth got on her knees and crawled between Jerome's legs. Her hair was now loose and flowing down her shoulders. Jerome's hand was replaced by Elizabeth's as she stroked his dick slowly with a worshipful look in her eyes. She considered his phallus a work of art. She bent her head and flicked her tongue back and forth over his scrotum. Jerome's groans competed with the sounds of the African drums resonating from the hidden speakers. He gasped loudly when her hot mouth finally claimed his throbbing manhood. She sucked him languidly, expertly working her way down to the base of his shaft. She impressively held him in her mouth for several seconds before coming up for air. Elizabeth then reached over and retrieved a condom from the wide variety that was in a container next to the rug.

After unsuccessfully trying to put on the first two, she rummaged through and found an extra-large magnum. Breathing heavily, she quickly rolled it on and positioned herself over his robust erection. She held it with her right hand and slowly inserted the head. She then released it and lowered her body gently, whimpering softly as she slid down his shaft. She wondered if she would ever stop sliding. His dick seemed to go on forever.

"Oh my god...don't move...yet," Elizabeth whispered, as she adjusted to the feel of the gargantuan phallus that was embedded inside her. She had never felt anything like it. She was so filled.

Jerome caressed her breasts as she slowly began to gyrate. Elizabeth then squatted instead of sitting, and they both watched, one with pleasure, the other with disbelief, as his long shaft disappeared inside her depths over and over again.

Richard pulled up at the Suite promptly at eleven. He knew his boss would chew him out if he was late. He had been her personal driver for the past fourteen months. The previous driver had retired after being with the Rhodens for ten years. The pay was good, and Mrs. Rhoden was a nice enough person, one just had to be careful not to get on her wrong side, as Richard had learned in embarrassing fashion on a few occasions. She was a very attractive woman and her husband was a handsome fellow as well. Richard wondered what the story was with those two. They had been married for over fifteen years and in the relatively short time that he had been with them, he had never even seen them argue, yet he knew that they both cheated on each other incessantly. *The beautiful and wealthy, Richard mused philosophically, who can understand them?*

He watched as they exited the Suite and noted with a low chuckle that Mrs. Rhoden was walking gingerly. Young boy fix yuh business man, Richard thought with much amusement, though he was careful to keep a stoic expression on his face.

Jerome helped Mrs. Rhoden into the SUV and she promptly rested her head on his chest as Richard drove out of the property. Elizabeth sighed and snuggled up against Jerome. She was tired and her body ached, though not unpleasantly. She was totally satiated. The evening had culminated with a torrid doggy-style session in the steaming 'grotto'. At one point she was positive the steam had been emanating from her and not the 'grotto'. She had climaxed so hard that she almost fainted. The nine hundred and fifty US dollars that she had paid for the Suite was money well spent. It had been quite an experience. She had been to the Prometheus on several occasions with different men, but to say those nights paled in comparison to this night would be a gross understatement. Now all she wanted to do was to crawl into bed and get some much needed rest. Fucking Jerome had made her feel every inch the forty-eight year old woman that she was. Her personal assistant would have to cancel her meeting in the morning with the representative from the Ministry of Sports; there was no way she'd be able to get out of bed before midday.

Jerome told Richard to drop him off in New Kingston. He didn't feel like going home. He kissed a sleepy Elizabeth on the cheek and hopped out of the SUV in front of Smooth, a popular watering hole for the young and hip. A quartet of attractive young girls who were standing outside of the bar waiting on a cab flirted with Jerome as he went inside. The place wasn't jam packed, but there was a good amount of people in there hanging out. Jerome acknowledged some acquaintances as he looked around. He walked over to the main bar and the bartender gave him a pound and told him he could have a drink on the house. Jerome ordered a Hennessy on the rocks and looked in the large mirror that spanned the length of the bar behind the bartenders, and that's when he saw her.

CHAPTER 6

In the coming months, Jerome would remember every single detail about the first time he laid eyes on Angela. He would recall looking in the mirror and seeing the prettiest, warmest smile he had ever seen, on a beautiful young woman who had an unassuming air about her that suggested she either wasn't aware of her beauty or she simply was unaffected by it. He would remember that he was staring with his mouth slightly open, not even realizing that the bartender had placed his drink in front of him.

"Jerome!" the bartender said, looking behind Jerome to see what had him in a trance.

Jerome grinned sheepishly, somewhat embarrassed by his reaction to the woman. He took a large sip of the strong drink. It calmed him and his swagger slightly returned.

"You know her?" he asked the bartender, gesturing discreetly to where Angela and Jean were sitting.

"The one in the blue top?" the bartender asked, frowning as he tried to place her face. "No sah, first I'm seeing her. Pretty girl."

Jerome watched her through the mirror. She seemed to be enjoying herself. Talking and smiling frequently with her friend. For the first time in his life, Jerome felt nervous about approaching a woman. He took a deep breath and walked over to where they were seated. The table could seat four and they were the only ones sitting there.

They looked up when he approached the table.

The plain one's eyes registered recognition when she looked at Jerome. The beauty merely looked at him with a pleasant if quizzical look.

"Good night, how are you ladies doing?"

"We're fine, just hanging out. How are you?" the beauty responded.

"I'm good. I'm Jerome, Jerome James," Jerome said expectantly, extending his hand.

She shook it; firmly and quickly.

"I'm Angela and this is my best friend Jean," she replied.

Jerome was annoyed that she was pretending that she didn't know him. At the very least his face should look familiar to her. He was currently featured on several large billboards across the island in advertisements for a popular mobile phone company, and he was in a television commercial for a major sporting goods store. Matter of fact, he was on a billboard right across the street from the bar.

"I knew your face looked familiar," Jean enthused. "You play for the Reggae Boyz. You scored that goal against the US the other day!"

"Please, join us! Angie, you don't know him?" Jean asked incredulously. "There is an article in today's gleaner about him going to London this week to try out for two major clubs."

Angela took a sip of her vodka and cranberry juice, and wondered why Jean was acting like a groupie. "No, sorry, I'm really not into sports." She smiled politely at Jerome who had graciously accepted Jean's invitation to join them at the table.

"Wow, it's really nice to meet you, Jerome," Jean said excitedly. "I'm a huge fan of yours and I totally love football."

"Thanks, Jean, I appreciate the love," Jerome replied, looking at Angela. Damn, she's even more beautiful up close.

Jean realized that Jerome was absolutely taken by Angela who was either unaware or inexplicably not interested. Jean decided to give them a moment alone, she found the whole scenario quite exciting.

"I'm going to the ladies' room, be right back," Jean announced and grabbed her purse.

"So," Jerome began, thanking Jean mentally for the opportunity to speak with Angela alone. "Tell me a little about yourself Angela."

"Oh, there's not much to tell," Angela responded, "I'm a physiotherapist and I really love my work."

"Ok, interesting," Jerome responded, thinking quickly. "Perhaps you could give me a session before I leave for London. You know, to loosen me up for those tryouts."

"Oh. I'm sorry. I don't think that would be possible. Didn't Jean allude to you leaving this week?"

"Yeah, I leave on Thursday."

"I'm booked solid for the next two weeks," she told him with an apologetic smile.

"There's no way you can slot me in?" Jerome asked, miffed at her response. This girl was something else. Almost anyone else would've most certainly accommodated him.

"Unfortunately, no," Angela said as Jerome's cell phone rang.

He checked the caller ID. It was Patricia.

"Hey, what's up?"

"Hi baby," Patricia said; she was in bed watching a movie and thinking about Jerome. "I miss you."

"I'll call you back in a bit," Jerome said and hung up without waiting for a response.

Two skimpily clad girls came over to the table and asked Jerome to take a picture with them. He complied and signed an autograph for the busty, tall one as she flashed Angela a dirty look. Angela ignored her and sipped her drink. She was going to kill Jean for leaving her alone with Mr. Celebrity. Angela knew she did it on purpose. She decided to leave as soon as Jean returned.

"That's really hard...and inflexible," Jerome said to her, sipping his drink.

"Well, others would call it professionalism," Angela replied.

Things were not going as Jerome would've liked. He took another sip of his drink.

"May I have your number? I'd love to take you out sometime," Jerome said, looking into her eyes.

"No, I'm not dating right now," Angela replied, maintaining eye contact.

"Are you a lesbian?" Jerome asked exasperated. He was not used to women turning him down.

Jean returned to the table and immediately noticed the tension. "Everything ok?" she asked as she sat down.

"Everything is fine," Angela replied. "Are you ready Jean? I'm feeling a bit tired."

Jean knew better than to argue. Angela was such a strange creature. Jean sighed and chalked it up to Angela's inexperience on the dating scene. If it had ever been her that Jerome was interested in...

"Well it was a pleasure meeting you Mr. James," Angela said as she stood up, extending her hand.

Jerome, his handsome face in a slight scowl, nodded and shook her hand.

Angela walked off ahead of Jean who shrugged her shoulders apologetically.

"Give me her number Jean... please," Jerome said. Angela seemed to be a tough nut to crack and he was never one to back down from a challenge.

"Sure," Jean replied and handed Jerome one of Angela's business cards after scribbling Angela's private mobile number on the back. "Don't take it personal ok? She was hurt really bad in her last relationship so she has her guard up."

"Ok, thanks for the heads up," Jerome told her.

"Ok, bye," Jean said and hurried out.

They had parked a few doors down from the bar, and Angela was in the car waiting with the motor running when Jean got there.

"What happened when I went to the bathroom Angie?" Jean asked as Angela pulled off.

"Nothing happened...he asked me out and I refused," Angela replied, "and please don't do that again. I don't need you to try and set me up with anybody."

"I didn't try to do anything," Jean retorted. "I really needed to use the bathroom."

"Yeah, sure," Angela snorted sarcastically.

"Whatever Angie, the guy is fine as hell and has something going for him," Jean said, annoyed at Angela's attitude. "You could do much worse on a rebound from Brian."

"You take him then, Jean," Angela replied. "What makes you think I would want a man like that? Women always sweating him and in his face...no thanks...I'm a simple girl...don't need all that drama."

"I'd take him in a heartbeat but unfortunately you're the one he wants."

They looked at each other while they waited for the light to turn green.

"I'm sorry, girl," Angela said as they both burst out laughing. "I know you just want me to meet someone and have some fun...I was just a little overwhelmed...you know?"

Jean patted her hand. "It's ok Angie...I understand. He's hot though isn't he?"

"Hot like fire!" Angela agreed, laughing. "But seriously, a guy like that is trouble Jean; definitely not what I need right now."

"I hear you girl."

"I'll never see him again anyway."

"Yeah," Jean agreed.

"By the way, what were you doing in there so long?" Angela asked suspiciously.

"Nothing girl, was just telling him goodbye," Jean replied.

"Yeah right, you gave him my number didn't you?"

"Angie please...I see you trying to hold back that smile...you know you're glad I did!"

They laughed hard as Angela turned onto Jean's street. They knew each other so well.

"Whatever," Angela said smiling.

"Ok, talk to you tomorrow," Jean said as she exited the car. "Bye."

Angela drove off and took a shortcut to get back onto Old Hope Road. She was immensely attracted to Jerome but she vowed to fight it. She was not getting involved with someone like him. She wasn't into the limelight and the hype life. He'd better not call me, she thought as she turned onto Lady Musgrave Road. She was almost home.

After Angela and Jean had left, Jerome was joined by three girls who had come over to meet him. He flirted with them for the next twenty minutes but his mind was on Angela. She was a cold fish, Jerome mused. He should just forget about her. She probably thought that she was better than him. He sighed as he flicked her business card between his fingers.

"So, Jerome," the dark one with the low, spiky hair cut was saying, "What yuh doing later?"

"Not sure yet," Jerome replied, getting up. "I gotta make a call...be right back."

Jerome went into the restroom and dialed Angela's cell number. She answered on the fourth ring.

"Hi, Angela. It's Jerome."

"Hi, Jerome...I don't recall giving you my number," she said, as she turned off the living room light and went into the bedroom.

"A good Samaritan helped me out," Jerome replied, "realized I was in need."

"I see. Need is a strong word. Are you sure you didn't mean want?"

Jerome laughed. "I always say exactly what I mean Angela...and what I'm saying now is that I like you... a lot."

"You don't even know me."

"All I know is that from the moment I saw you I can't stop thinking about you...I just want you to give me a chance to get to know you." His tone was earnest.

"Jerome. As I told you earlier...I'm not dating."

"Are you in a relationship?"

"No, I'm not."

"What is it then...you don't like me? I'm not your type?"

"Yes, that's it. You're not my type."

"And what type is that? What type am I?"

"Look, Jerome, it's late and I'm going to bed. I'm flattered but no thanks. Take care and good night."

Jerome couldn't believe it. He put his cell phone in his pocket and left the bathroom. Oh well, fuck it, he surmised. Too many women out there were going crazy over him for him to be sweating this uppity chick. He'd just forget about her.

Laura was bored. Lenky wasn't back yet and when she had called to see what time he'd be back, he told her not for another couple of hours as he was over in Portmore taking care of business.

Laura put on a pair of hipsters with some trendy Gucci sandals and grabbed the keys to her BMW X5. She decided to go to New Kingston and have a drink. She called her friend Michelle to find out if she wanted to hang out.

"Michelle, what's good?" Laura drawled in her transplanted Brooklyn accent.

"Hey L," Michelle replied sleepily. "When you got back?"

"Just today, you sound like you're in bed."

"Yeah, fighting the flu. Just took some meds and trying to get some sleep."

"Ok, girl, I'll come by and see you tomorrow. I bought the pink razor and those silver Manola Blahniks that you were going crazy over."

"Great! Thanks so much L," Michelle replied, sneezing. Laura was the best. Those boots cost eight hundred US dollars.

"Ok, see you tomorrow."

She contemplated calling Khianna but it wouldn't be the same without Michelle there. The three of them frequently hung out but she was much closer to Michelle.

Fuck it; let me go by Smooth and have a couple of drinks, Laura decided, as she climbed into her truck. Lenky had bought it for her as a wedding present. She planned to change it in another eleven months. Laura didn't think that she should drive the same vehicle for longer than two years.

The hip strip was bustling with activity when Laura got to New Kingston. The gate to the private parking lot across the road from Smooth was closed but a man quickly beckoned to Laura and hurried to open the gate. She figured he must have recognized that she was Lenky's wife.

"Yes, pretty girl," the man said as she paused by the entrance, "Just go straight down. Ah empty spot dung deh."

"Thanks," Laura told him and headed down to the end of the relatively small lot.

She parked, activated the alarm and strutted sexily towards the gate.

"Just gimme a small t'ing pretty girl," the man said when she reached the gate.

So he didn't know Lenky, Laura surmised; just a little hustler trying to make some money.

Laura gave him a five hundred dollar bill and walked off.

"Thanks, de ride safe, enjoy yuhself!" the man shouted as Laura crossed the street.

Jerome was leaving Smooth when Laura was walking in and they almost collided at the door. Jerome was looking down at his cell phone as he read a text message that Tara had just sent him. He looked up at the woman and froze in his tracks.

Maybe the night was not lost after all. The three girls he had been hanging out with were unable to shake the despondency he felt from Angela's rejection, despite his best efforts. Not even their offer of sharing his bed at the same time could cheer him up. So he had told them that he had something important to deal with and left abruptly. Laura returned his lustful gaze boldly as she slowly attempted to go around him.

Jerome held on to her hand gently.

"I know you're not just going to walk pass me like that," he said looking her up and down. She was the sexiest woman he had seen in a long time. A very long time.

Laura smiled. "Give me one good reason why I shouldn't?"

They were standing very close to each other. He was wearing Versace Dreamer, Laura noted appreciatively. God, she loved that scent.

Jerome smiled and discreetly placed her hand on his crotch. Laura gave it a firm squeeze before removing her hand. *Oh my god*, she thought. No fucking way that thing is real.

"You're a naughty boy," she whispered, leaning even closer to him. "Making me fondle you in public... I'm a married woman, you know."

"In that case, let's go somewhere more private and have a drink," Jerome replied.

"Is that right...where do you have in my mind?" Laura asked, stepping back a bit as she sized him up. He was fine. And that dick. Goodness gracious. It had felt so big and powerful.

"How about my apartment?" Jerome suggested. "I've got Alize... Hennessey... Hypnotiq....Remy...you name it."

Laura chuckled. "And what makes you think I'd just pick up and go home with a complete stranger?"

Jerome smiled. "I'm no stranger...look behind you."

Laura looked where he was pointing. His handsome face was plastered on a large billboard at the bus stop across the street. He was shirtless and holding a cell phone.

"Are you a model?"

"I'm a man of many talents," Jerome replied, looking directly into her eyes.

"Yo! Jerome!" someone shouted from a blue Lexus sedan that pulled up to the curb. It was Twitch, a singer from Jerome's old neighbourhood.

"Don't move a muscle," Jerome said as he went over to the car. Jerome stuck his head in the car and gave Twitch a pound.

"What's up man? Long time nuh see," Jerome said, nodding a greeting to the two girls and three men that Twitch had rolling with him.

"Yeah, fi real," Twitch replied. "Mi just come back from tour ah Europe."

Jerome looked up to see the woman he had been flirting with crossing the street. Damn, look at her ass! Jerome thought inwardly.

Twitch followed his gaze.

"Bloodclaat, 'Rome, dah one deh fit nuh rass!" he exclaimed, much to the annoyance of the girl seated in the front of his car.

"Trust mi rude boy," Jerome said. "Yo, we will link up a next time."

With that he hurried across the street to catch up with Laura. She was already through the gate.

Laura walked quickly to her vehicle. She wasn't sure why she was going to her truck instead of going inside the bar to have a drink as she had planned. Was it because she wanted the guy to follow her...or was it because she wanted to get away from the situation and drive off before she got herself in trouble? She suspected it was the former. She was in absolute heat. Never before did a complete stranger have such an aphrodisiac effect on her.

"Yes, balla," the man at the gate greeted Jerome. "Ah your girl dat?"

Jerome nodded at him and walked down to the end of the lot where the lights on a pearl white BMW X5 had just come on. He went around to the driver's side and flung the door open.

Laura looked at him in surprise. What the hell was he doing? Jerome grabbed her and kissed her passionately. After a moment's hesitation, she opened her mouth and allowed his insistent tongue to enter. She moaned in his mouth as she clutched him by his blazer. This was what her life was missing. Passion. And here she was, feeling it with a complete stranger.

They were both breathless when they finally broke the kiss.

Laura decided to throw caution to the wind. Maybe this guy was what she was looking for to ease her sexual frustration.

"How far is your apartment?" she croaked.

"Five minutes away," Jerome replied as he walked around to the passenger side.

He got in and Laura quickly exited the parking lot.

"You don't drive?" she asked on she turned onto Holborn Road.

"Yeah, but it's at the garage," Jerome replied. He owned a used Honda Prelude that he had purchased a little over a year and a half ago but he had decided to sell it as he didn't think it was a hot enough car for a guy like him. So it was parked with a For Sale sign at his friend's garage. Problem was; he couldn't afford to buy what he really wanted just yet so for the moment he was without his own ride. But he didn't think the girl needed to know all of that.

"Shit," Laura said as they reached his apartment.

"What?" Jerome asked. He fervently hoped that she wasn't getting cold feet.

"We don't even know each other's name," Laura said, chuckling as she switched off the engine.

Jerome laughed in relief. "I'm Jerome."

Laura grinned. "I'm Mystique."

"Now that the pleasantries are out of the way, let's go up to my apartment and pick up where we left off."

"Sounds good to me," Laura breathed.

They exited the SUV and Jerome held her hand as they strode purposefully up the stairs to his apartment. He noted with pleasure that Angela had receded to the very back of his mind; Mystique was the perfect distraction. Laura's cell phone rang as they entered the apartment. She retrieved it from her handbag and checked the caller ID. It was Lenky.

CHAPTER 7

"**W**here yuh at baby? Mi jus' call de house phone an' it ring without answer," Lenky asked.

"I'm over by Michelle," Laura told him, standing just inside the door of Jerome's living room. "Catching up on some girlie stuff."

Jerome returned from the bedroom and turned on the blue shaded night light.

Laura gasped. He was naked as he paraded to the kitchen to pour them some wine. His erection was enormous and looked as hard as granite. It hurt just to look at it. She leaned against the door for support.

"Yuh alright babes?" Lenky asked.

Laura coughed. "Yeah, Michelle has the flu and it seems as if she's passing on her germs to me."

Jesus Christ Lenky! Get off the damn phone, Laura thought irritably.

She wanted Jerome now.

"Nuh badda get sick enuh," Lenky warned. "Remember say mi big dance is coming up soon."

"I'll be fine, honey. See you later, ok?"

"Alright and nuh stay ova deh too late," Lenky said, and was about to tell her that he loved her when he realized Laura had already hung up.

Laura threw the phone and her handbag down on Jerome's couch and moved swiftly towards him. She kissed him hungrily as she braced him against the kitchen wall. Jerome placed his drink on the counter and cupped her voluptuous ass as he returned her kiss ardently. He spun her around against the wall and she put her hands in the air as he quickly removed her top. Their breathing was ragged as he deftly unhooked her bra and freed her 36 Cs. Laura moaned loudly and threw one leg around

Jerome as he sucked on her breasts.

"Mmmm...ohhh...." she moaned as Jerome pulled off her jeans. She stepped out of them quickly. She didn't have on any panties.

"God you're sexy," Jerome breathed as he admired her hour glass figure.

"Admire me later, fuck me now Jerome!" Laura declared wantonly as they tumbled onto the couch.

"Oh... god...don't... leave... any... marks... Jerome," Laura warned breathlessly as Jerome sucked and nibbled on her neck and breasts. Jerome reached down and palmed her fleshy vagina before inserting a finger. He was amazed at how tight she felt. And hot. Her pussy was on fire. He groaned and quickly put on a condom. Laura spread her legs wide and watched as Jerome inserted his dick.

"Oh shit....Jesus Christ...your dick is too big," she protested, placing her hands on his hips to hold him back.

"I won't give you more than you manage baby," Jerome assured her as he lay on top of her with half of his dick inserted.

"Ohhh...goddamn..." Laura swore as Jerome began to gyrate slowly, inching his dick in a little deeper with every move. It was an intricate mix of pleasure and pain. She couldn't tell where one ended and the other began.

Laura bit and scratched him as he fucked her at a slow, deliberate pace.

"Sweet ...Jesus...I think you're in my womb..."

Jerome flipped them over and entered Laura doggy style. Again he did not give her the full length of his dick.

"Fuck... yeah...you're hitting my spot Jerome!" Laura shouted as Jerome settled into a nice, even rhythm. Her luscious ass bounced with each stroke. He struggled to delay his climax. He knew if he wasn't wearing a condom he would've been a goner. Inside of her felt so good.

"Just ...like...that...oh...god...don't... stop...don't ...fucking... stop..."

Laura started bucking back against Jerome as she felt her orgasm rushing to the fore. Jerome was slapping her ass so hard she was sure the wings on the butterfly that she had tattooed on her right ass cheek had fallen off.

Jerome gritted his teeth as he felt his climax approaching.

He was about to explode.

"Ohhhhh...ohhhhh...ohhhh!" Laura squealed as she came violently, her ass a big blur as she moved it against Jerome's dick rapidly.

"Argghhhhh," Jerome grunted unintelligibly as he ejaculated while Laura was in the throes of her orgasm.

They crumbled to the sofa.

"Wow," Laura said softly, trying to catch her breath. "That was the bomb."

"It sure was," Jerome agreed, "I've never experienced a simultaneous orgasm before. Matter of fact, that's the quickest I've ever climaxed."

"Guess I'm too hard on my poor husband then huh?" Laura joked. "He never lasts longer than five minutes."

Jerome laughed. "You have the high-grade nookie for real babes."

Laura gave him a mock glower before cracking up. "Jerome, seriously though, where the hell did you get that dick? My god! That's too much dick for one man to have. I don't think I could ever take all of it."

Jerome merely laughed. He got up and went inside the kitchen to get them a drink.

Laura was sitting up on the couch when he returned. She looked at his dick swinging when he stood in front of her with the two glasses of wine. She took a glass from him and pulled him closer with her free hand. She rubbed her face sensuously against his genitals. She wanted to taste him. To drain him. To swallow everything that he had to offer. She took a sip of the wine and then placed the head of his shaft in her mouth. Jerome groaned as she sucked him sensuously. Her mouth ached as she attempted to take him deeper and deeper but she was determined to milk him dry. *Mystique is off the chain*, Jerome thought, savoring the sensations that were electrifying his body. He wondered which poor schmuck was her husband.

Lenky was fast asleep when Laura got home. She quietly went into the bathroom and took a quick shower. She would have loved to go to bed with Jerome's scent all over her but no can do. She climbed into the queen-sized bed beside a heavily snoring Lenky and fell asleep almost instantly. Her last conscious thought was of Jerome.

The next morning, Jerome arrived at the British Embassy a few minutes early for his 9 o' clock appointment. It would be his first visit to the UK and because the system had changed, Jamaicans now needed a visa to enter the country. He was confident he wouldn't be denied. He had letters of recommendation from the national coach and the Prime Minister, and he also had the letters of interest from the two British clubs who were interested in procuring his services.

He met with the dour-faced immigration representative who warmed to him when he realized that his favourite club, Manchester

FC, was interested in signing Jerome. He gave Jerome a multi-entry visa valid for three years, advising him that he would have to apply for a work permit if he indeed signed with one of the clubs. They chatted about football for a few more inutes and Jerome went out to the lobby where Tara was waiting on him. He had called her to give him a ride to the embassy and Tara, though tired from hanging with the girls late the night before, had gladly obliged.

"I take it all is well," she remarked as they went out to the parking lot. She snorted derisively at an unkempt taxi driver who had the audacity to ask them if they needed a cab.

"Yeah, everything criss," Jerome responded as Tara started the car using the remote and they hopped in.

"What do you want for breakfast?" Tara queried as they turned onto Knutsford Boulevard.

"Something heavy," Jerome replied. "Some dumpling and banana with either liver or ackee and saltfish would definitely hit the spot." He was famished. The two intense rounds with Mystique had thoroughly drained his body of all its nutrients. He wondered what she was doing. She had refused to give him her number, saying her husband was a very jealous and dangerous man, but she had taken his. He hoped she called before he left for England.

Tara grinned.

"Ok, we'll go to Terra Buena. They have a fabulous breakfast buffet every morning until eleven."

After breakfast, Tara dropped Jerome off at the Jamaica Football Association headquarters for his 12 p.m. meeting with the President, reminding him before she sped off about the party he had promised to accompany her to on Tuesday night. Jerome assured her he had not forgotten and went inside.

Stephanie, the receptionist, grinned when she saw Jerome.

"Hi Jerome, how are you?" she asked, instinctively taking a quick glance in the small mirror on her desk to see if she was looking her best. Rumour had it that Leo Barnes, the President, was screwing her. If he was, he was getting some good sex, Jerome mused.

Stephanie was very nimble. She had given him some positions in the small broom closet on the second floor that he hadn't thought possible in such a confined space.

"Sup Steph," Jerome replied, "Tell the boss I'm here, although I'm a few minutes early."

He plopped down on the sofa in the waiting area and began thumbing through an old issue of Sports Illustrated.

Stephanie buzzed the President's office and he told her to send him in. Jerome winked at her and knocked on the thick cedar door once before going in.

He was surprised to see that Leo was not alone.

"Jerome, good to see you, man," Leo enthused, getting up to shake his hand. "This is Ralph Rhoden; his Sports Apparel Company is one of our major sponsors. When I told him you were coming here today, he insisted on meeting you."

Elizabeth's husband, Jerome thought. He had seen the man several times but they had never officially met. He was a tall, fairly handsome man, and always impeccably attired. He carried himself with the self-assured ease that men born in wealth normally had.

"How are you, young man?" Ralph Rhoden shook his hand firmly, almost painfully. "I've heard a lot of good things about you. Apparently everyone thinks you are the second coming."

Jerome smiled modestly. "I'm just trying to do my part in making the team successful, sir."

"Humble!" Rhoden said to Leo. "How refreshing...athletes nowadays are so full of themselves."

"Jerome is a good kid," Leo said like a proud parent, adding, "and quite the ladies man."

"Hmm. Well, I've got to get going, Leo. I'll send that cheque over tomorrow." He grabbed his Louis Vuitton attaché case. "Good to meet you Jerome. My wife is a big fan of the Reggae Boyz. She never misses a game. You should meet her sometime."

Jerome swore that the man had a twinkle in his eye. Ralph Rhoden patted Jerome's shoulder and left. Jerome was a bit perturbed as he sat down in one of the comfortable leather chairs in front of Leo's large mahogany desk. He was willing to bet that somehow, Ralph Rhoden knew that he was messing with his wife.

"Hi baby," Laura said to Lenky as she made her way to the kitchen. Lenky was in the living room with two men she had never seen before.

"Hey, babes," he replied. "Mi think say yuh neva plan fi get up today."

It was now 12:15 p.m. and Laura was just venturing out of bed.

"Just felt like sleeping late," she replied as she poured a cup of coffee. "Gotta get my beauty sleep, boo."

Lenky grunted and resumed discussing business with the two men from Rocky Point in Clarendon. They were fishermen who had found close to twenty kilos of cocaine one morning when they went out to sea. Apparently the drugs had been thrown overboard by a boat that was being pursued by the Coast Guard.

They had made discreet enquiries and someone told them Lenky was the best person to see. The person had a cousin who knew how to get in touch with Lenky, so a meeting was set up and they came to Kingston.

Lenky chatted with the men for fifteen minutes, sizing them up. He surmised that the two men were out of their depth sitting in his upscale mansion discussing business. They were just simple fishermen who wanted some money for their find. They had brought a sample of the cocaine with them and it was pure, high quality Colombian. It was a damn good find; worth a lot of money. No way was he going to pay them the full value. Not even close.

Lenky stroked his goatee and made them an offer. The two men looked at each other and shrugged. They accepted and plans were made for Lenky to send someone to take the money to them in Rocky Point in exchange for the drugs. Lenky shook their hands and walked them to the door. He picked up the phone and called two young policemen that were on his payroll and told them that he had a job for them later that night.

He then went into the kitchen to join Laura who was eating a granola bar and watching a talk show.

"Yuh come home late last night," Lenky remarked as he poured himself some sour-sop juice and joined her at the kitchen counter.

"Yeah," Laura agreed, grinning at the antics of the two female guests on the talk show. The topic was *I'm sleeping with my sister's husband.* "Michelle and I had loads of things to talk about. Next thing I know it was late as hell."

"I have to go to Ocho Rios today," Lenky told her. "Yuh coming?"

"Nah, I'm going to the gym and then I have some errands to run," Laura replied, her eyes still glued to the screen. The Jerry Springer show was a guilty pleasure.

"Alright, later then; mi ah go get ready to leave." Lenky kissed his wife on the lips and went upstairs.

Angela was at the office having a chicken salad for lunch when her cell phone rang. She had just finished a session with her favourite patient – a nine year old boy that had endured a very bad spinal injury in a car accident. Fortunately his parents were well-off and could have afforded the expensive surgery that was necessary to ensure that their son would walk again, as well as the extensive physiotherapy that was needed post surgery. Angela thought he was so adorable.

"Hello."

"Hi, it's Jerome." Jerome was seated in the lobby of the JFA headquarters waiting on Lenky to pick him up. Lenky had called during his meeting asking if he wanted to go with him to Ocho Rios.

Angela sighed. She was hoping he wouldn't have called her again. Persistent bastard.

"Hi, Jerome. How are you?"

"I'm good, just had a meeting. About to go to Ocho Rios in a little while."

"Ok, have fun." Probably going with some hoochie.

"I just called to say hi...you know...see how you were doing." While waiting in the lobby for Lenky, she had crossed his mind and stayed there; prompting him to call despite his vow to forget her.

"That was nice of you. I'm fine...having a quick bite before my next patient arrives."

"I'm going to London on Thursday for a few days...I'd like to see you before I leave."

Here we go again, Angela thought.

"I don't think that's a good idea, Jerome...I mean...I don't want to lead you on in any way."

Jerome sighed.

"Ok, Angela, you take care."

Angela was thoughtful as she ate the last of her salad. Was she being too hard on him? Should she give him a chance? No, she decided. It was for the best. No way was she getting hurt again.

CHAPTER 8

L enky called Jerome at 1 p.m. informing him that he was outside in the parking lot. Jerome waved bye to Stephanie and headed out. He bumped into Paul, Gary and a couple other members of the national team when he got outside. Lenky's Lincoln Navigator was idling a few meters away.

"What's up, Jerome?" Paul said, "Everything cool?"

"Yeah, man, Leo wanted to see me to discuss some things," Jerome replied, giving hi-fives to all the guys.

"We just came by to look at the new gear that our sponsors sent over," Gary said. "When yuh leaving for England?"

"Thursday," Jerome told him. "Probably stay for only a week."

"Cool, you participating in the light training session tomorrow?" That was Tito, the lanky goalkeeper.

"Yeah man, see you guys tomorrow." Jerome walked off and hopped into the luxurious SUV where an impatient Lenky was waiting.

"Waddup Lenky," Jerome greeted as he slouched in the comfortable tan leather seat.

"Nutten much," Lenky replied, as he exited the parking lot and joined the Monday afternoon traffic streaming down St. Lucia avenue. "Have a meeting with a youth from Brixton. Him come down fi a short vacation so mi ah go link him fi sort out some business. After dat we can have some fun before we come back up. A new massage parlour open pon Content Avenue, mi hear say de gal dem look good."

"Ok, sounds like a plan," Jerome agreed. Eat some of that nice lobster and shrimp at the popular seafood restaurant on Main Street; then get a nice massage and whatever else the girls had to offer.

Laura met Michelle for a late lunch at a trendy new Japanese eatery in Constant Spring. Laura loved Japanese food and as Michelle knew absolutely nothing about Japanese cuisine, Laura ordered for the both of them.

Laura ordered sashimi with soya sauce for herself and chazuke with green tea for Michelle, who though feeling better, was still a bit weak from the flu.

"I have your stuff in the truck," Laura told her as they waited for the food.

"Great! Oooh, I can't wait to wear those Manola Blahniks," Michelle enthused.

"You can wear them to Lenky's big party next week," Laura suggested.

It was a courtyard style restaurant and they were seated in a shaded area a couple of seats away from three businessmen who kept looking at the two attractive women. Laura was wearing a tight fitting Burberry polo-style top with Dolce & Gabbana shorts that showcased her hour-glass figure in all its glory, and trendy Christian Louboutin sandals. She topped it off with aviator Gucci shades and a Louis Vuitton pocketbook.

Michelle had her long curly hair – courtesy of her Indian mother – tucked under a Hermes cap and wore a Prada peasant blouse with skin tight True Religion jeans.

They were a formidable pair.

"Girl, I had so much fun last night," Laura told Michelle.

"Ok, you went on the road with Khianna?"

"Nah, went by myself," Laura replied as the waiter who appropriately resembled a sumo wrestler, presented their meals.

"Where you went?" Michelle asked; her face made up as she looked at the dish in front of her. "Eww! This looks disgusting, L!"

"Girl please...just try it....pretend its oatmeal," Laura said dismissively. "Anyways, I had a one night stand last night."

"What! For real?" Michelle was incredulous. Laura was known for stringing guys out for a long time and getting what she wanted out of them before giving up the coochie, if any at all.

"Yep...I can't explain it Michelle." She paused as she searched for the right words to articulate her feelings. "There was just this ridiculous chemistry between me and this guy. I mean...we connected."

"Damn...so how was it?" Michelle tasted the chazuke and was pleasantly surprised to find it quite tasty. Different, but good.

"Oh my god...Michelle...best sex I ever had. We had simultaneous orgasms! It was awesome. And his dick...it was fucking enormous!"

Michelle laughed. "This guy sounds like something special."

"He's fine too...apparently he's some model or something...I saw his picture on a billboard in New Kingston advertising cell phones."

"Hold on...you mean that billboard across the road from Smooth and he's shirtless?"

"Yeah, that's the one," Laura concurred.

"I know him!" Michelle said excitedly. "My cousin Gary plays for the Reggae Boyz and your stud muffin is the star player on the team. He scored the winning goal against the US in that crucial World Cup qualifying game."

"Shit. If he plays football Lenky must know him. You know Lenky never misses a game," Laura said thoughtfully.

"Well, it was a one night stand...right?"

Laura sighed. Hell no, but it was best to keep that to herself. Actually she was sorry she had mentioned it to Michelle.

"Yeah, it was...I'll never see him again."

"Well I don't know about that girl," Michelle remarked. "You probably will see him around but if you know what's good for you, don't let on that you know him if you're with Lenky. You know how jealous he is and trust me...Jerome is a known 'cocksman'."

Michelle chuckled. "So it's true what they say about his dick, huh?"

"Trust me...whatever you heard multiply it by two," Laura replied, still deep in thought. *Good thing I had given him a fake name,* Laura surmised; *and he doesn't have my number. I am in control.*

Jerome and Lenky made good time on the road. A little over an hour after leaving Kingston, they were almost at Fern Gully, just four miles outside of Ocho Rios. Lenky took out his phone to check up on his wife.

"Hi baby," he said when she came on the line.

"Hey, what's up?" Laura replied, sipping a glass of red wine, which went so well with the sashimi.

"Almost reach Ochie, me and one of mi brethren ah spar since yuh neva want fi come wid me."

"Don't say that babes. I told you I had things to do."

"Just troubling you baby....anyways you will meet him later when we come home. Ah big star."

"Is he now...what kind of star?"

"Later yuh will find out baby...yuh go gym already?"

Laura did not like the sound of that. Her instinct told her that it was Jerome. Once Jerome's identity had been established, she distinctly remembered Lenky having mentioned to her during one of their daily telephone conversations while she was in New York that he was hanging out with the best footballer that this side of the world had ever seen. She hadn't paid it any mind because for one she wasn't a sports fan and two, Lenky was forever babbling about football like an excited child. Wow, it was such a small world. She would have to call Jerome before he came to the house and prepare him so that he wouldn't give them away.

"No, not yet; having a late lunch with Michelle before I go."

"Alright, later then."

Michelle ate the last of the chazuke and dabbed her pouty lips with a napkin.

"What's wrong?"

Laura looked perturbed.

"Lenky does know Jerome. They are actually on their way to Ocho Rios now."

"Fuck! Yuh sure?"

"Not a hundred percent...but...I'm positive because Lenky said he's going to introduce me to a big star when he comes back to Kingston this evening. I remember him telling me a few weeks back that he was hanging out with this star football player so..."

"Yeah, you might be right. What are you going to do? You have to call him L. If you don't have his number I'm sure I can get it from Gary."

"I have it but he's with Lenky now...probably it's best I send him a text message."

"Ok, do that then."

Laura whipped out her Blackberry and sent Jerome a message: *Hi Jerome, it's Mystique. Please call me urgently but don't do it until you are alone.*

Jerome's phone beeped as they entered the bustling tourist oriented town of Ocho Rios. He frowned when he read the message.

He would call her while Lenky was discussing business with the guy from England.

"What happen?" Lenky asked as he headed to the hotel where the guy was staying.

"Oh nothing...just a message from this chick I met last night."

"Fuck her?"

"Yeah, man."

Lenky laughed loudly. "Yes, star boy...ah so de t'ing set up."

Jerome chuckled and turned up the volume on the CD player. They were listening to a mix CD with the latest dancehall hits and his favourite new song just came on.

Jerome's cell phone rang as Lenky conferred with the security at the entrance of the Full Moon Resort and Spa. The security guard wrote down the fake name that Lenky gave him and the license plate number of the vehicle and waved them in.

It was Dimples calling from Miami.

"Hi baby," she gushed. "How yuh doing?"

"I'm good babes, when yuh coming down?"

"Friday, supposed to arrive at 7 p.m."

"Ok, I won't see you until next week though...going to London on Thursday."

"Ok, for the tryouts with the clubs right?"

"Yeah."

"Alright baby, good luck and make sure you choose right."

"Yeah, man."

"I bought some really nice stuff for you. Roberto Cavalli's new line is wicked and I got you some Ed Hardy gear as well."

They entered the crowded lobby and Lenky walked over to one of the representatives who were assisting the many guests who had obviously just arrived and were checking in, while Jerome sat down on one of the few empty chairs and continued his conversation with Dimples.

"That sounds good baby," Jerome said. Dimples could always be counted on to get him the hot stuff. Too bad he wouldn't get them before his trip to London. No worries though. He still had a few new pieces he hadn't yet worn.

He listened to Dimples tell him how much she missed him and couldn't wait to feel him inside her as Lenky beckoned towards to the elevator. The guy was staying in room 3D on the third floor.

A fat Caucasian couple with a German accent rode with them to the third floor. The man was wearing one of the ugliest floral shirts Jerome had ever seen. They exited the elevator and Jerome wrapped up the call with Dimples after she promised to send him some money to purchase a few hundred pounds for spending money while he was in England. Lenky knocked on the door and a British accent shouted that it was open. Lenky opened the door and they went in.

The guy, whose name was Gunner, greeted them warmly and introduced them to his cousin, who lived in Jamaica, and his girl-friend, a slender girl with large, oval-shaped eyes who was also from Brixton. When Lenky and Gunner went out on the balcony to discuss business, Jerome excused himself and went out into the corridor to call Mystique.

She answered on the first ring.

"Hi sexy, what's up?" Jerome asked.

"A helluva lot," Laura replied. "You're alone right?"

"Yeah, man," Jerome answered impatiently; he was anxious to find out what was going on.

"Ok. First of all...do you know anyone named Lenky?"

"Yeah..."

"He's my husband."

"Oh Shit!" Jerome couldn't believe it.

"And my name is Laura, not Mystique."

"Rass...I'm in Ocho Rios with Lenky right now! He's my good friend...I can't believe this shit," Jerome bemoaned.

"Listen, it is what it is...what's done cannot be undone. The main thing now is not to let Lenky find out," Laura told him forcefully, taking command of the situation. "He's going to bring you by the house tonight so you had better start practicing your poker face."

"Damn," Jerome muttered, still in disbelief.

"Listen, Jerome, snap out of it!" Laura said. "Don't tell me you are so scared of Lenky that you can't think straight."

That got Jerome's attention. "Aint nobody scared girl...I'm just shocked...I mean...what are the odds of this happening?"

"Well, I don't give a fuck if it's a million to one...fact is it has happened and I need to know you'll play your part in keeping this under wraps."

The initial shock was beginning to wear off and Jerome analyzed the situation.

"Its all good...I'll play it cool when I come by the house later."

"Good."

"So...what does this mean...we won't hook up again?"

"You tell me...you're the one who couldn't even breathe when I told you who my husband was..."

"Stop trying to diss me. I was just shocked. Of course we can still see each other...just have to be really careful."

"Good boy...thought you didn't want anymore of this sweet, tight pussy..."

Jerome laughed. Laura was crazy. He did want some more though, despite the danger. A death warrant if Lenky found out. Maybe they were both crazy.

"You know I do...and I know you want some more of this big, thick sugar cane..."

"Got that right," Laura replied with a laugh.

"We won't be back in town for awhile yet anyway," Jerome told her. "Lenky's in a meeting now and we have some rounds to make afterwards."

"Ok, so I guess I'll see you later."

Jerome remembered something.

"Laura..."

"Huh?"

"Lenky really never lasts longer than five minutes?"

Laura laughed.

"Bye Jerome..."

Jerome slipped the phone in his pocket after Laura hung up and went back into the room.

"Yuh play for Jamaica right?" Gunner's cousin asked when Jerome came in and took a seat on a chair by the large dresser. Lenky was still on the balcony in an animated discussion with Gunner.

Yeah," Jerome replied.

"Mi tell yuh say is him!" he exclaimed to his cousin's girlfriend. "Trust me him wicked man!"

Jerome merely smiled. He wished Lenky would hurry up. He was getting very hungry.

Angela met her dad at his favourite restaurant on Dumfries Road after she left the office at 4 p.m. It was a small, quaint establishment, known to people in certain circles as Kingston's best kept secret. Her father loved it and had been eating there for as long as Angela could remember.

"Hi daddy," Angela said greeting him with a kiss on his freshly shaven cheek.

"How's my little girl?" David Charlton asked as he hugged his favourite child. He loved Sara too, but Angela was his heart.

"I'm good. Today was a pretty easy going day," Angela told him. They tried to have dinner with each other at least once a week. Her mother, who had a doctorate in economics, was currently in Barbados doing a series of lectures at the University of Barbados on globalization and its ramifications for the Caribbean region. Angela had a relatively good relationship with her mom but she was much closer to her father.

"Good, I'm famished and I took the liberty of ordering for both of us the moment I arrived," David told his daughter. "I ordered steak for me and grilled salmon for you."

"Ok cool, that's fine daddy."

Their food arrived fairly quickly and they immediately dug in.

"I'm going to South Africa with your Uncle Greg in another year and a half," David commented.

"What for?" Angela licked her lips. The salmon was divine.

"World Cup!" her dad exclaimed excitedly. "Didn't you know that Jamaica qualified?"

"So I've heard, but it's not a big deal to me," Angela replied.

"Well big deal it is my dear daughter," David told her. "It's going to be an historic moment when the Jamaican anthem is played on that pitch and the flag is raised. Where is your civic pride?"

Angela made a face at him.

"That Jerome James is something else, he is so talented," her daddy continued.

"I met him the other day," Angela remarked casually.

"Really," David replied, arching his bushy, grey eyebrows. Jerome James had quite a reputation as a ladies man. Football star or not, he didn't want him anywhere near his little girl.

"Yeah, Joan and I were having a drink and he came over to our table." Angela sipped her carrot juice.

"And..." David prompted.

"And nothing...he invited me out and I refused. There's no way I'd date someone like him. Too much drama."

"Well, that's good. He seems like a nice enough fellow but he has a certain reputation." David was satisfied. Angela was generally level headed, except for her failure to see that creep Brian for what he was before it was too late. He wanted her to meet a nice, Christian young man and get married. He wanted some grandkids. He had given up on Sara and they rarely spoke. She had turned out to be a promiscuous, selfish and immoral young woman. He cringed anytime he thought of what she had done to her sister. Sleeping with Angela's boyfriend had been such a low and disgusting act. After a long list of atrocities that had blemished the family name, that had been the final straw. David had been tempted to cut her out of the will; only her mother's intervention had saved her. He had envisioned great things for his two lovely daughters, and while Angela was on the right path, Sara was a great disappointment to him. Last he heard she was an air hostess with a British airline. David sighed as he remembered a line from one of his favourite movies, Forrest Gump. *Life is like a box of chocolates. You never know what you're going to get.* So true.

Jerome's stomach growled angrily as he and Lenky exited the hotel. He was famished. Lenky was in high spirits after his meeting with Gunner. The Brixton youth had agreed to purchase fifty kilos of cocaine from Lenky, and if the shipment arrived safely and all was well, he would only purchase from Lenky in the future. Also, the two policemen he had instructed to go to Rocky Point to pick up the drugs were on their way. He had left four hundred and fifty thousand dollars at the house for them to take as payment. It was only half of the amount he had agreed to pay the fishermen. Lenky figured that was enough and most generous on his part as it would've been quite easy for him to take the drugs from them without paying a cent. But he considered himself to be a fair man. They hopped in the truck and Lenky drove to King of the Sea, one of Ocho Rios' most popular seafood restaurants. The place was packed, but it was large, with indoor and outdoor seating, and the waiters were plenty and efficient. They received their order of lobster served with the special house sauce, shrimp and festival in twenty minutes.

Their meal was interrupted several times by ardent football fans but Jerome didn't mind and happily signed a few autographs. They lingered at the table for awhile after eating; Lenky enjoyed a small spliff while Jerome thought about Angela. He decided he was going to have her. He didn't know why he liked her so much but he did, and he would not stop until she gave in. When he got back from England he would turn up the pressure. After all, he was Jerome James. Lenky finished his spliff and they made their way to the parking lot. It was time to visit the new massage parlour.

CHAPTER 9

T he massage parlour was situated in a lovely nine bedroom, six bathroom dwelling on Content Avenue. There was no sign, and the gate was manned by a slightly overweight, armed security guard. He opened the automatic gate when they drove up and they entered the premises and parked in the expansive driveway. Four other vehicles were parked on the premises. They were all expensive cars, underscoring the fact that this was an up-scale parlour. They were met at the door by the hostess. She was a matronly woman of about fifty, dressed in a navy blue business suit. She smiled pleasantly at the men and welcomed them in.

"How are you gentlemen doing today?" She queried as she led them to the living room which served as the reception area. They sat down on a large leather couch and she sat opposite them and offered them something to drink. The men declined and they got down to business.

She handed them two folders which consisted of the type of massages offered and photographs of each available masseuse, along with a brief biography. Prices were not displayed. It was implied that if the price had to be asked, one was in the wrong place.

Lenky was right, Jerome mused as he examined the photos. The girls, none of whom looked a day over twenty-five, were all very attractive. He selected Isabel, a voluptuous twenty year old from Cuba, and Natalie, a tall, svelte nineteen year old from St.

Mary. He chose the Wet Set Massage which consisted of the two women in the shower with him, titillating his body using foamy, scented bath gel. That would be followed by a sensuous massage, including stimulation of the genitals to orgasm, with fragranced oil.

Lenky selected, Cora, a tall, thick, light-skinned, twenty three year old cutie from Cuba, and he selected the French Massage, which consisted of his masseuse performing a striptease before giving him a sensuous massage.

The hostess smiled when they made their selections and went over to the lovely antique desk where she spoke quietly into the telephone. The three selected women appeared almost immediately into the living room. They all wore wide smiles, tiny bikinis and stilettos. Lenky gave the hostess a credit card, and the women came over and introduced themselves to the two men. Once the payment was processed, the hostess told them to enjoy, and the women led them around to where the first floor bedrooms were situated. All the ones upstairs were presently occupied.

The ladies took them into adjoining rooms. Jerome looked around appreciatively; the room was spacious and sparsely furnished, but tastefully decorated. He stood in the middle of the room next to the bed and the two women undressed him slowly. Isabel, the Cuban, eyed him seductively as she unbuckled his jeans and pulled them down to his ankles, kneeling as she did so. He stepped out of his jeans and Natalie hung them in the closet along with his shirt. Isabel reached up to gently tug off his boxers. Her eyes were wide when his dick sprang free. She looked at Natalie wide-eyed and they both grinned.

"Now that is what you call a dick!" Natalie exclaimed.

"Si," Isabel agreed, nodding her head enthusiastically as she removed her bikini set.

Jerome sat on the bed and admired the two women. Iasbel was short and curvy, with beautiful skin. Her breasts were large and firm, and her vagina was cleanly shaven with a little landing strip above it. Her clit was prominent and juicy. Natalie was all legs, leading up to the one of the plumpest vaginas Jerome had ever seen. Her pussy looked as if it had been stung by an entire hive of bees. She smiled when Jerome kept staring at her crotch.

"You thought you were the only one blessed in that department?" She asked saucily.

Jerome grinned. It was certainly a pussy to be proud of, he thought. She could win a 'fat kitty kat' contest held anywhere in the world. They took him by hand and led him into the shower. Isabel turned on the tap and Jerome moaned as the women lathered him from head to toe with scented bath gel and gently rubbed him all over. They did not miss a spot. It was an exhilarating feeling. He was extremely horny. His dick was so hard it was almost painful. The veins bulged and the head of his dick was an angry red; anxious for release. He knew he wouldn't take long to climax once they started to give him the sensuous massage. After being in the shower for fifteen minutes, they went into the bedroom and Jerome relaxed on his back on the bed. Natalie massaged his upper body while Isabel concentrated on his dick. Her small hands gripped his pulsing phallus almost lovingly as she stroked him languidly. She skillfully brought to him to the brink of orgasm three times before pushing him over the edge. His ejaculation was forceful and powerful. Yet, despite shooting such a torrid load, he remained rock-hard. The women were suitably impressed.

"Lets get down to real business," Jerome said, getting up to retrieve his wallet from his jeans in the closet.

"How much for extras?" he asked, standing with the wallet open in his hand, his dick in front of him, waving like an iron flag.

When the women took too long to answer, he extracted two hundred US dollars and placed it on the bedside table. "This should cover everything," he said, putting down his wallet. Jerome sat on the bed and Isabel slid to her knees and placed his swollen shaft in her hot mouth. Natalie sucked on his nipples, eliciting loud groans from Jerome. That was his spot. He reached over and played with her fat vagina, again marveling at its plumpness. It was so juicy and fleshy. And wet. He wanted to be inside it. Now. He gently held Isabel's head, and indicated for her to stop. Jerome then got up and quickly put on a condom. Natalie, eager to be filled by his massive tool, scampered to her knees and positioned herself doggystyle on the edge of the bed. Though she hadn't let on that she knew him, she was a huge football fan and would've fucked him for free. Any time. Any place. She loved money though, and a hundred US dollars wasn't a bad tip.

Her luscious vagina gaped obscenely in the air. Jerome groaned and got behind her. He slid his dick inside her slowly until he was balls deep. Isabel positioned herself in front of Natalie with her legs spread, and Natalie licked her between groans as she savoured the unfamiliar feeling of her pussy being stretched to capacity.

Lenky collapsed on the bed after his third orgasm in the past hour. Everytime he ejaculated quickly and thought that was it, Cora would resume tantalizing his body with that hot knowledgeable tongue of hers, and bring him back to life. *Dah gal yah is something else*, Lenky thought breathlessly. *Ah need a spliff an' a well cold Guiness yah now.*

Lenky got to the lobby a few minutes before Jerome and conversed with the hostess while he waited.

"I trust you had a good time," she said sweetly, sitting opposite him on the couch.

"Yeah, man," Lenky replied, "definitely coming back anytime mi deh ah Ochie."

"That's good to hear," she responded, as Jerome came into the living room. He had taken Natalie's phone number, promising to call her whenever he was in the area.

Lenky rose from the couch and they thanked the hostess and went out to the driveway. It was now 5:15 p.m. and the sun was getting ready to hide behind the clouds.

"Jah know," Lenky said as they exited the premises, "Dat ah de best fuck mi ever spend money pon."

Jerome laughed and nodded in agreement. "Yeah, man. De gal dem gwaan good, trust me."

Lenky stopped at a weed spot that was run by a Rastafarian he knew called Diplomat, and purchased a bag of marijuana. He deftly rolled a big spliff and they headed out of Ocho Rios. Jerome relaxed in his seat and admired the beauty of Fern Gully in the sunset as Lenky cruised the luxurious vehicle towards Kingston. He yawned contentedly. It had been a good day. His mind drifted to Laura. They would have to be extremely careful not give any sign of recognition when they 'met' later that evening. If Lenky even suspected that they knew each other there would be hell to pay. Jerome wasn't scared of Lenky, or so he tried to convince himself, but he knew Lenky would kill him if he found out he was fucking his wife. Even before he had become friends with Lenky he had heard stories about him. Lenky was not a man to cross. *Oh well*, Jerome surmised, *he won't find out and in another couple of months, all being well, I'll be playing in the English League and Laura will be a distant memory.*

"Yuh alright rude boy?" Lenky asked, taking a deep drag of the potent weed.

"Yeah, man," Jerome replied, "Everyt'ing criss."

CHAPTER 10

Officer Cuthbert, one of the policemen on Lenky's payroll that he had sent to retrieve the drugs from the fishermen in Rocky Point, slowed the squad car as he neared an old, white Toyota pick-up truck that was parked by a dilapidated house a few meters away from the fishing village. He had called the fishermen half an hour ago and they had agreed to wait for him by the roadside just past the fishing village. The area would not be crowded at that time in the evening as most of the fishermen would already be home after hauling in the day's catch. He pulled up behind the vehicle and honked his horn twice. The two fishermen alighted from the truck and walked over to the police car.

Officer Cuthbert and his partner, Officer Radcliffe, also known as 'Wolf' for his predatory attitude and appearance, watched as the two fishermen nervously approached the vehicle.

"We shouldn't even give dem country bwoy yah ah cent enuh," Officer Radcliffe murmured, his face in a harsh scowl.

"Fi real," Officer Cuthbert agreed. Lenky didn't have to know. On the way to Clarendon, they had pulled over on the side of the road on highway 2000 a few minutes after exiting the toll booth, and counted the money. Four hundred and fifty thousand in cash. *I'll just give them a hundred an' mi an' mi partner keep de rest*, he surmised, stroking his thin goatee thoughtfully, wrinkling his nose at the pungent odour of fish in the humid air.

"Evenin'," Brownie, the taller of the two fishermen respectfully greeted the policemen when they got to the car. The other man remained silent. His face was stoic but his mind was churning. He knew one of the policemen. 'Wolf' had been originally stationed in Clarendon before being transferred to Kingston where he had further enhanced his reputation as a dirty cop who would do anything for money. Calvin's gut instinct told him they would try and cheat them out of the money. He couldn't have that as he was depending on his share of the money to pay for his common-lawwife's badly needed surgery. She had developed a rare eye condition and was rapidly going blind. It could be corrected by surgery in Cuba but it was expensive. His share of the eight hundred thousand that Lenky was supposed to pay them for the drugs would go a long way in coming up with the amount needed.

"Weh de drugs deh?" Officer Radcliffe demanded rudely, attempting to intimidate the two fishermen.

Brownie flinched at the venom in the cop's tone and stammered a response that it was in the back of the pick-up disguised as bags of chicken feed. Radcliffe noted that the quiet one did not seem to be scared of him. He took offense to that. He, who had made so called 'shottas' in Kingston quake in fear, would not condone being eyeballed by a fucking country bumpkin – conveniently forgetting the fact that he too, hailed from the country – deep rural country at that, a hilly, bushy community known as Trout Hall in the hills of Clarendon.

He came out of the squad car and walked around to where the men were standing.

"Hey bwoy," he snarled, holding on to the butt of his service weapon. "Ah who yuh ah look pon so like yuh a bad man?"

"Chill out, Wolf," Officer Cuthbert said to his partner, as he grinned and stepped out of the vehicle. "We nuh come yah fi dat."

Officer Radcliffe ignored his partner and gave Calvin a vicious back-handed slap that rocked him and stung his face mightily.

"You!" Radcliffe shouted, pointing at Brownie, who was now shaking in fear and wondering just what he had gotten himself into. "Go get the drugs and put it inna de car trunk. We nuh have nuh more time fi waste."

"Where is the money?" Calvin demanded calmly, looking directly in the policeman's eyes. He was ready for anything. He would not allow them to leave with Pat's surgery money.

"Hey bwoy yuh want fi bloodclaat dead?" Officer Radcliffe asked in disbelief, he couldn't believe the man had the audacity to challenge him. He reached for his firearm.

Laura was by the poolside with Michelle, having drinks and playing a game of dominoes when they heard the unmistakable roar of the powerful V12 engine of the Lincoln Navigator in the driveway. Lenky was home.

"Ok, girl," Laura said, smiling. "This is the big test. How's my poker face?"

"You gwaan joke around," Michelle replied, feeling nervous excitement. She just loved drama.

"Whatever," Laura said, taking a sip of her white wine. "I've got this covered like insurance."

Michelle gave her the 'hand' and sat back to watch the drama unfold. Lenky and his friend, presumably Jerome, had entered the house talking loudly. Michelle watched them through the large glass door as they strolled through the living room and made a beeline for the pool when Lenky realized that's where his wife was.

"Hey baby," Lenky said as he reached them, bending to hug Laura from behind. He nodded at Michelle. "Feeling better? Mi hear say yuh did have flu."

"Yes, much better, thanks," Michelle replied, but she was staring at Jerome. He didn't seem to be nervous at all.

Laura twisted in her chair a bit. She decided that the best defense was a good offense. "So where's your friend you wanted me to meet?"

"Si di star boy yah," Lenky proudly replied as Jerome stepped around to stand beside Laura. "Baby, meet Jerome, best footballer ever fi come out ah Jamaica. 'Rome meet mi wife, Laura."

Jerome was surprised at how at ease he felt. The moment of guilt had passed long ago when Laura had first told him the news.

"Hi, Laura. Nice to finally meet you." He shook her hand, holding on to it a tad longer than necessary. Her eyes told him to chill and not get cocky.

"Same here," She replied, relieved that he seemed to be in control.

"An' dis is her good friend Michelle," Lenky added, gesturing at Michelle.

Jerome and Michelle shook hands and exchanged pleasantries as Lenky shouted for the chef. He felt for a snack. The delicious seafood he had devoured in Ocho Rios had worn off.

"Yuh hungry 'Rome?" he asked, as he pulled a chair up beside his wife.

"Nah," Jerome replied, "could use a drink though."

"Baby, bring a bottle of henessey and two red bull come,"Lenky instructed his wife.

She rose to do his bidding.

"An' bring a bucket of ice!" He shouted to her departing back.

Michelle sipped some more wine and looked at the two men. She was a bit disappointed that the 'meeting' had gone so smoothly. Of course she hadn't wanted them to give away themselves, but at the very least she had been hoping for some tension.

"So how was Ocho Rios?" she asked, staring at Jerome and suppressing a grin as she remembered what Laura had said about Jerome's dick and sexual prowess.

"Ochie was ok," Jerome responded coolly, extracting a cigarette from the pack in his shirt pocket and lighting it. He took a deep drag and exhaled into the cool night air.

"So how does it feel being the subject of so much hype?" Michelle queried. Mmmm, nice lips. Nice arms. Nice everything it seems. No wonder Laura had gotten caught up. The man was the poster child for the cliché: tall, dark and handsome. She had seen him before but had never been so close to him. He had this animal magnetism and she could feel herself being drawn to him. *Calm your little self Michelle*, she said inwardly. *Can't be sharing men with your best friend, that's a no no.*

"It's cool," Jerome replied nonchalantly. "I don't really let it get to my head...just try and be the best player I can be...playing at the highest level."

"Ok...its exciting to watch you play," Michelle said, "I was at the game against the US the other day. That was a rass move you made to secure the penalty."

The men laughed boisterously. There was nothing sexier than an attractive woman who understood and loved sports.

"Too bad yuh can't get Laura fi appreciate the game," Lenky lamented. He loved when his wife accompanied him places and he loved to attend football games. Laura wasn't interested and would not go to any games with him no matter how much he begged.

"What you guys out here saying about me?" Laura asked, as she placed the tray with the liquor and ice on the table.

She sat in Lenky's lap.

"Be careful baby, I might have to lock you out of the bedroom... put you on suspension," She teased, as everyone laughed.

"How come you know so much about football?" Jerome asked, enjoying the conversation with Michelle. She was really cool. Cute too. Reminded him of that R&B singer, Amerie.

"Football has always been a big part of my family. Matter of fact, my cousin, Gary, is your teammate on the national team."

"What!" Jerome exclaimed. "Gary never told me he had such a pretty cousin."

Michelle was surprised to find herself blushing. What the hell?

"Look like is a matchmaking t'ing ah gwaan yah so," Lenky teased as he poured himself a drink.

Laura grinned but she was seething inside. She couldn't believe Jerome was flirting with Michelle and that Michelle was lapping it up. If she ever...

"But wait, mi never call de chef 'bout fifteen minutes ago? Weh de rass him deh?" Lenky growled. "Him nuh know say him fi deh pon call roun' de clock?"

"Calm down, Lenky," Laura said. "What do you want to eat? I'll call and order some food. Bigga told me he was going on the road."

Lenky sucked his teeth but he relented. "Order some pizza...ground beef, pepperoni and extra cheese."

"Lenky, I'm about to roll out," Jerome told him, standing and stretching his lanky frame.

"How yuh ah go reach home?" Lenky asked. "Yuh want mi fi drop you down?"

"No man, don't worry yourself," Jerome replied, "I'll call a cab."

"I'll drop you home," Michelle offered, avoiding Laura's eyes. She could sense that Laura was not pleased with her. *Whatever. I'm just giving the guy a ride home for fuck sakes! It's not like I'm going to sleep with him or anything.* "I need to get going anyway."

"All right, dat is settled then," Lenky said, getting up as well. He knocked fists with Jerome and told him he would see him tomorrow.

Jerome waved bye to Laura who waved back with a warning in her eyes. Jerome grinned inwardly. She was jealous!

"Bye, L, talk to you later," Michelle said, as she gathered her things.

"Yeah, I'll definitely be calling you later," Laura replied, looking at Michelle pointedly. *If you think you're gonna take my new found spoogie away from me, you've got another thing coming darlin',* she thought. *Damn white liva coolie gal.* Michelle smiled at the veiled warning and walked off to catch up with Lenky and Jerome who had gone ahead. Laura was acting as if Jerome was hers. Not that she was planning to act on her attraction to Jerome, but if she did, Laura had no reason to be upset. She was a fucking married woman. Lenky went upstairs to take a shower while a silently fuming Laura picked up the phone to order the pizza. Michelle and Jerome let themselves out and walked slowly to Michelle's Silver Rav 4.

"The view up here is so nice," Jerome said, casually draping his arm around Michelle's shoulders. "When I sign my big contract, I'm going to buy a house either up here or in Beverly Hills."

Up until that point, Michelle had been undecided as to whether she would yield to temptation and sleep with Jerome, but from the moment he touched her, her body made the decision for her. A simple hug and there she was, creaming her panties.

She cleared her throat.

"Yes, it's really nice," She managed, fishing for her keys when they got to the car. She deactivated the alarm and they got in. Jerome reclined comfortably in the passenger seat and placed his hand on Michelle's left thigh, rubbing it gently through her Capri pants. She didn't object as she exited the driveway and turned onto the main road. The only question now was his place or hers.

Calvin sprang into action quickly to prevent the rogue cop from pulling his firearm. As fast as he moved, however, Radcliffe was still able to get a good grip on his gun. They wrestled as Calvin tried to disarm him.

"Yo! Weh yuh a do?" Officer Cuthbert shouted as he pulled his firearm. "Release the officer and step away!"

Brownie was rooted to the spot, watching in terror as his friend struggled with the cop. The commotion had attracted a gang of teenagers from the community and they walked slowly towards the scene. One of them, Pat's sixteen year old brother, realized that it was Calvin and Brownie in trouble.

"Mek wi stone dem rass," he said to the group of boys and grabbed two rocks from the roadside. He sailed the first one in the back window of the squad car, smashing it to pieces.

Officer Cuthbert spun around with his gun trained on the approaching youths.

"Oonu want fi dead? Go home now!" He shouted. "Police business!"

A rock sailed dangerously close to his ear in response. He fired two shots in the air. Radcliffe paused momentarily at the sound of the gunshots and Calvin used that split second to his advantage. He elbowed Radcliffe in the nose and was rewarded with a popping sound and gushing blood.

"Yah fool Babylon bwoy!" One of the youths shouted as they all rained large rocks on the squad car and on Cuthbert who got hit by one in the head. He angrily fired at the group of boys and a loud scream indicated that one of them had been hit. Angry shouts were heard coming towards them and Officer Cuthbert dashed to the car, shouting for Radcliffe to follow him. He hopped in and started the car but didn't drive off when he realized that the fisherman had disarmed Radcliffe and was pointing the gun at him. Radcliffe was on his knees clutching his bloody face in agony.

"Pass the money!" Calvin said to him calmly but forcefully. Cuthbert obliged, throwing the large bag of money out the window. They had to go quickly before the mob descended on them. He couldn't believe the situation had deteriorated into this. He couldn't call for back up due to the circumstances, and anyway, the nearest police station was some fifteen miles away. Calvin shouted to Brownie to take up the bag. Brownie responded jerkily as if suddenly awakening from a deep stupor and snatched the bag off the ground. Calvin kicked Radcliffe and told him if he didn't want to be beaten to death he'd better get going. Radcliffe grunted in humiliation and pain, and staggered to the vehicle. Cuthbert drove away hurriedly as several items pelted the vehicle. How the fuck was he going to explain the destruction of the car to headquarters? He would have to run the vehicle off a precipice or something and report that he had an accident. Then there was the matter of Lenky. How would he explain to Lenky that he didn't have his money or the drugs? This was a fucking nightmare.

CHAPTER 11

Angela curled up in bed with the novel she had purchased from a bookstore in the plaza where she had bought lunch earlier that day. It was a spy thriller and was quite riveting. However, her mind kept drifting. Jerome kept penetrating her thoughts. Admittedly, she liked him. He was handsome, out-going, athletic, and apparently, going places. On the flip side, he was also young, flashy, popular and clearly in the fast lane. Not exactly her cup of tea. She was lonely though, and longing for stimulating, long-term male companionship. Maybe she should give him a chance to prove that he wasn't just trying to get in her pants. Angela sighed as she gave up and closed the book. The action taking place in Moscow was losing out to the battle waging in her head. She was actually supposed to be on a date. Her dad had set her up with a thirty year-old accountant who attended his church. 'Nice Christian fellow' according to her dad. The guy seemed nice enough but came across as stuffy and boring. He also was not very easy on the eyes. She didn't consider herself a surface level thinker – there was more to it than mere looks – but she liked handsome men. Brian had turned out to be a bastard but he was a cute bastard. She just wanted a good looking guy for herself that she could share something meaningful with. She was an independent woman and all, but she wanted a guy who she felt safe around. One who could protect her. This guy – Steven was his name – looked as though if they were getting mugged on the street, he would run off screaming and leave her at the mercy of the criminals. So she had gently turned him down.

Angela decided she wouldn't completely shut the door on Jerome the next time he called. She would open it just a crack; easing it open a little more as time passed, as long as he demonstrated that he was serious. Her mind now clear, she resumed reading the novel.

"Weh de rass yuh really ah tell mi say?" Lenky asked incredulously, looking at Officer Cuthbert as though he was an apparition. They were standing by the poolside at Lenky's home. Lenky had been in bed relaxing after having sex with his wife when Officer Cuthbert called to say that he was on his way to see him. "Yuh nuh have mi money or de drugs?"

For the fifth time, the policeman tried to explain what happened.

"De fishermen an' dem cohorts rob us Lenky," He implored. "Dem ambush we an' tek de money. We lucky fi escape alive. Radcliffe deh ah hospital right now. Him face mash up."

Lenky took a deep breath and paced the length of the pool. He was trying to reconcile his impression of the two fishermen with the image of them beating up two armed cops and relieving them of the money. His money. It wasn't happening. Either the men were the biggest fools on earth to think they could take his money and live to spend it or this cop was trying to play him. Either way, he wasn't having it. A lucky funeral parlour was about to get some business.

Fuming, he whipped out his cell phone and dialed the number for one of the fishermen. The one called Brownie.

"Who yuh calling Lenky?" Officer Cuthbert asked apprehensively.

"Shut de fuck up!" Lenky responded, "An' don't try mi patience. Mi soon deal wid yuh."

The phone rang without an answer and went to voicemail.

"Dis is Lenky, call me back as soon as you get dis message."

He then called Mikey, who answered his phone saying he was playing pool at a sports bar in Constant Spring, and told him to report to him immediately.

"Go to de hospital fi yuh partner an' come back here," Lenky instructed Officer Cuthbert without turning around.

"Alright," he replied and hurried off.

"If yuh nuh come back within two hours mi ah go hunt yuh dung and introduce yuh to pain dat will mek yuh beg mi fi kill yuh an' tek yuh out ah yuh misery."

Officer Cuthbert shuddered as he left the house. He had to get himself out of this mess. He knew that Lenky was serious. It was Radcliffe's fault anyway. Why should I have to suffer for Radcliffe's greed, he reasoned, conveniently forgetting the fact that he had welcomed the idea of robbing the fishermen. By the time he had gotten in his personal car - the damaged squad car was now at the bottom of a deep ravine in St. Catherine - and exited Lenky's property, he had decided to tell Lenky that Radcliffe's greed was the cause of the operation going awry.

Elizabeth Rhoden was in the bathroom applying a facial mask when her husband came to stand by the door. He watched her without speaking. She was wearing a very short, silky nightdress. It turned him on despite the gook that she had on her face. He loved to see her in red. He felt himself getting an erection.

"Good night, Ralph," Elizabeth murmured, looking at him through the oval mirror. "How was your day?"

Instead of responding, Ralph stepped up behind her and pulled his erect dick from his trousers.

This marriage is such a strange one, Elizabeth mused as she spread her legs and allowed her husband to penetrate her. She winced slightly as she was dry and he was rough in his entry, but the pain was minimal as her husband was not well hung. Handsome, rich and powerful with a small dick. They had been married for twelve years, and for the last six, it had been an open marriage. They had gone on a vacation to Italy six years ago and while there, they had indulged in swinging with a very attractive, sophisticated Italian couple. When they returned to Jamaica two weeks later, Ralph had informed her that he was going to openly have sex outside the marriage and she was free to do the same, but discreetly. She had been ecstatic to hear that as it meant she would no longer have to sneak around. She had been cheating on her husband since their first year of marriage. Her husband was just too small to satisfy her and while she had tried to supplement her sexual needs with a wide variety of toys and other sexual paraphernalia, after six months of sexual frustration, she caved in and sought satisfaction elsewhere. She couldn't leave Ralph, however. She had had to sign a prenuptial agreement when they got married. She had several lawyers look at it over the years but they all told her the same thing. It was ironclad. She would get nothing of consequence if she divorced him. Besides, she was accustomed to the lifestyle that she led. She loved being Mrs. Ralph Rhoden. Ralph's family was like Jamaican royalty, their history dated back to the days when Jamaica was a British colony. Ralph's great grandfather had been a wealthy, influential planter who had owned one of the largest banana plantations on the island.

Elizabeth, despite her beauty and excellent physical condition, was wary of a younger woman snatching her husband and consequently, her way of life away from her. She kept tabs on who he was fucking and if he was in contact with anyone that she considered a threat, she would call them and warn them off. Like that gorgeous physiotherapist that Ralph had started going to. The possibility had existed that her exotic beauty and youth could have made Ralph lose his head. She had nipped that in the bud by calling her and giving her a stern warning.

"I know you fucked Jerome James the other day," Ralph said in her ear, breaking into her thoughts.

His admission caught Elizabeth off-guard. It had never occurred to her that Ralph kept tabs on her extra-marital activities. They maintained eye contact in the mirror as he increased his tempo.

His breathing was ragged.

"Does he have a big dick?" Ralph asked his wife as he freed her left breast from the nightdress and squeezed the nipple.

Elizabeth was surprised. He had never asked her about anyone before and it seemed to excite him. His dick swelled inside her. He squeezed the nipple painfully when she didn't answer.

"Ouch!" she cried out, though she could feel her moisture level increase when she thought about Jerome's dick.

"Answer me!" he demanded, thrusting mightily.

"Yes!" Elizabeth shouted. "It's fucking enormous!"

"Did you like it? Did he fuck you good?"

"Oh yes! It was so good. I came so many times I lost count. I could hardly walk when he was through with me!"

That pushed Ralph over the edge. He grunted loudly as he erupted inside his wife. He had masturbated to the videotape of Jerome having sex with his wife at the Prometheus several times. It was better than any porno movie that he had ever seen. The sight of that big dick penetrating his wife turned him on immensely. Maybe he would show it to her one day. Shock her out of her sensibilities. Getting a video camera placed in the suite had been relatively easy. There were few things that money couldn't buy.

"Your apartment is nice," Jerome commented as he sat down on the couch in Michelle's small living room. The apartment was brightly decorated and utterly feminine.

"Thanks," Michelle replied. She had gone into the bedroom to change into something more comfortable. She was nervous. She wanted Jerome but it felt wrong because of the Laura angle.

She was standing by the bed about to slip into her sexy boy shorts when Jerome came to the bedroom door.

"Where is..." he began, his voice trailing off when he looked at Michelle. She had on a tank top but her bottom half was naked. The shorts she was about to put on was in her hands. She looked at him. Her face was a torturous mix of desire and restraint. Jerome's dick lurched as he admired her. He forgot all about using the bathroom. He walked swiftly over to her and removed the clip that was holding her hair in a loose ponytail and her long mane tumbled free.

She turned around and kissed him deeply, gasping in his mouth when she felt his powerful erection straining against her stomach. Now *that* felt like a dick that she could ride all night. The house phone rang as she rubbed Jerome's head while he sucked her large breasts hungrily. The phone rang to voicemail and then her cell phone started ringing while she hurriedly unbuckled Jerome's jeans, desperate to get to his dick. She was sure it was Laura. Oh well, she sighed lustfully as she took Jerome inside her mouth, Laura would just have to get over it. There was no turning back now.

Officer Cuthbert returned to Lenky's home with his injured partner in tow an hour and a half after leaving there. Lenky was still by the poolside but was now accompanied by Mikey and four of his street soldiers. If possible, Lenky was even more upset than he was prior to Cuthbert leaving. When the rogue cop had left to do his bidding, the fisherman from Rocky Point had returned his call. It had been the one named Calvin, calling from Brownie's phone. He told Lenky what had transpired and informed him that they were still willing to do business with him but he had to come himself and he had to bring the rest of the money seeing as he had only sent a little over half of the agreed sum. Lenky was incensed. How dare this nobody fisherman dictate to him? Lenky had gritted his teeth and agreed to drive down to Rocky Point the following day so that they could tie up the deal, vowing inwardly to teach them an unforgettable lesson.

Lenky eyed the two cops as they came up to him. Cuthbert opened his mouth to say something and Lenky quieted him by putting a solitary finger to his lips. The large diamond ring on his pinky glistened in the light.

"Don't say a fucking word," Lenky told him in a gruff, low tone. "De fisherman dem tell mi exactly what happened so mi know de truth."

He lit his spliff that had gone out due to the light breeze and continued. "I am not going to kill de two ah yuh even though dat is what oonu deserve."

Lenky paused and looked steadily at them as the two cops nervously awaited their fate. He took a deep drag of the potent weed and theatrically blew out a large cloud of smoke before continuing.

"De two ah oonu going to work for me for free from now on. Any little thing ah want done, oonu will take care of it at no cost to me. Dead man caan make mi any money."

His cell phone rang and he checked the caller ID and ignored the call. It was Jada. He would call her back later.

"Now get outta mi sight. I'll call when mi need oonu," Lenky said, dismissing the two policemen.

They nodded and made their way out to the parking lot. Officer Cuthbert shook his head in disbelief as they neared his car. He would sorely miss the extra cash he earned engaging in illegal activities for the gangster. Depending on the job, it sometimes was a tidy sum. Now he would have to risk his life and job for free. He took his keys out of his pocket and opened the car. He fervently hoped his papers came through sooner than later. His mother had been filing for him to be able to live in the US for a couple years now and had recently told him that her lawyer said that he would soon get through. It was time to go. Radcliffe, reclined in the passenger seat, was in incredible pain. The left side of his face was bandaged and badly swollen. It throbbed with pain relentlessly.

The medication the doctor had given him was not strong enough to combat the pain. He grimaced and thought about the situation. He decided to ask for a transfer to the other end of the island, as far away from Lenky as possible. Maybe a little country post in Hanover, where he could start over. Nobody ever requested to be sent to those locations so the transfer would be easily approved.

Laura checked the time. It was now 1 a.m. She couldn't sleep. Images of Jerome having sex with Michelle kept dancing before her eyes. She couldn't believe those two. She had called Michelle and Jerome three times each during the course of the night and neither of them had picked up. She had left a scathing message on Michelle's voicemail on the third call. She was more upset with Michelle than Jerome. She knew Jerome for what he was - a sexual predator. He just couldn't help himself. Michelle, on the other hand, should have resisted and not disrespect her like that, Laura reasoned as she got up and went out on the balcony. She looked down at the poolside. Lenky and his goons were still out there drinking, smoking and conversing about God knows what. She sighed and went back into the bed. Michelle deserved to be slapped. She couldn't believe that she was contemplating fighting over a man, but it was a matter of principle. She decided to swing by Michelle's apartment in the morning.

Michelle stirred, and sleepily got up to pee. She grimaced as she sat on the toilet. Her vagina was burning. She wiped gently and returned to bed. She spooned comfortably into Jerome's sleeping arms and sighed contentedly. If ever she had a gotten a proper screw in her life it had been tonight. Jerome had fucked her every which way all over the apartment. She had an extremely sore pussy and a broken bedside lamp to show for their frolicking, but it had been well worth it. After a lengthy second round she had tried to resist when he pulled her to him an hour later. Aghast, she had told him she couldn't possibly endure another bout for the night or even the next few days for that matter. Jerome hadn't listened and the result had been two mind blowing orgasms in the shower. Her last thought before falling back in slumber was how what had transpired with Jerome would affect her friendship with Laura.

CHAPTER 12

Jerome, after catching a cab home from Michelle's apartment at 7:30 the next morning, hurriedly took a shower and quickly made a protein shake of raw eggs, guiness stout, and a little bit of milk, all blended up. The team bus was coming to pick him up at eight. The team had a light training session scheduled from 8:30 to 11 a.m. No sooner had he finished the frothy shake and placed the glass in the kitchen sink, he heard the annoying sound of the Reggae Bus' horn. Jerome grabbed his gym bag and exited the apartment.

Michelle, who had gone back to bed after Jerome had left early that morning, was awakened by incessant knocking on her apartment door. Groggy, she climbed out of bed and went to investigate who the hell was beating down her door like she owed them money. She looked through the peephole before opening the door. It was Laura. Now fully awake, Michelle took a deep breath and opened the door.

The three cars consisting of Lenky and six of his henchmen, including his brother, Mikey, were twenty minutes away from Rocky

Point. Lenky had placed a call to Brownie, advising the fisherman that he would meet him at the abandoned school building, located off a pothole-filled road just a few minutes from the small town center at 8:30. Brownie and Calvin were already there, and Calvin, much to Brownie's chagrin – he didn't want any more problems with Lenky – had enlisted the help of three of his close friends and fellow fishermen to help with security. They were armed with machetes and fish-guns, and were strategically located close by – two in the bushes and one in the small room at the back of the main room where the meeting was to take place. Calvin was determined that the gangster from Kingston not be allowed to rob them. There was no way he was missing this opportunity to pay for Pat's surgery. If it wasn't corrected soon, she would go completely blind.

Lenky, under the guidance of Cowboy, one of his men who knew the area, having used it as a hideout a few years ago while on the run from the cops before lucking out in meeting Lenky who had employed him and paid off the police to get the illegal weapons charge against him dropped, drove through the center of the town and made a left turn beside the old, dirty concrete structure which housed Maas Ken's Grocery Shop. A few meters up, he made another left turn, and drove until Cowboy told him to slow down.

"Don't stop but see de 'ouse deh," he said pointing through the tinted window of the non-descript Nissan Sunny that Lenky had decided to use for the excursion. He knew that they would be looking out for luxury vehicles so he had decided the crew would travel in three regular sedans. The house Cowboy was gesturing at was a three bedroom dwelling in large yard dominated by a lot of fruit trees. It was where Calvin lived with his common-law-wife and three children. Lenky, realizing that Calvin was determined in getting the full sum agreed on, had correctly surmised that the fisherman most likely had taken precautions at the venue where they were supposed to meet and so, once it had come up at the meeting by his house that Cowboy knew the area well, he had decided to go to Calvin's house and get the fisherman to come to him there with the drugs. Lenky was positive he wouldn't want to risk any harm coming to his woman and children. The two other cars carrying Mikey and the rest of the men had stopped along the side of the road leading up to Calvin's house, awaiting further instructions from Lenky.

Lenky drove past the house and they looked around the neighbourhood as he made a U-turn further up the road. Cowboy had informed him that most of the men would be either at sea or down by the seaside, and that only mostly women and children would be around, doing household chores and such. True enough, in the yard of the small one bedroom house next door to Calvin's, there was an obese woman seated in front of a large, metal wash pan, heartily plowing her way through a stack of dirty laundry. Two little boys, clad only in briefs, were playing a game of marbles.

Lenky stopped the vehicle almost in front of the woman's gate and he and Cowboy got out of the vehicle. They waved to the woman, who waved back and wished them a hesitant good morning, thinking to herself that the tall one with the bald head looked familiar. She wondered what the two men were going to see Calvin about. She didn't like their aura. She kept on washing but kept a suspicious eye on the two men as they walked into Calvin's yard like they owned the place. One went on the verandah and knocked on the front door while the other looked around casually. She hastily looked down at her washing when he caught her watching him. Despite his smile, he seemed cold and menacing. Her instinct told her something bad was about to happen.

"Hi," Michelle said to Laura when she opened the door.

"What's up?" Laura responded. "Didn't you see me calling you last night?"

"Oh, sorry, I was busy," Michelle told her, leaning against the door-jam.

"Doing what?" Laura asked, taking off her Dolce & Gabbana aviator shades and slipping them inside her pocket book.

Michelle laughed a mirthless, nervous laugh. "I'm a grown woman L, what kind of question is that?"

Michelle shifted on her feet and Laura noticed the hickey on the left side of her neck.

"You were busy fucking Jerome weren't you," Laura growled, moving forward until her face was mere inches from Michelle's.

Michelle stepped back involuntarily, stumbling as she did so.

"It's none of your business who I fuck Laura!" she retorted. "You forget that you're a married woman?"

"You forget that you're my friend?" Laura countered as she stepped inside the apartment and pushed Michelle.

"Laura, just calm down," Michelle said, not liking the direction things were going. She did not want to fight Laura over anything, especially a man. Michelle was rewarded with a hard slap to her right cheek as Laura continued to advance on her.

Michelle held her jaw in shock. She couldn't believe Laura was serious about fighting her. Another hard, quick slap to her other cheek, which she was sure left a handprint on her face, confirmed that was indeed the case.

Sobbing, Michelle attacked Laura with her arms swinging wildly and they grabbed each other and stumbled to the floor. Laura, being bigger and stronger, maneuvered herself on top of Michelle.

"Slut! Traitor!" she cried as she administered a hard punch to Michelle's face. Michelle squealed in pain and found the strength to push Laura off of her. They wrestled around the living room, knocking over furniture as they clawed, grabbed and pulled each other's hair. Michelle's neighbour, a gym instructor on his way to work, saw the fight through the open door and rushed in.

Canute, Calvin's eleven year old son, opened the front door and looked at the two men.

"Mi father not here," he stated, assuming that the men must have come to see his dad.

Cowboy and Lenky stepped into the house and closed the door behind them.

"Where is yuh mother?" Cowboy asked, as the boy suddenly afraid, turned to run. Cowboy grabbed him and held him roughly.

Pat, her vision blurred, stepped into the living room.

"Canute! Who is there?" she asked, eyes squinting. She had been worried since last night. Calvin, who never kept anything from her, had told her what had transpired the first time they had attempted to sell Lenky the drugs. She had barely slept last night, worried that this time Calvin might get hurt. She had tried to convince him to just leave it alone but he was adamant that it was the only way that they would be able to come up with the money for her much needed eye surgery.

"Easy Pat, have a seat on the sofa and nuh worry yourself," Lenky said to her. "We not going to hurt yuh...unless yuh man force us to."

Cowboy rounded up the other two kids who were playing with dolls in the back room and bundled all of them together on the large, well worn sofa. Lenky then made a call to Brownie.

"Hello," Brownie said in a nervous voice when he answered. Lenky was late and everyone was tense.

"Give Calvin the phone," Lenky instructed.

Brownie handed the phone to Calvin, who was standing right next to him.

"Yeah," Calvin said when he got on the phone.

"Calvin, mi ah give yuh 10 minutes fi get yuh rass over yuh yard wid mi drugs. Mi deh yah wid yuh girl and pickney dem. If yuh tek longer dan 10 mins...dem dead."

Lenky then terminated the call.

Calvin looked at Brownie with a pavid expression. It was a look that Brownie had never before seen on Calvin's face. Whatever he had heard on the phone had injected him with the kind of fear that sapped the energy from a man.

"Dem over mi yard," he said to Brownie, adding tearfully, "him say if we nuh show up wid de drugs in ten minutes 'im going to kill Pat and de children."

"Lawd, God!" Brownie exclaimed. They were in way over their heads, Brownie, thought mournfully. They were simple fisherman...not gangsters.

"Come on then," Brownie said, galvanizing Calvin, who seemed paralyzed by the fear of losing those dearest to his heart, into action.

They shouted to the other men to hurry on, and they hopped into Brownie's dilapidated pick-up truck and sped off to Calvin's home.

Dennis, Michelle's neighbour, managed to get between the two women and part the fight but received a nasty gash on his nose, courtesy of Michelle's long fingernails.

"What is going on here?" Dennis asked breathlessly. It hadn't been easy stopping the two angry women from fighting. "I thought the two of you were good friends..."

"So did I," Laura responded, fixing Michelle with a hateful look. She pushed away Dennis' hand which had been holding her back and went into her pocketbook. Dennis and Michelle thought she was taking out a weapon of some sort but Laura removed her cheque book and looked around at the damage to the apartment. She wrote Michelle a cheque for fifty thousand dollars and threw it at her.

"That should take care of the damage, slut," Laura said derisively and turned to leave. She noted with much satisfaction that she had definitely kicked Michelle's ass. The area around her right eye was swollen and already black and blue. Her lips were also swollen and bloody.

Laura stopped at the doorway and slipped on her shades. She turned her head dramatically and told Michelle to forget her number.

She then stepped off towards the parking lot. When Laura got in her SUV she quickly looked at her face. Thankfully it was unmarked, just sweaty and flushed. She did have two scratches on her neck though, and she had a really bad headache, due to Michelle's hard pulling of her hair as well as the whole drama of the situation. Everything that had happened seemed surreal to her. From meeting Jerome and fucking him on the first night, to fighting her best friend over him...it was all so crazy. She gunned the engine and headed home. A long, warm bath and some breakfast should go a long way in helping her to feel better. Thankfully Lenky wasn't home to see her disheveled appearance. She was in no shape to concoct a story at the moment.

"Michelle, I think you should go to the doctor," Dennis told her as he examined her face. Sobbing, Michelle had yet to utter a word since he came in the apartment and stopped the fight. She moved away from him and sat on the couch, cradling her head in her hands.

Dennis figured it was best he leave her alone, besides he had to get going. He was supposed to get to work at 10 and it was already 9:45. He touched her gently on her shoulder and promised to check on her when he got back from work. He then left and closed the door behind him. When Dennis left the apartment, Michelle got up and went into the bathroom to examine her face. She gasped audibly at her reflection. She looked horrible. Laura had really done a number on her. Bitch, Michelle thought, as she tentatively touched her right eye and mouth. She would really have to go to the doctor. She still couldn't believe that things had come to this. Maybe she was wrong for sleeping with Jerome after Laura slept with him but Laura had taken it too far. She was a married woman and had no claims on Jerome. To come to her home and fight her was just ridiculous. *End the friendship if you feel compelled to do so but don't put your hands on me,* Michelle reasoned as she turned on the tap and prepared to take a bath. The more she thought about it the angrier she got. She decided the best way to get back at Laura was to continue seeing Jerome. And God help Laura if she thought she was going to get a chance to beat her up again. Let her try.

"Good shot," Paul said to Jerome after he sank a free-kick from fifty yards out beating the long arms of Tito, the first choice goal-keeper for the national squad. They had been training since 8:30 and only had another hour and a half to go. They were now practicing to take free-kicks and penalties.

"Thanks, man," Jerome replied, adding, "You know my right foot is like a compass...can't miss."

Paul laughed. "Whatever, man."

They both knew Jerome was only joking. He never bragged about his prowess on the football field. He was very humble when it came to his prodigious talent. Not so when it came to his personal life though, Paul mused as he watched Jerome take another shot, this time hitting the crossbar but the ball still went into the back of the net. Jerome was very flashy and loved attention. One thing Paul respected about him though, no matter what was going on in his personal life it never affected his stellar play on the pitch. He always performed at a high level and gave it his all.

The coach, an Argentinean who had guided the Argentina youth squad to the world youth finals a few years ago and who was hired with much fanfare – and at too high a cost some critics had said – by the Jamaica Football Association, signaled for the team to take a 10 minute break. Those critics were now silenced, as he had guided the Reggae Boyz to an historic berth in the upcoming World Cup finals.

Jerome grabbed a bottle of Gatorade and plopped down next to Paul. He wiped the sweat off his face with a towel and then placed the towel over his head to provide a little shade from the bright late morning sun. He wondered what Laura was up to. If she didn't call him before he got back home, he would call her. He had seen three missed calls from her when he got up this morning and checked his phone. He knew there was no way she would believe that he wasn't with Michelle last night. He'd just tell her the truth and let the chips fall where they may. His mind then wandered to Angela. He wondered if he should attempt to see her before leaving for London on Thursday. Most likely she would refuse but he resolved to try anyway. He'd call her later and invite her out to dinner. He had a party to attend with Tara but that would be much later that night so there wouldn't be a problem juggling both dates – if by some miracle Angela actually said yes. Jerome sighed and got up as the coach signaled the resumption of training.

Brownie pulled into Calvin's yard and Calvin stumbled out of the van without waiting for it to come to a complete stop. He ran up the steps of the verandah and burst into the house, perhaps never even hearing his neighbour, Miss Mattie, calling out to him that some strange men were in his home. Pat and the kids were seated close together on the sofa and they all wore the same expression. Fear. The youngest child, Mabel, his three year old daughter, was sucking her thumb and sobbing quietly. Cowboy was standing behind the sofa, smiling at Calvin. Calvin remembered the tall, dark man. He had lived in the area for a few months, shacking up with Berta, a fifty-two year old vendor who lived a few houses up the road. Calvin was mad at himself for putting them in this situation. It was entirely his fault they were in danger but he was just trying to help.

"Yuh mek it," Lenky said from behind him, breaking into his thoughts. Lenky was leaning against the wall holding a handgun equipped with a silencer. He held it downwards to the floor.

"Weh de drugs deh?"

Calvin sighed. No drugs, no money, Pat would surely be blind by the end of the year. "It's in de van."

Lenky called Mikey and told him that both cars should come around to the house.

He then looked at Calvin. "Yuh was going to ambush mi and try something around the meeting place, innit?"

Calvin looked at him for awhile before responding. "No, just took precautions so that we would get what we were supposed to."

"Where is my four hundred and fifty thousand yuh tek from the police?" Lenky asked him.

"It inna de bedroom," Calvin replied.

Lenky looked at him steadily. "I respect yuh. Ah nuff man wouldn't try and stand up fi dem self the way yuh did. But at the de same time, yuh haffi watch who yuh ah stand up to cause look how yuh family coulda dead today. Wipe out."

Calvin remained silent. The man was right. His woman and children could've been dead right now. Victims of a drug deal gone bad.

Vehicles were heard pulling up outside. Mikey ran up the steps and came in. He looked at Calvin and administered a vicious back-handed slap to his face, eliciting a loud gasp from Pat and screams from the children.

"Ah dah country bwoy yah ah give 'imself so much trouble?" he asked rhetorically.

"Mikey! Weh de bloodclaat wrong wid yuh. Just go outside and go load up the drugs inna de car dem!" Lenky said to his younger brother forcefully. Mikey always had to do something stupid. At times like this Lenky wondered why he bothered with him.

Mikey went back outside slamming the door behind him. He could be heard rudely telling Brownie, who had remained seated in the van to 'come and help load up de drugs'.

Lenky then sent Cowboy out to the car and told him to bring the bag that was in the trunk.

"I'm going to give yuh de whole ah de money," Lenky told a surprised and very grateful Calvin. "Don't tek mi kindness for weakness...mi only doing it because mi respect yuh. But trust mi, if yuh did ever take longer than the ten minutes mi did give yuh..."

Cowboy returned with the bag and lenky gestured for him to give it to Calvin.

Lenky then turned abruptly and went outside; telling the men that it was time to go. Cowboy caught up with him at the car.

"Why yuh give him the money boss?"

Lenky looked over at the house for a moment before responding.

"Even in dis cut-throat business...if yuh conduct yuhself right, good blessings will follow yuh."

He went in the passenger seat and allowed Cowboy to take the wheel. He reclined the seat way back and closed his eyes. The three cars then sped through the dingy town, their occupants anxious to get back to Kingston.

CHAPTER 13

"Oh my god!" Dr. Blair, Michelle's personal doctor for the past four years exclaimed when she saw her face. "What happened to you?"

"Hi Dr. Blair," Michelle responded taking a seat. "I had an altercation...don't really want to talk about it."

She hadn't even spoken to Jerome about the incident yet.

"Ok, I won't pry," Dr. Blair said, thinking that domestic abuse seemed to be on the increase in Jamaica. Poor girl. She got up and gestured for Michelle to lie down on the examination table. "Let's see if there's any serious damage."

Half an hour later, with her face bandaged and armed with a prescription, Michelle went to the pharmacy on the same complex to fill the prescription. Dr. Blair had placed her under the xray machine to ascertain if any bone was fractured. When she was through examining her, she had admonished Michelle not to suffer silently and let any man beat up on her. If only she knew.

Jerome got home at 12:30 and promptly took a shower. The light training had been good. Tomorrow he would just go to the gym and work out for a few hours; that should keep him loose for his tryouts in England. His phone rang as soon as he got out. It was Lenky.

"What's up, man?" Jerome said, slipping on a pair of sweat pants.

"Mi deh yah 'Rome," Lenky replied, "Mi over Nannyville spending some time with my son." After getting back to Kingston, Cowboy had taken Lenky over to Nannyville while Mikey had gone up to the house to retrieve Lenky's Lincoln Navigator to take to him.

"The son or the baby mother?" Jerome teased.

"Yuh gwaan man," Lenky responded with a grin. Jada wasn't even there when he arrived. She was at the hairdresser and had left her younger sister to keep an eye on Nathaniel, who was playing video games with one of his friends, as usual. "So what yuh up to?"

"Just got home from training," Jerome told him, as he got some juice from the refrigerator. "Gonna relax for a little while and make a few calls."

"Alright, link me up later," Lenky responded and hung up.

Jerome turned on the TV and settled on watching a repeat showing of the BET hip hop awards. He hadn't gotten a chance to see it when it first aired a few days ago. He scrolled through his phone book and dialed Laura's number.

"You fucking bastard!" Laura shouted in his ear. "You just had to fuck the tramp didn't you? Ignoring my calls and shit! Fuck you think you are?"

Jerome half listened as he allowed her to vent and get everything off her chest. The rapper T.I. was now on stage performing.

"That's why I had to fuck her up, the little slut!"

She got Jerome's full attention with that one. "Whoa...what you mean you fucked her up?"

"I beat her ass this morning. It's the principle of the whole thing. She disrespected me."

"You fought Michelle this morning?" Jerome was incredulous. He couldn't believe Laura would fight her best friend over him. That was crazy. Suppose word of the fight got out and Lenky heard about it?

"Yeah and I swear Jerome, if you continue to see her she's not going to like it. I'm not sharing you with that tramp."

Jerome scratched his head. He figured the best course of action was to calm Laura down and assure her that he had no interest in Michelle.

"It was just a spur of the moment one time thing babes," Jerome cooed in his most charming tone. "I'm not interested in anything with Michelle...you know you're my boo."

"Whatever...you just make sure you leave her alone. Where are you?"

"I'm home, just got back from training," Jerome replied. He wondered if Michelle was ok. Laura was a lot bigger than her. He wanted to know the details but didn't think it was a good idea to ask Laura anything about it.

"Ok, I'm gonna come by for a little while. Lenky isn't here," Laura told him. She was horny. She had fought because of him and now she wanted to fuck him.

"Ok, baby," Jerome replied, not minding the idea one bit. Especially knowing that Lenky was by his baby's mother house and wouldn't just pop up at his apartment.

"See you in a bit," Laura told him and hung up the phone.

Jerome was about to call Michelle, but decided to wait until later. He dialed Angela's number instead. She answered on the third ring.

"Hello."

"Hi, Angela...its Jerome," Jerome said, surprised at how good it felt just to hear her voice. "How are you?"

"I'm good, just had lunch...clearing my email before my next patient arrives in a few minutes," Angela replied pleasantly.

"Are you ok?"

Jerome was very surprised at how gregarious she was being with him. Normally she would just be brutally polite.

"I'm ok, just got in from a light training session."

"Ok, nice talking to you but I've got go," Angela told him.

"Angela...before you go...would you like to have dinner with me tonight?"

There was a pregnant pause as Angela toyed with the idea. While she had decided to be a little more receptive to him she hadn't banked on spending any time with him yet.

"Ok, where and what time?" she finally replied.

Jerome couldn't believe that she actually said yes.

"7 o' clock would be a good time. How about the Rib Shack?"

The Rib Shack was a hip new eatery on Chelsea Avenue. Angela hadn't been there yet though she had planned to catch up on all the new restaurants soon. Kingston's annual restaurant week was coming up in two weeks.

"Ok, I'll meet you there at 7. See you later. Bye." Angela hung up and logged out of her email. She was glad that she had said yes. It was nice to be going on a date, especially with such a handsome, sexy man.

Jerome put the phone down with a bemused expression on his face. He didn't even mind that she didn't want him to pick her up at home. At least she seemed to now be open to giving him a chance. Goes to show, nothing beats persistence, he mused as he resumed watching the awards show. He needed to call Lenky and get a vehicle for the night. He would do that later. He checked the time. Laura should be getting there in another twenty minutes or so.

aura knocked impatiently on Jerome's door when she arrived at his apartment. Jerome was in the kitchen making one of the three protein shakes that he usually drank a day, when he heard the incessant banging. Relax, girl...I'm coming, he said to himself as he strode quickly to the door. He opened it and Laura stepped in.

He closed the door behind him and they stood looking at each other in silence. Laura then suddenly gave him a hard slap to the face. It stung mightily, but Jerome took it in stride, and merely rubbed his jaw. He would allow her that one slap so she could let off some of the steam over the Michelle incident. But that was it. Laura tried to slap him again but Jerome grabbed her hands and she struggled vainly to get free as he spun her around and pushed her up against the door. Still restraining her, he lowered his head and kissed her roughly. Laura bit his lip but relented and slipped her tongue in his mouth when he didn't stop kissing her. They kissed passionately as they practically ripped each other's clothes off. Eschewing any further foreplay, Laura, panting heavily, turned around and braced herself on the door, arching her back and spreading her legs invitingly.

"Take me hard Jerome! I want you inside of me so bad!" Laura told him, turning her head and fixing him with a look that made Jerome lose it. He growled and rammed his dick inside her with a brutal thrust. Laura squealed like a stuck pig. It was painful at first, and she couldn't believe all that dick was inside her, but her pussy was so wet, that she quickly adjusted to his size and started giving as good as she was getting. Jerome fucked her mercilessly and she loved every intense minute of it. His long, thick, unsheathed dick felt so good inside her. In between the violent waves of pleasure wracking her body, she made a mental note not to let him ejaculate inside her. Her period was due to start today and she had used her last pill for the month yesterday.

Her jealously and extreme reaction to the Michelle incident had shown her that she was inexplicably falling in love with Jerome; just like that. It was foolish, dangerous, irresponsible and futile. But she couldn't help it. She just wanted him.

"Oh god Jerome...you're hurting me so good...mmmm... fuck me baby...it's yours...it's all yours...fucking hell...coming again..." Laura babbled, caught up in the throes of primal ecstasy as she came again and again.

Jerome held Laura tightly around the hips as he continued to pummel her with deep, long strokes, struggling to delay his climax as her hot depths bathed him with its juices continuously. He loved the way how her large, full breasts shook mightily with each stroke.

"Oh baby...you feel so tight...hot...can't hold it anymore...oh fuck..." Jerome grunted through clenched teeth as he shook uncontrollably and emptied his seed inside Laura's wetness.

"Ooohh Jerome...that feels so good...mmmm....yes baby...fill me up," Laura moaned, climaxing again as she clenched her buttocks and held Jerome inside her until his erection subsided and he slowly slipped out of her wetness.

"Sweet Jesus...that was so fucking good," Laura whispered, still crouched in the same position. She stood up and made her way to the bathroom when she felt Jerome's juices begin to trickle down her thighs. Jerome followed behind her, sighing as he watched her ass. He was sure it was the eighth wonder of the world. They got into the shower together.

"As crazy as it sounds, I'm falling in love with you Jerome," Laura confessed as she lathered Jerome's body, looking up at him as she pulled his foreskin back to clean his dick. "We have no future but I can't help the way I feel about you...can't explain it..."

Jerome looked at her thoughtfully. She actually had tears in her eyes. He couldn't think of an appropriate response so he kissed her softly on her forehead and then her eyelids. It seems he did the right thing. Laura, tears flowing freely now, pressed her body against his and kissed him with a quiet, intense passion. They didn't get out of the shower until an hour later.

Michelle had just taken two more painkillers and was reclined on the couch listening to the new John Legend album when her cell phone rang. She checked the caller ID. It was Jerome.

"Hi," Michelle said softly.

"Hi Mich," Jerome said, "How come you didn't call and tell me what happened?"

"I was going to call you eventually," she told him. "Everything happened so fast and was so shocking...then I had to go to the doctor and stuff..."

"I understand," Jerome responded. He didn't like how she sounded at all. "How bad is it?"

Michelle sighed. "Well I'm in a lot of pain...my face is badly swollen and mentally I'm a mess...it's just crazy Jerome...nothing like this has ever happened to me before."

She started sobbing.

"Hush baby," Jerome said, trying to console her. "I have an appointment at seven but I'll try and come by afterwards ok?"

"Ok," Michelle mumbled. "Call first though...the pills make me drowsy so I might be asleep."

"Alright, later babes...and I'm sorry about the whole thing."

"Its ok...not your fault...Laura is just a crazy bitch," Michelle replied.

Jerome told her bye and terminated the call. Time was going, it was now 6 p.m. and he needed to call Lenky to get a vehicle to borrow. His date with Angela was at 7:30 and he didn't want to be late. He dialed Lenky's number.

"What's up?" Jerome asked him when he came on the line.

"Nutten much, on my way home," Lenky replied, "Mi nuh see mi wife all day."

"Ok, I need a wheels tonight...have a big date," Jerome told him.

Lenky laughed. "Which bird that now?"

"Met her a few days ago...very nice girl," Jerome told him.

"Alright...I'll send down the Lexus RX 300," Lenky told him. "It just come back from the garage today."

"Thanks, man," Jerome said gratefully. He knew the truck. It was a very nice ride as were all of Lenky's vehicles. Mikey had badly scratched the right bumper and Lenky had sent it to his trusty mechanic to have it repaired. "I need it by 7:15."

"Dat soft man," Lenky replied. "I'll call Blacka and have him bring it down to you right now."

They chatted awhile longer and then Jerome got off the phone and went into the bedroom. He selected a black pinstripe blazer, a trendy black designer T and a pair of distressed True Religion jeans to go along with black Prada sneakers. He then went into the bathroom to take a shower.

Angela checked the time as she turned onto Lady Musgrave road. It was 6:30. She had an hour to get to the restaurant. Good thing she was almost home. The hairdresser had taken a little longer with her hair than expected but she couldn't complain. Her hair looked fabulous. She drove into the complex where she lived and parked hurriedly. She wasn't one of those women who liked to play stupid games and keep men waiting so she wanted to be at the restaurant on time, or at the very least, just a few minutes late. She waved to Mrs. Trought, her obese neighbour who was out walking her dog - or maybe it was the other way around - and rushed inside to get ready.

Laura was by the poolside when Lenky came home. She was sipping on a glass of champagne listening to love songs on her iPod. She was in a mellow mood. The visit to Jerome had helped her release a lot of the tension and stress that she had been feeling since the incident. And intensified her feelings for him.

"What's up baby?" Lenky asked as he gave her a hug and joined her by the poolside. "Don't see yuh from morning."

"Hi babes," she replied, taking another sip of the bubbly. "Whose fault is that...you left in the wee hours of the morning and you are just now returning."

"I know baby...just ah trouble yuh man," Lenky replied, helping himself to a glass of the champagne. "So what yuh did today?"

"Nothing much. Went to look for store space and a few other things," Laura told him nonchalantly.

"Found anything?" Lenky asked. Laura wanted to open a clothing store but she wanted it in the heart of half-way-tree where the best malls were and it was very hard to get space there. Lenky owned several plazas around the city but they were mostly in the ghetto areas. Laura had plans for an upscale boutique so those plazas were out of the question.

"No, not yet but hopefully something will become available soon," she replied. She really wanted the store as she was very much into fashion and would like to be able to help wealthy Jamaicans find quality high fashion clothing without having to travel abroad to shop. She saw a niche and was determined to fill it. The make-up she had applied to cover the scratches from the fight with Michelle was working like a charm. Lenky didn't notice a thing.

Blacka arrived at Jerome's apartment at 7 p.m. Jerome was getting dressed when he heard a horn beeping downstairs. He pulled on his jeans and went outside shirtless. Blacka was standing by the Lexus SUV and Ping Pong was behind the wheel of the Toyota Tundra that Lenky had assigned to his two senior soldiers.

Jerome waved to Ping Pong and gave Blacka a pound.

"What a gwaan balla," Blacka said, greeting Jerome enthusiastically.

"Nutten much, have a little one a way flex to make, yuh si mi?" Jerome replied.

"Alright, tek it easy," Blacka told him and handed him the keys.

They left and Jerome went inside to finish getting dressed.

Jerome arrived in the parking lot at the popular restaurant at 7:28. He parked quickly and made his way inside. He was greeted at the door by the lovely hostess who immediately recognized him and led him to a table for two as requested. The restaurant was doing brisk business. The place was nearly full, which on a Tuesday night, was a clear indication that the restaurant had been a big hit since its opening two months ago. As soon as Jerome sat down, a soft hand came to rest on his right shoulder.

"Expecting someone are we?" a sultry, cultured voice asked.

Jerome knew who it was without turning around. Elizabeth Rhoden.

"Hi Elizabeth," Jerome replied, still staring in front of him. He noted that a few glances were being thrown in their direction and Elizabeth must have noticed too as she removed her hand from his shoulder. "Matter of fact I am."

He turned his head slightly.

"How are you?" he asked. They hadn't contacted each other since their tryst at The Prometheus.

"I'm great," Elizabeth responded. "I'm having dinner with two of the board members of my favourite charity organization."

"Ok," Jerome responded, noting that she looked absolutely stunning as usual. "You look lovely."

"Thank you," she responded, lowering her voice and adding, "You look quite dapper yourself. I felt a surge of moisture when I saw you walk through the door."

Jerome grinned and his smile became even wider when he saw the hostess pointing him out to Angela. She walked gracefully towards the table.

"So that's your date," Elizabeth murmured. "That physiotherapist. I hear she likes married men. Old married men."

With that Elizabeth bade him goodnight and left the table. Jerome got up and seated Angela, wondering why Elizabeth had made that comment.

"Hi, you look very pretty," Jerome told her as he sat down across from her. And she did. The minimal makeup she had applied complemented her skin beautifully and the simple but sexy black dress fitted her slender but curvy frame to perfection.

"Thank you, Jerome," she responded. "You look positively handsome as usual."

They were both surprised at her statement. Angela grinned sheepishly.

"Thanks," Jerome said, smiling. "I was happily surprised when you said yes to dinner. Made my day."

Angela smiled sweetly and was about to respond when they were interrupted by the pleasant, diminutive waiter. They quickly scanned the menu and Jerome ordered roasted prime beef sirloin served with finely chopped mushrooms in red wine, along with white rice and sautéed potatoes. Angela decided to try the fresh asparagus wrapped with slivers of smoked chicken served with a Cajun mustard cream sauce. They both decided on the gingerbread soufflé with chocolate strawberry sauce for desert.

When the waiter left, Angela resumed their conversation.

"I'm glad I said yes. I'm enjoying your company immensely."

And she was. Now that she had decided to give him a chance, she could relax and just allow things to flow naturally. She felt excited and wanted. The way he looked at her made her nipples harden. But no matter how Jerome made her feel, she was definitely going to take things slow. Make him prove that he really wanted her as his woman. Her mind ran on her dad briefly. She knew that he wouldn't approve of her being in a relationship with someone like Jerome. Anyway, she decided to cross that bridge when she got there, if she ever got there. It was still early days yet.

"Who is that lady that was by the table when I came in? She keeps looking at me," Angela remarked, taking a sip of her white wine.

"That's Elizabeth Rhoden...her husband's sports apparel company is one of the team's major sponsors," Jerome replied without looking in Elizabeth's direction. He took a bite of the succulent well-done steak.

Angela chuckled.

Jerome looked at her quizzically.

"Her husband is a patient of mine," Angela explained, "and when I first started treating him, Mrs. Rhoden had deemed it necessary to call me with a stern warning not to try anything inappropriate with her husband."

Jerome laughed. Now he understood why Elizabeth had made that catty remark about Angela. "Really?"

"Yeah. I was not amused. She was very arrogant and rude." Angela patted her lips daintily with her napkin. "But anyway, enough about that old biddy. So you're leaving on Thursday?"

"Yeah, think I'll be staying for a week," Jerome replied, leaning forward and taking hold of Angela's hands. She didn't pull away.

"So these are the magic hands that help to ease the pain of so many," he teased. "My back hurts..."

Angela laughed. "Nice try Mr. James."

They talked for quite some time, so engrossed were they in their conversation that they didn't realize that they had been in the restaurant for three hours. They were the last of the patrons to leave when the place closed at 10:30.

They strolled to the parking lot holding hands and joking with each other. Angela could not recall the last time she had so much fun in the company of a man. Jerome was funny and witty, and there was always that strong undercurrent of sexuality that she could feel emanating from him which both excited and scared her simultaneously.

There were now only four cars in the parking lot and two of them were over the section clearly labeled *Staff Only*. They stopped at Angela's car and Jerome stood very close to her. Angela cleared her throat nervously.

"You smell really good," she told him. "What are you wearing?"

Jerome chuckled. "It feels a little bit funny saying this but it smelled so good I had to get it..."

Angela was curious. "Come on tell me..."

"Paris Hilton for Men."

Angela laughed. "I understand your hesitation but it's very nice."

Jerome lowered his head and kissed her without warning. Caught with her mouth slightly open, Angela could do nothing about the warm tongue invading her mouth. Things were moving a hell of a lot faster than she would've liked – she had not planned on giving him such an intimate kiss on the first date – but it wouldn't do to push him away. Nor did she want to. She returned his kiss with her hands by her sides and her eyes tightly closed. Their tongues did a slow and sensuous waltz as they stood in the bright moonlight in the empty parking lot and enjoyed their first foray into intimacy. When Jerome finally broke the kiss, tugging her bottom lip gently as he did so, Angela was flushed and breathless. She had to lean against her car for support. She had not masturbated in some time but there was no question that the pink vibrator that she had bought on a whim but had only used once was going to be called into action tonight. She was soaked.

"I had a really good time, Angela," Jerome told her softly. "I liked you a lot before I knew anything about you and now that I know you a little better, I definitely know that I want you in my life. I want you to be my woman."

He held her hands in his and rubbed them gently.

"You're the girl for me Angela. Someone I could see myself with for a very long time."

The words were just pouring out of Jerome.

Angela didn't know what to say. He was saying all the things she wanted to hear but was it genuine? Her heart being broken would be a very steep price to pay to find out. Angela sighed.

"I like you a lot too Jerome," Angela finally responded. "But I'm so scared of my heart being broken. When I give, I give my all and then some. I was hurt really bad in my last and only serious relationship so it's a little hard for me to throw caution to the wind. Then a guy like you...that's out in the public eye and looking the way you look...that's trouble Jerome....I just know it is."

Jerome remained silent. He had already made his intentions clear. She would have to meet him the rest of the way on her own.

"But, I do like you and if a man is going to give me trouble... I'd prefer he looks like you."

They both laughed heartily at that.

Jerome placed a solitary finger under her chin and lifted her face up to his.

"I promise I'll never deliberately hurt you. Let me in Angie... you won't regret it."

"I-" Angela never got to finish that sentence as Jerome devoured her mouth again. This time his kiss was hard and passionate. Bruising even. It left Angela flustered and in heat.

"I'll call to make sure you got home safe," he said to her, stepping back so that she could open the door and get in the car.

Angela could only nod. She didn't trust herself to speak. She got in and smiled at him before driving off. She couldn't wait to get home. She needed to have an orgasm like she needed air. She hoped fervently that the batteries in her rarely used vibrator were still good. She glanced in the rear view mirror. Jerome was still standing in the same spot watching her drive away.

Jerome took his cell phone from the inside pocket of his blazer as he walked to the truck. He had placed the ringer on silent as he hadn't wanted his date with Angela to be filled with any distractions or interruptions. Good thing he had. There were 10 missed calls and three text messages. There were two calls from Tara and a text message reminding him about the party that he was supposed to be attending with her later that night. The other calls were shared between Laura, Patricia, some girl named Charlene, two numbers that he didn't recognize and Elizabeth Rhoden had sent him a text: Having Fun? I know your flight is 8 p.m. Thursday night. I want to give you a 'ride' to the airport. Jerome smiled. That woman was something else. He sighed as he opened the SUV and got in. He pulled out of the empty parking lot as he returned Tara's call. He really liked Angela and absolutely wanted her to be his main girl but the show must go on. Jerome wondered idly if it was even possible for him to be with one woman. He didn't think so.

CHAPTER 15

Jerome called Michelle after talking to Tara and was mildly surprised when she answered the phone. He thought she would've been sleeping.

"Hi Mich," he said when she came on the phone. "What are you doing up?"

"Hey...I had fallen asleep but woke up to use the bathroom a few minutes ago," she replied with a yawn.

"Ok, I'm on the road...I want to come and see you." Tara had told him that she would pick him up at twelve but Jerome told her he was driving and would meet her there instead. It was only 11 o' clock so he decided to swing by Michelle and chill until it was time to go.

"Sure, that's cool," Michelle responded as she poured a glass of water. Her throat felt really dry. She hated taking medication but they seemed to be working. The swelling on her face had receded slightly and it wasn't hurting as much as it had before.

"Alright, I'll be there in a little while."

Michelle hung up and unlocked the front door so she wouldn't have to get up again when Jerome arrived. She then curled up in the couch and waited for Jerome. He got there in five minutes. He knocked on the door then tried it and the door swung open.

He went over to Michelle and hugged her carefully, avoiding the bandaged area on her face. Jerome was startled when he saw the state that she was in. He hadn't expected it to be this bad. Laura had really put it on her.

They hugged for awhile and Michelle started sobbing again.

"How bad is the pain?" Jerome asked.

"I'm feeling a little bit better," she told him. "The medication seems to be helping."

"Damn...still can't believe Laura actually came over here and attacked you," Jerome said, shaking his head.

"Well you better believe it...she even said that if I continued to see you its gonna be worse next time but Jerome, mark my words, if that bitch thinks that she's going to touch me again she has another thing coming," Michelle said with conviction.

"Just chill baby, don't talk like that...can't let this thing spiral out of control," Jerome chided gently.

"Easy for you to say...no one came to your house and destroyed your belongings and gave you a trip to the doctor," Michelle retorted.

Jerome didn't respond. What could he say? She was right.

"Anyway, I'm going back to bed...you spending the night?" she asked as she got to her feet.

"No, but I'm staying with you a little while longer," Jerome replied as he stood up and removed his blazer and shirt, and kicked off his sneakers. They went into the bedroom and Michelle curled up in his arms and promptly fell asleep. Jerome then called Angela to make sure that she got home ok. She told him she had just arrived and was on the phone with Jean. He told her goodnight and that he would talk to her tomorrow.

"Oh that's great!" Jean exclaimed, as she listened to Angela tell her how much she had enjoyed her date with Jerome. Jean had called Angela about two minutes after she had gotten home and grilled her mercilessly. Jean had been so excited when Angela had told her that she was going out with Jerome, one would've thought that she was the one going on the date.

They chatted for another 15 minutes before Angela told Jean she needed to get some sleep and finally got her off the phone. Angela undressed and hurriedly extracted the slender vibrator from her lingerie drawer. She put on her favourite R&B CD, Mary J. Blige's My *Life*, and got down to business. Jerome's searing kiss lingered in her mind and she had her first orgasm before the first track on the CD was finished. That was a record for her. By the time she had her fourth orgasm she was screaming Jerome's name and the bed was drenched. She had also discovered, much to her astonishment, that she was a squirter. It had never happened to her before though she used to experience orgasms with Brian, her ex. *I guess there are orgasms, and then there are orgasms*, Angela mused as she got up to change the sheets. When she wondered what it would be like when she finally made love to Jerome, she was almost tempted to go for another round.

Lenky went upstairs after swimming a few laps in the pool. After drinking and talking with Laura, she had told him that she was going to lie down for awhile so he had decided to take a swim. Laura was curled up underneath the comforter seemingly fast asleep when he went into the bedroom. Lenky removed his wet boxers and finished drying off his body. He then stood by Laura's side of the bed and gently removed the comforter, exposing Laura's sleeping form. She was sexily clad in a barely there white T-shirt with no panties. Immediately erect, Lenky climbed into the bed and started to fondle his wife. Laura woke up and sleepily told him to chill. In response Lenky tried to position his head between her legs. Laura, now fully awake, kept her legs firmly closed.

"Lenky, stop!" she protested, as she tried to get up. "I'm not in the mood. I just want to go to sleep. I'm not feeling too well."

Lenky looked at her in the semi-darkness. Lately she always seemed reluctant to have sex with him. Ever since she got back from New York. He wondered again if she was cheating on him.

"Yuh was fine just now when we were downstairs," Lenky retorted. "I am not a fool Laura so watch yuhself. If mi ever find out say yuh a cheat pon mi yuh an' de bloodclaat man dead like dog!"

"I'm not cheating on you Lenky," Laura told him, not liking the direction the conversation was taking. "I'm really just not up for any sex right now."

"Yuh seem to never be up for any sex these days," Lenky replied, mimicking her tone. "But yuh ah get fuck tonight whether yuh want it or not. Bloodclaat man! Mi tired haffi ah ask yuh fi pussy an' yuh is mi wife."

With that Lenky pulled her legs apart and climbed on top of her. Laura tried to fight him off and Lenky lost it. He grabbed her hair in a vicious twist and growled for her to stop. She didn't and was rewarded with a hard slap to the face. She stopped struggling immediately. She couldn't believe Lenky had actually hit her. She knew that he was a violent man but he was always very gentle with her no matter what.

She held her jaw and looked at him in disbelief as he defiantly threw her legs apart and inserted his member inside her dry pussy with a hard thrust. Upset that she was dry – clearly she really didn't want to have sex with him – he fucked her as hard as he could, twisting her hair in the process and eliciting screams of pain from Laura.

"Lenky ! This is rape!" Laura cried. Then she started screaming at the top of her lungs. "Rape! Rape! Help! Rape!"

Lenky smothered her with one of the pillows as he continued to have his way with her. It was over in three minutes. He climaxed with much fanfare and removed the pillow from her face.

He spoke with his face mere inches away from hers. "If yuh ever refuse to have sex with mi again ah de same t'ing ago happen to yuh. Maybe worse next time. Something is up with you and since yuh decide say yuh ah go start deal with mi certain way, I am going to deal wid yuh accordingly. No more pet up business and if yuh spend one dollar, mek sure yuh ask permission. Mi ah lock off yuh unlimited access to mi money until yuh start behave yuh rass self. Yuh also will have a driver from now on to take yuh anywhere yuh want to go at anytime, until mi decide otherwise."

Laura couldn't believe what she was hearing. All because she wasn't in the mood to have sex he had deemed it necessary to start acting like a monster. She got up from off the bed and was about to go into the bathroom when Lenky's gruff voice stopped her. He had rolled over and was lying with his back to her after his brutal act. He spoke without turning around.

"Where yuh going?" he asked in a hostile tone.

"To the bathroom," she replied.

"If ah shower yuh ah go shower, come back inna de rass bed. A wash yuh want to wash mi off like say yuh is a rape victim?" he snarled. "Yuh ah mi wife. Mi caan rape yuh. If yuh did ah perform yuh sworn duty dat woulda never happen to yuh. Come back inna de bed!"

Laura looked at him incredulously. But, to avoid further confrontation, she did as she was told. She went back into the bed and was careful not to touch him. She couldn't believe that things had disintegrated so quickly and easily. No way was she going to put up with this. She had to leave him. Her mind made up, she plotted the best way to do just that. She knew she had to be careful though, because if Lenky caught her trying to leave, there was no telling what he might do.

CHAPTER 16

Jerome called Tara when he got to the Azzuri Pub. He had quietly let himself out of Michelle's apartment a few minutes to twelve and had gotten to the party venue five minutes later.

"Hi Jerome," Tara said when she came on the phone. "Where are you baby?"

"I'm outside in the parking lot...just finished parking," Jerome told her as he activated the alarm and made his way towards the club. The parking lot was filled with luxurious SUVs and sedans. *Rich, spoiled kids* Jerome mused as he listened to Tara tell him that she was coming outside.

"That was Jerome, I'm going outside to meet him," Tara said to Marianne, the host of the party.

"Ah, Mr. Stud is here...good," Marianne replied, gesturing for Tara to lead the way.

Tara didn't like the sound of that. Marianne seemed a bit too enthused to meet Jerome. Marianne loved to be in competition with her in every way and Tara knew that she would try to fuck Jerome. She didn't mind sharing, but not with Marianne. If it happened she wouldn't make a big deal about it though, that would only give Marianne more ammunition. They got outside just as Jerome was nearing the entrance.

"Hi baby," Tara gushed, giving him a big hug. She was genuinely happy to see him.

"Sup T," Jerome replied coolly, holding on to her ass as she hugged him.

"This is Marianne," Tara said, as she broke the hug. "Marianne meet Jerome."

"Hi, Jerome," Marianne said, giving him a soft kiss on both cheeks. "It's a pleasure."

"Same here," Jerome replied, amused at the predatory way in which she was looking at him.

Mmmm, he looks even more handsome in person, Marianne mused. *I definitely want a piece of that.*

The two women walked on either side of Jerome as they entered the club. The party was in full swing. The DJ was spinning the latest hip hop tracks and the young affluent crowd was dancing up a storm.

"What would you like to drink?" Tara asked him over the din of the music.

"Hennessey and red bull," Jerome replied.

Tara nodded and walked off to get the drink.

Marianne slipped into Jerome's arms and started to gyrate sensuously.

"Give the birthday girl a dance," she whispered, giving his right ear a light flick of her velvety tongue.

Jerome smiled and their bodies moved in sync to the stripclub-comes-to-mind beat of Akon's hit single *Smack That*. Marianne pressed her slender body against his even more when she felt his phallus along the length of her thigh.

Fucking hell, she thought. *Gina definitely was not exaggerating about his size.*

Tara returned with a small bottle of Hennessey, a can of red bull and a cup with ice. She mixed Jerome a drink and handed it to him, then she placed the can and bottle on one of the many small, cone shaped tables that were scattered throughout the club. She then went behind Jerome and started dancing, running her hands through his low, curly hair as she gyrated against his ass. Jerome took a sip of the strong drink as he enjoyed the attentions of the two women. Gina and the rest of the gang came over a few minutes later when the three of them had taken a break from dancing.

"Hi Jerome," Gina said as she greeted him with a warm hug. "Having fun I see..."

Jerome grinned. "Yeah, the party is tight."

Gina introduced him to the other two girls and they all took turns dancing with Jerome as the DJ switched to soca music. About twenty minutes later, Jerome asked Marianne where the bathroom was and she grabbed his hand and told him that she would take him there. Tara shook her head as she watched Marianne make her move. *Cunt!* She fumed resignedly as she lit a cigarette and took a deep drag. She hoped that Jerome wouldn't enjoy it.

Jerome trailed Marianne as they navigated their way through the throng of party-goers, some of whom Marianne stopped briefly to acknowledge. There was a short staircase to the rear of the club that led to a thick oak door. Marianne led him up there and removed a key from the pocket of her fashionably frayed designer denim skirt.

She opened the door and they went in.

"The club belongs to my cousin,"she explained, "and this is his private office."

Marianne switched on the antique desk lamp and bathed the room in a soft glow. The room was relatively large and consisted of a very expensive-looking antique desk which housed a small flat screen computer monitor and a lovely penholder. There was a large leather couch and a mini bar to the right of the room. To the left was a small bathroom which Jerome immediately went to. He flicked on the light and left the door open.

Marianne turned on the air conditioning and turned to watch him pee.

Jesus H. Christ! Marianne gasped inwardly as she looked at the huge piece of flesh Jerome was currently shaking dry. It was by far the biggest dick she had ever laid eyes upon. She removed her top without even realizing she was doing so and was standing by the desk nude by the time Jerome washed his hands and exited the bathroom.

His dick was still hanging from his fly as he strode over to her purposefully.

"You want to help me put this back in my pants?" Jerome asked teasingly as he stood close to her.

Marianne's breathing was ragged and she bit her quivering lips as she grasped his dick with both hands. She ran her hands along its length, marveling at the bulging veins and its weight as it grew in her hands.

"I can think of a few better places to put it...or at least some of it," she replied, licking her lips. "I don't think there's anywhere on my body that can accommodate all of this..."

"Let's see how much you can take..." Jerome said; his dick now fully erect.

Marianne looked at him steadily as she kissed him softly on his lips and worked her way down to his genitals. She squatted and cupped his testicles as she ran her tongue along his shaft before placing the head inside her mouth. She sucked him languidly, concentrating on the tip, eliciting groans of approval from Jerome who began to gyrate slowly, working his dick further down her throat. She was only able to take half of him in but her technique of sucking while twirling her tongue in such a way that it seemed like it was wrapped around his dick, drove Jerome crazy. He gripped her hair and uttered sounds similar to that of singing in falsetto. Aching to feel Jerome inside her, Marianne then got up and led him to the couch by holding onto his dick. It felt like a steel rod. Jerome sat on the couch and she shoved his jeans and underwear to his ankles. Jerome told her to retrieve a condom from his pocket. He quickly rolled it on and Marianne climbed on top of him.

She maintained eye contact with him as she positioned herself over it and slid down slowly. She gasped and proceeded even more slowly when the bulbous head entered her.

"Oh fuck...you're so big...and thick...mmmm...stretching me..." Marianne moaned as she stopped her descent when about half of his dick was inside her. She then bounced slowly, careful not to pass the midway point. Jerome groaned. He could literally feel the plush tightness of her walls. He knew a lot of that had to do with his size but he could tell that she had a tight vagina, which he found surprising given her apparent promiscuousness.

Marianne squeezed her nipples and rode Jerome with her eyes tightly closed.

"That's it...ride it girl...show me you're not scared of this dick... fuck me..." Jerome growled as he slapped her small ass and urged her on.

Marianne liked the dirty talk. Jerome could feel her getting wetter. He started meeting her downward movements by thrusting upwards. Marianne wailed like a banshee but didn't back down. Jerome got up from off the couch while still buried inside her and stood with her in his arms as he continued to stroke her. He went deep but slowly so as not to hurt her.

"Oh god...no...too deep...fucking hell...put me down.... can't manage this position...too painful..." Marianne told him breathlessly, her face a study of discomfort.

Jerome put her down and she stretched out on the couch and spread her legs widely.

"Give me some good old missionary," she told him. "I don't think I can manage anything else...I want to be able to have children when I'm ready."

They both laughed at that. Jerome got on top of her and reentered her slowly. He tucked her legs under his chest and ground his way into her with slow circular movements.

"Yes Jerome...oh yes...that feels good...ooohhh....don't stop... just like that...oh yes...yes...hitting my g-spot...oh god I love it...fuck me!"

Marianne was a screamer. One of those women who let it all out when they climaxed and tonight was no exception. Jerome's ears rang as she experienced two gut-wrenching orgasms a minute apart. Jerome then pulled out and ripped off the condom. Inside of her felt really good but he couldn't fuck her the way he wanted to so he positioned himself over her mouth and let her suck him off the rest of the way. He wondered if she swallowed as he felt his climax approaching. She did.

Calvin tossed and turned in his sleep. He was too excited to get a good night's sleep. It had been a very busy and productive day for him. He had gone to the black market and purchased ten thousand US dollars - a bank would have wanted to know where the hell he had gotten so much cash - and he had also gone to the travel agency to book a flight to Cuba for himself and Pat. Arrangements had also been made for Pat's older sister to stay with the kids for the week that they would be away. Brownie would look in on the house as well and make sure that everything was ok. The flight was in the morning and the agency had booked them a room at a small hotel in downtown Havana. He looked over at Pat who had no trouble sleeping. He was so happy that things had worked out. Now his darling would not go blind. God bless Lenky. Calvin's mind was made up to marry her when they got back from Cuba. No more shacking up. It was time to make it official. He had purchased an affordable engagement ring earlier that day at a jewelry store in May Pen. He kissed her on the cheek and closed his eyes. Sleep was far away but he had to try. Tomorrow would be a long day.

"That was quite an experience Jerome," Marianne told him as they sat on the couch, both enjoying a cigarette. "It would take a lot more sessions for me to even begin to get used to your size...that thing is too big man."

Jerome laughed.

"But it did hit some spots previously untouched...those back to back orgasms were simply divine. I usually only climax from oral sex," Marianne continued as she put the cigarette out in the ashtray and got up to get dressed.

"I know you probably think I'm just a rich, loose girl but I'm just having good clean fun until its time to settle down and get married. You are the first guy I've let penetrate me in over a year. I usually just engage in oral sex but I just had to feel that monster of yours inside me. Anyways, lets head back downstairs, I'm sure Tara is quite pissed...she's always in competition with me...I think she has an inferiority complex where I'm concerned."

Jerome thought it wise not to comment. He pulled his pants and boxers up and went into the bathroom to freshen up. They made their way back down to the party a few minutes later. The party was still jumping and they found the girls at the same spot dancing and talking to a couple of guys.

"Look who's back," Tara slurred, taking another sip from her ninth glass of wine since Jerome and left with Marianne. "Had fun?"

Jerome responded by gently taking the glass away from her and placing it on the table. "I think you've had enough."

She didn't resist when he took away the glass and pulled her in his arms.

"It was boring...she's nothing like you..." Jerome whispered in her ear.

This prompted a huge smile and a series of giggles from Tara.

This clique is something else, Jerome mused as he noticed the perplexed look on Marianne's face, no doubt wondering what Tara had found so funny. These rich, privileged girls are so screwed up.

Jerome told the girls goodbye and arranged for Gina to give Tara a ride home. She was too tipsy to drive and her car would be secure if left in the club's parking lot until she was able to retrieve it later. Tara wanted to spend the night with him but Jerome decided he needed to get some rest and had gently told her that he would make sure to spend some time with her later that day. Marianne hugged him bye and kissed him on the cheek. Jerome exited the club and quickly made his way to the vehicle. He ignored the couple kissing against the car next to his and hopped in. It was now 3 a.m. He figured that he could get six hours sleep and then get up and take care of everything he had to do on the road. He didn't plan to give Lenky the vehicle back until Thursday. Angela crossed his mind as he drove home. He wondered if she was dreaming about him.

CHAPTER 17

Bigga, Lenky's chef, was up earlier than usual. It was 6:30 and he usually didn't get up for work until 8 a.m. He was in the kitchen making breakfast. He was preparing Johnny cakes, ackee & saltfish, roast breadfruit and peppermint tea. Every morning, he prepared a huge breakfast so that the occupants of the house or any one who came there before 11 a.m. could have breakfast if they so desired. His mind was on Laura as he cooked. He had heard her screams last night and was worried sick. He couldn't imagine Lenky doing Laura harm based on the way he doted on her, but obviously something went wrong last night. Laura was very dear to him. She always treated him with respect and whenever she traveled, she always bought him a gift. Sometimes he felt guilty when he told her about Lenky's various women but he did it any way. He just loved sitting around and talking to her about any and everything. He hoped that she was ok and anxiously awaited her arrival to the kitchen for breakfast.

Angela was in a very good mood that morning. She sang Ne-yo's hit song *Sexy Love* as she showered, and blushed furiously whenever she remembered how many times she had masturbated and called out Jerome's name the night before. She had a quick breakfast of lucky charms cereal and a grapefruit – she had over-slept – and rushed off to the office. Her first appointment was at 8:00 a.m. and it was now 7:50. She usually didn't schedule appointments before 9, but the client in question was going abroad today and wanted a session before the long flight. The client, a prominent business woman, was going to Korea on business and would be flying all day across four time zones. Angela thought of Jerome as she got into her car and sped off to the office. He was leaving tomorrow and had asked her when they just met to give him a session to loosen him up before he left for his try-outs. She had refused then, as she was all booked out, but under the current circumstances she would have to accommodate him. He's kinda my new man after all, she giggled to herself as she turned into the complex where her office was located. Angela knew what the tingly feeling she felt whenever she thought of Jerome was, and it scared her to death. She just prayed she'd be able to stick to the plan and not sleep with him too quickly.

Brownie pulled up at the departure area of the Norman Manley International Airport at 8:15. Calvin assisted Pat in getting out of the dilapidated pick-up truck which was the beneficiary of a few snide remarks by the security guards who were responsible for keeping the traffic flowing. Once your drop-off had been completed, you were to leave the area immediately.

The guard with the bull-horn, a stubby big-breasted woman with long extensions, pretending not to know who drove the vehicle though she was standing right there when Brownie pulled up, shouted, "The driver for the pretty red pick-up truck please remove your vehicle or it will be towed!"

Her co-workers laughed dutifully as Brownie, a bit embarrassed, quickly bade his friends goodbye and wished them the best of luck. He then hopped in his truck and drove off noisily, leaving his tormentors in a cloud of smoke.

Calvin waved off the porter – he could easily manage the two small suitcases –and Pat held on to his arm, as they made their way into the airport to check in. They would be flying on a small plane that provided chartered flights three times a week to Cuba. Pat thought about how lucky she was to have a man like Calvin as they waited in the short line. The plane could only hold thirty people and most of them had already checked in. He had been a tower of strength to her ever since they had gotten together thirteen years ago. He was a good provider and father to his children, and he was totally devoted to her. He had taken her sudden sickness hard, and when he had found out that it could be corrected by surgery, he had trouble sleeping at night because he knew that he couldn't afford it. She had been so scared when he found the drugs and decided to sell it to raise the money, but there was no telling Calvin that it wasn't an act of God. She was ecstatic that she was going to be able to have the surgery though; being able to watch her children grow was a great source of joy for her. They got to the front of the line and Calvin handed their tickets to the agent.

Bigga had just finished eating and was enjoying a strong cup of coffee when Lenky came downstairs fully dressed. He nodded a greeting to Bigga as he talked on his cell phone.

"Alright, so be here in another half an hour," Lenky instructed. "And if she giving you any problems just let me know."

Lenky terminated the call and turned his attention to the chef.

"What yuh cook?" he asked gruffly, scowling as he looked at Bigga. Bigga told him.

Lenky sucked his teeth and grabbed the keys to his Navigator from the rack of keys above the kitchen door.

"I'll get something on the road, mi nuh feel fi nuh rass ackee right about now," he snapped, adding, "A youth name Snapper

will be here soon. Give him some breakfast and give him these."
Lenky threw the keys to Laura's X5 on the counter. Bigga nodded
and Lenky left the house. Bigga wondered what that was all about.
He couldn't wait until Laura came downstairs.

Jerome got up at 9 and immediately went into the bathroom
to take a shower. He had a lot of errands to run before he left for
England and he wanted to do them all today so that tomorrow he
could just relax. He was pleasantly surprised to receive a call from
Angela while he munched on an egg and cheese sandwich.

"Hi baby," he gushed. He had figured she would have been
busy at work and had planned to give her a call about midday.

"Hi Jerome," she replied, "What's up?"

"I'm here, getting a quick bite before I go on the road," Jerome
replied, taking a swig of fruit juice. "Have a few errands to run."

"What time is your flight tomorrow?"

"8 p.m."

"Ok, I'm going to be nice and give you a therapeutic massage
tomorrow in the afternoon...say about 2?"

"Thank you baby," Jerome replied, with a wide grin. "That
would be great."

"Ok, I'll talk to you later. My next client just arrived."

Angela hung up the phone and told Suzzette, her receptionist,
to send in Mr. Baldwin. She was glad that she had offered to give
Jerome a massage, he sounded really excited about it. She hoped
he didn't get any ideas. That's all he was getting.

Laura got up at 9:30 and went into the bathroom to take a long
shower. She had been awake for the past hour but wanted to be
sure Lenky was out of the house before she got up. She got out of

the shower twenty minutes later and slipped on a tank top with a pair of denim shorts and went downstairs.

A rough looking young man that she had never seen before was sitting at the kitchen counter stuffing his face with ackee and readfruit. Bigga was at the sink taking dishes out of the dishwasher.

"Morning Laura," he said, looking at her with concern. Her eyes looked puffy from either crying or lack of sleep.

"Hi Bigga," she replied but her eyes were on the stranger.

"Who is this?" she asked, gesturing to the guy who looked at her with a smirk as he ate.

"That's Snapper," Bigga replied. "Lenky sent him here. Said he's your driver?"

Laura shook her head in dismay. She couldn't believe that she would be stuck with this ugly criminal any time she needed to go on the road. How would she get to see Jerome?

"You want some breakfast?" Bigga asked.

"No, I've lost my appetite. Bring me some tea out by the pool." Laura sat under the large umbrella by the poolside and reclined comfortably in the lounge chair. She would miss this house. It was such a lovely home. She wondered how she would o about leaving Lenky. It would be extremely difficult. Even if she managed to slip away and go back to the US, Lenky had contacts all over the States and would leave no stone unturned in finding her. Laura sighed. Bigga bought her the tea along with some crackers and cheese and was about to sit down beside her but she told him that she wanted to be alone. Her grandmother used to tell her it was easier to catch flies with sugar than with vinegar. She decided that the best thing to do was to get back in Lenky's good graces. That would be child's play compared to trying to get away. She never loved him, and now, after what he did the other night, didn't even like him anymore, but she could do whatever it takes to have him wrapped around her little finger once again.

Feeling better now, Laura sipped her tea and nibbled on the snack that Bigga had given her.

After leaving the house, Lenky had stopped by one of his business places over on Hagley Park road. It was an auto parts store that specialized in Honda and Mitsubishi parts. It was a cash cow. Lenky got a lot of his parts at cheap prices from car stealing rings both in Jamaica and abroad. The place was filled with customers as usual. He nodded a curt greeting to the staff and went around to the private office in the back that he allowed Raymond, the general manager to use. Raymond was there handling some paperwork. He looked up when Lenky entered without knocking.

"What's up boss?" he greeted, shaking Lenky's hand.

"Nutten much," Lenky replied sullenly. The incident with Laura had left a sour taste in his mouth. He loved her to death and hated having to be so hard on her, but there was no way he was going to tolerate her behaving like that. He hoped she realized the error of her ways and made an attempt sooner than later to get her act together because he was dead serious about everything he had said. He'd be damned if he allowed a woman to take him for a fool. Even one as sexy and desirable as Laura. Lenky sat down and listened to Raymond as he brought him up to date on the happenings with the business.

Jerome left the Western Union outlet in New Kingston and made his way over to the commercial bank that was next door. Dimples had called him just before he left the house letting him know that she had sent some money for him as promised. She had sent him seven hundred US dollars. Jerome used some of it to purchase two hundred and fifty pounds. He knew that he wouldn't need much pocket money while there. He wouldn't need to do any shopping, he still had new clothes in his closet that he could take with him and Dimples would be here with a lot of new clothes for him by the time he got back – she was coming down from Miami on Sunday. Also, Gunner, the drug dealer Lenky was doing business with, had told him to make sure he gave him a call when he got to England. He was sure Gunner would see to it that his needs were well taken care of. All he would probably have to spend his own money on was a gift for Angela. And perhaps Michelle – she could use a little cheering up. Jerome swung by the Jamaica Football Association's offices to pick up his certificate of fitness that the team physician had left there for him – he needed to have it with him when he went for his tryouts though any team he chose would conduct their own physical. He chatted with Leo, the President, for a few minutes and then he made his way to his favourite barbershop at Kingville Plaza in Constant Spring to have his weekly grooming done.

Lenky went to Nannyville after he had made a few more stops checking on his various businesses. Nathaniel wasn't there; he was over by his grandmother's house where two of his cousins were visiting from the country. That was ok with Lenky. He really had come by to see Jada. They hadn't spoken since the last time he was there, but despite what had transpired he knew that she would be happy to see him. He felt for some of that love right now. The vibes with Laura had him feeling really out of sorts. The front door was closed but not locked – he had a key anyway – so he opened it and stepped in.

Jada came out of the bedroom when she heard the door open and shut.

"Sup?" Lenky asked as he walked over to her.

Jada didn't respond. She leaned against the wall with her arms folded.

"Yuh still vex with me?" Lenky asked as he reached her and pulled her in his arms. She allowed him to pull her to him but didn't return his hug.

"Ah me yuh ah give silent treatment?" Lenky asked softly, whispering in her ear. He kissed her on the neck and nibbled on her ear. He spun her around and hugged her from behind.

"Miss yuh baby," Lenky continued, as he slipped his right hand underneath her T-shirt and rubbed her crotch through her panties. Jada moaned involuntarily. "Give me some that hardcore fuck that only you alone can give me."

Jada turned around and kissed him hard. He was a bastard and didn't treat her well at times but he was her bastard. She loved him and always would. He could have her any time he wanted and that's just the way it was. She moaned and unbuckled his pants while he hurriedly took off his shirt. Lenky then ripped Jada's panties off and they tumbled on the bed in absolute heat.

"Miss yuh too boo," Jada told him as he sucked her breasts ravenously.

Jada spread her legs and reached down for his throbbing dick. She knew he didn't last long and wanted to get at least a few strokes in before he ejaculated. She inserted his dick inside her pulsating wetness and wrapped her legs around his back.

"Fuck mi Lenky!" Jada implored. "Fuck out mi bloodclaat!"

Lenky loved how Jada behaved in bed. Hardcore and raw. Real ghetto slam.

"Who ah fuck yuh?" Lenky growled as he threw Jada's legs unto his shoulders and increased his tempo.

"Yuh Lenky! Yuh know say ah your pussy this baby! Fuck it like ah fi yuh own!" Laura shouted as she flashed her fingers and screwed up her face like she was doing the 'hot wuk', a risqué dance move that was taking the dancehall by storm.

It excited Lenky to no end and he groaned loudly as he bucked like a bronco and spilled his seed inside Jada's willing orifice. Jada stroked his back as he shuddered in her arms. She hoped that she got pregnant. Having another baby for Lenky would be a good thing. Especially if it happened before he got that bitch Laura pregnant. And especially if it was a girl. She knew that he wanted a daughter really bad.

Jerome spent close to two and a half hours at the barbershop. Besides the fact that he and the guy who always cut his hair had become good friends, he also liked it there because they offered a full range of services. Two very nice girls worked there as nail technicians and beauty care specialists. He got a shave, a haircut, a facial and a manicure.

After leaving there he called Michelle to see how she was doing.

"Hi Mich," he said when she came on the line. "How are you feeling?"

"Not too bad I guess," she replied. "I'm here, looking at my diary and checking to see if I need to cancel any of my overseas jobs. No way am I showing up on anyone's set looking like a mummy."

Michelle was a make-up artist who after doing some outstanding work on a Sean Paul video set shot in New York, had been scoring a few gigs with high profile artistes. She had jobs coming up for Missy Elliot's new video, Shabba Ranks' new comeback video and she was scheduled to work on a photo shoot for the September issue of King Magazine.

"You're the make-up artist Mich," Jerome chided gently. "Not the model or video girl…it doesn't matter if you look like Godzilla. They're just interested in the magic you work with that make-up kit of yours."

"I know…but I'm so self conscious right now Jerome," she complained. "I just couldn't go looking like this."

"Ok, hopefully you'll be better by the time the first one rolls around." He lit a cigarette as he went into the parking lot. "When is the first one?"

"Missy's new video…that's two weeks away in Miami," Michelle told him.

"You'll be good as new by then babes. Hungry?"

"Yeah…kinda…I'd eat a chicken salad."

"Ok, I'll stop at Wendy's and get you some. See you in a bit."

Jerome hung up and exited the plaza. He then rang Lenky. It was strange of Lenky not to touch base with him all day.

Lenky answered on the first ring.

"What's up 'Rome," he said through a mouthful of food. Jada had happily prepared a meal of dumplings and boiled bananas with curried chicken for him. "Mi deh yah ah eat some food."

"Everything alright?" Jerome asked as he waited at the traffic light at the intersection of Constant Spring road and Dunrobin Avenue.

"Yeah man, everyt'ing cool," Lenky responded. He didn't want Jerome to know about his marital problems. The reason was a just a tad bit embarrassing. How could he tell Jerome that Laura didn't want to have sex with him anymore and he suspected that she was cheating on him? Hell no.

"Cool. I'm on the road running some errands...link you up later."

"Yeah man," Lenky replied and terminated the call. He looked at Jada who was sitting across from him watching him eat. "Gimme two more dumplings baby."

Jada smiled and got up to do his bidding. Lenky had always loved her cooking. *I'm going to fuck, breed and cook my way back to my rightful spot*, she vowed to herself as she went into the kitchen.

Jerome purchased the chicken salad for Michelle and got himself a double cheeseburger along with fries, a baked potato stuffed with bacon, and a large cherry juice. He was at the New Kingston location so he got to Michelle's apartment in six minutes. They ate and talked while they watched Serena demolish Sharapova in the Australian Open tennis finals.

"Thanks Jerome," Michelle told him, wiping her mouth with a napkin. "For everything. You've been really cool."

Jerome just smiled and blew her a kiss.

"I'm feeling horny," Michelle confessed. She was surprised as since the fight with Laura she had felt drugged up and listless. "No oral though...at least not from my end."

They both laughed at that. It would've been some sight watching her try to blow him with a swollen, bandaged jaw.

Jerome took a sip of his cherry juice and then made love to Michelle on the couch.

At 4 p.m., Laura, having figured out how she would go about blowing Lenky's mind and get him back in line, got dressed and went downstairs. She told Bigga to cook steamed fish with okra and crackers - Lenky loved that - and she selected a bottle of Moet & Chandon Brut Imperial from the bar and told Bigga to get it chilled. She then went into the living room where Snapper had made himself at home smoking weed and watching porn. he switched off the TV and snapped her fingers for him to follow her. Scowling at her attitude, Snapper got up slowly and followed her to the car. He deactivated the alarm and Laura climbed into the back.

"Take me to Premier Plaza," she instructed airily. She was going to buy new lingerie and give Lenky a show that he wouldn't be forgetting any time soon.

Tara called Jerome to ask if he could take her to pick up her car from the parking lot at the club where she had left it last night and to remind him that he had promised to spend some time with her today. He had just finished having sex with Michelle and was in the bathroom taking a leak when she called. She told him that she had slept for most of the day and her hangover was pretty much gone. He told her that he would pick her up in half an hour.

He wouldn't stay there long. Maybe an hour or two then go home and relax.

Calvin was in good spirits as he and Pat enjoyed the lively Latin sounds of the street band that was playing in a park close to the hotel in downtown Havana. The flight to Cuba had been quick and uneventful and after checking into the hotel, Calvin had immediately called the clinic for which the doctor back in Jamaica had recommended. He was able to book a time for Pat to have the surgery done the following day. After dinner at the hotel, Calvin had suggested that they take a walk and they had come upon a small but appreciative crowd listening to the band in the park. Calvin liked Cuba, the people were extremely friendly and the island was beautiful. Calvin thought the people seemed very happy living in a country where he had always heard they didn't have many rights. Guess communism works in some cases, Calvin mused philosophically as he tapped his feet to the infectious beat. He found it ironic that Cuba had some of the best doctors and one of the best health care systems in the world. Pat would be in good hands.

Bigga was putting the finishing touches on dinner when Laura returned home at 6 p.m. She advised Bigga that she was having a candlelight dinner with her husband on the bedroom balcony and that he should quickly arrange the table. Bigga wondered for the hundredth time that day what the hell was going on with Laura and Lenky. Half an hour later, with the table set and Bigga instructed not to come into the main house under any circumstances for the next three hours, Laura, looking a like a Victoria Secret lingerie model, dialed Lenky's cell number. Lenky was on his way to Dumbarton

Avenue to speak with the owner of one of the sound systems that he was using to play at his upcoming party when his phone rang. He knew it was Laura immediately as she had a special ring tone. One of his all time favourites, The Isley Brothers hit *For the Love of You.*

"Hello," he answered gruffly, instead of his usual mushy greetings whenever she called.

"Baby! Come home now! Something's terribly wrong! Oh god!" Laura wailed in the phone and then hung up.

Perplexed, and alarmed, Lenky called back continuously but the phone went straight to voicemail. He called Snapper who told him that he had taken Laura on the road but had taken her back home around 6 and she had sent him home saying she wasn't going back on the road. Lenky then called Bigga but his phone rang without an answer. Lenky quickly detoured and made his way home as quickly as possible. He prayed that Laura was ok. He didn't know what he would do if something happened to her.

Laura smiled to herself as she turned off every light in the house and went upstairs to the bedroom balcony to sit at the table and wait for Lenky. She would light the candles when she heard him enter the bedroom.

Lenky drove like a mad man as he moved as quickly as the traffic would allow. He had called Mikey and a couple of his soldiers but none of them were even close to the house at the moment, and wouldn't get there before him anyway. Another unbearable fifteen minutes and Lenky was screeching to a halt in his driveway. He pulled his handgun from the secret compartment in the dashboard and ran quickly but cautiously into the dark house.

"Laura?" Lenky said as he switched on the living room light. He quickly checked the kitchen and out by the pool. Seeing no sign of her, his heart growing heavier by the second, he dashed upstairs. Laura was lighting the second candle when Lenky burst into the bedroom with a wild look on his sweaty face. He stopped short when he saw her seated calmly at the table; smiling wickedly at him in the soft light. His expression registered relief, then anger, then lust when she stood up and he saw what she was wearing. The woman he married was a fucking goddess. She walked over to him.

"I'm sorry for tricking you honey," she said as she kissed him softly on the lips. "But I needed you to come home right now and I didn't know how...seeing as you are very upset with me."

His chest heaving mightily, Lenky didn't respond.

"Come and have dinner," she said, turning and leading him to the table. "It's your favourite." Lenky placed the gun on the bedside table and followed her meekly, as all the tension dissipated from his body and he allowed himself to feel the moment. Laura had never done anything like this before. She obviously had decided that she wanted to save her marriage and make things even better than it was before. He hadn't thought it possible, but at that moment, Lenky loved her even more. They sat and enjoyed their romantic dinner mostly in an expectant silence. Lenky was so excited by the ambiance, Laura's outfit and the devilish smile she had been wearing since he got home, that he climaxed right there at table. He wondered if Laura realized what happened. If she did, she wasn't showing any reaction. She sipped some of the champagne and continued to flash him that devilish smile.

CHAPTER 18

Laura smiled as she looked over at Lenky, fast asleep in a fetal position. She was very pleased with herself. After dinner, she had led Lenky to the bathroom where she had given him a sponge bath, and then treated him to his first blowjob by her on the love seat next to the bed. Lenky had been pleasantly surprised and was reduced to a mass of whimpering, quivering flesh when she pleasured him with her knowledgeable mouth. After he had climaxed and gotten up on wobbly legs, he wondered inwardly how was it that she was so skilled orally and had never given him a blow job before, but not wanting to start a fight and ruin the evening, he had decided to bring it up some other time. She had then taken him back out on the balcony where she had leaned against the railing and spread her legs, telling him to eat her from behind which he had done with much enthusiasm. In his eagerness, with his tongue moving briskly all over her vulva, she had actually climaxed, and the orgasm had been so sudden and unexpected that when it happened, she had screamed loudly, gripping the railing forcefully as she gyrated downwards onto his face.

Afterwards, they had retreated to the top of the staircase where she sat Lenky down and rode him like she wanted to uproot his dick. Despite climaxing twice in the past hour – she knew he had ejaculated at the table – he still hadn't lasted longer than his customary five minutes. *You're hopeless*, Laura thought as she got up and went into the bathroom, though she had to admit that it was the best sex they had ever had. They had a heart to heart talk when they went to bed to relax, and an emotional and satiated Lenky had professed his undying loving for her and had apologized profusely for the incident the other night. Well, mission was accomplished; Lenky was putty in her manicured hands once again. The way it was supposed to be. She peed and then retrieved her cell phone and went downstairs. She wanted to talk to Jerome for a few minutes. She missed him, especially knowing that he would be going to England tomorrow and she wouldn't be able to see him for at least a week.

Jerome was home relaxing and talking to Angela on his land line when his cell phone rang. He was in the bedroom while his mobile was in the living room. He made no attempt to get up.

"Aren't you going to get that?" Angela asked. She was curled up in bed in a T-shirt and panties with the lights off. After getting home from work, she had taken a long shower and had fallen asleep after lying down for a few minutes. Jerome had called her cell phone and woke her up, and she had given him the number for her land line as it was much cheaper to talk that way.

"Nah...couldn't be anyone more important than who I'm talking to now..."

Angela laughed. "Is that right..."

Jerome laughed. "It sure is...by the way do you have any idea how sexy you sound over the phone? If the physiotherapy hits a snag you can always fall back on being a phone sex operator..."

Angela found that image hysterically funny. She laughed until she had to get a glass of water. They didn't get off the phone until two hours later.

Calvin, excited and slightly nervous about Pat's impending surgery, had woken up very early. He watched TV for two hours until Pat got up, then they showered and had a light breakfast. At 8 a.m. they left the hotel and walked over to the clinic. It was only a few minutes away and the doctor had told them to be there at 8:30. Calvin didn't want them to be late.

Lenky felt energized when he woke up. He was pleased to find Laura curled up against him. He smiled fondly at her sleeping form. Everything was ok now. He checked the time and wondered if Jerome was up yet. He wanted to hang out with him for a bit today and make sure everything was ok for his trip to the UK. He decided to stay in bed until Laura woke up so that they could have breakfast together. He hoped she got up soon though. He was famished.

Angela thought about Jerome as she drove to work. After their lengthy conversation last night she felt a lot closer to him. She had been aghast when he told her what had happened to his mom and grandmother. She had never heard anything so horrible in her life. Poor Jerome. She was feeling very proud of him. He could have easily become a product of his environment but had, instead, chosen to use his talent and make something of himself. She was happy that she had decided to give him a chance. The more she got to know him the more she wanted him. She was suddenly nervous about giving him a therapeutic massage later that day. Things could easily get out of hand and she would never be able to look at her office the same again. She blushed at the thought.

Paul sighed when he saw Jerome pull up at the JFA's practice facility in Lenky's black Lexus SUV, hip hop blasting from the heavy speakers Lenky had gotten installed in the truck. *First Lenky used to drive him around now he's pushing Lenky's vehicles...what's next?* Paul thought as continued to stretch. The Reggae Boyz were having a light practice session and Jerome had decided to do some exercises and hang with them for a bit seeing as he wouldn't be practicing with them for at least a week. They had an international friendly with Peru coming up in three weeks. Jerome was excited about that as he had never been to that country and it would also be another chance for Jamaica to improve their world ranking if they won that game as well as the friendly against Ghana in seven weeks time.

Everyone greeted Jerome warmly and wished him the best at his trials for the English clubs. Jerome was genuinely liked by his teammates because he was always cracking jokes and despite his superior skills and popularity, never missed practice and always gave his all in any game the team played. An hour later, after Jerome had finished doing some laps around the field, he sat down with Paul as they took a break.

"What's good?" Jerome said, taking a long swig of Gatorade. "Everything cool?

"Yeah," Paul replied. "My girlfriend is pregnant. Found out yesterday."

"Congrats man!" Jerome told him, patting him on the back.

"Thanks," Paul replied. "I didn't want it to happen before we got married so we are going to speed up the process. We're planning a wedding in eight weeks. Her mom wants us to get married before the belly starts to show."

Jerome nodded in agreement though he didn't see what the big deal was. So what if the baby got born out wedlock? They were together and planned to get married anyway, so the child would've been in a family unit regardless.

Jerome and Paul talked for awhile longer and then they were joined by some of their teammates. The talk then turned to Jerome becoming a big star in the English league and what it would mean for other players hopeful of making it in the English Premiership.

Lenky called Jerome while he was on his way to the parking lot. Practice was over and everyone was heading out.

"What's up man?" Jerome said, as he opened the trunk and threw his sweaty clothes in there. He pulled a clean pair of sweats from the back seat and pulled them on along with a white tank top. "Can't hear from you...is which new girl have you weak?"

Lenky laughed. "Nutten like that rude boy...just had some things dealing with. What yuh up to?"

"Just leaving practice," Jerome replied as he hopped into the truck and drove out of the parking lot. "Going home to take a shower."

"Alright, mi deh home still," Lenky told him. He and Laura had been hanging out by the pool since breakfast, swimming and playing games like new lovebirds. "Might as well yuh come up here when yuh done so yuh can bring up the vehicle. Then mi and yuh touch the road and go hang out fi a bit."

"Yeah man," Jerome replied. "I'll do that."

Jerome checked the time. It was 11:30. He would go up there and have lunch and chill for a while then let Lenky drop him at Angela's for his session with her. He couldn't wait. He felt himself getting an erection as he imagined her hands massaging his body.

Jerome got up to Lenky's home an hour later. Lenky and Laura were still out by the pool. Lenky gave him a pound andLaura greeted him with a wave and a fake smile. Jerome figured she was pissed at not getting him last night when she had called. She got out of the pool and began to dry herself with a large towel. Jerome struggled to keep his eyes off her as he and Lenky conversed. Laura was looking ridiculously sexy in the Burberry two piece swim suit that she was wearing. Jerome was grateful when Bigga rolled a trolley out to the poolside laden with food. He immediately dug into the curry goat and white rice served with fried plantain. He focused on the food and laughed at Lenky's jokes as he pretended not to notice the satisfied smirk on Laura's face as she walked by to go upstairs, announcing that she was going to take a shower and dry her hair. She knew that Jerome wished he could give it to her right then and there. Hell, truth be told, so did she.

Calvin was elated as he enjoyed his lunch of paella with fruit juice. He was in his room at the hotel. He was seated at the small table by the window, while Pat rested in the relatively small but comfortable bed. They had been at the clinic for two hours, though the actual surgery had lasted only twenty minutes. The surgery had been declared a success and Pat was expected to regain full vision within six weeks. Calvin was anxious to go home but planned to enjoy the remaining five days they had left while Pat recuperated. He missed the kids though he knew Pat's sister and Brownie would ensure that all was well. Brownie was such a good friend. He had insisted that Calvin take all of the money because even though they had found the drugs together, if it wasn't for Calvin's bravery and determination they wouldn't have gotten a cent. Besides, the money was needed for a good cause, Pat would regain her vision and Calvin could finally afford to get married. He planned to propose to Pat sometime during their short trip but wasn't sure when to do it. He wanted it to be romantic even though Pat wouldn't be able to see the ring right away. He finished up his lunch and went into the bathroom. He wondered if Lenky would come to his wedding. He planned on inviting him.

Jerome got to Angela's office at 1:55 p.m. After chatting with the excited security guard and signing his autograph on a poster of the Regge Boyz that the guard had in his little station, Jerome and Lenky drove in. Jerome told Lenky that he'd call him when he was ready and then made his way around to Suite #7 where Angela's office was located. Suzzette, the receptionist, recognized him as soon as he stepped in, and greeted him with a bright smile.

"Good afternoon," she said. "Aren't you Jerome James?"

"Guilty as charged," Jerome replied easily. "Is Ms. Charlton in?"

"Yes, just a minute," Suzzette replied sweetly and dialed Angela's extension. Angela told her to send him in.

"You may go in," Suzzette told him. "Second door on the right."

Jerome smiled at her and went through the stained glass door that separated the back area from the lobby. *Yuh neva see smoke without fyah*, Suzzette said to herself. Now it was clear why her boss had rescheduled Mrs. Tucker's 2 p.m. appointment and had left the 2-3 slot free. She wanted to make way for Mr. Handsome himself. Suzzette wondered if there was something going on between them. In the time that she had worked there, she had never seen Angela reschedule an appointment just to facilitate someone else. *Go deh mi boss*, Suzzette grinned as she went online to check her email. Jerome is *so* hot.

Jerome knocked softly once and opened the door. Angela got up from around her desk and greeted him with a hug.

"Hi babes," Jerome said as he crushed her to him.

Angela grinned as she blended in his arms. "You gonna squeeze me to death?"

"Nah...just happy to see you," Jerome replied.

He lowered his head and gave her a kiss. He had meant to just give her a peck on the lips but the kiss quickly deepened.

Breathing heavily, Angela reluctantly pulled away.

"Bad boy...that's not what you came here for," she chided gently, trying to get a handle on the situation before things got out of hand.

Jerome raised his arms in surrender and she led him to the adjoining room where she conducted physical therapy sessions.

She led him to the bed and told him that he could pull the curtain and she would wait in the office while he changed into a towel.

"Its cool honey," Jerome told her. "You can stay..."

"Its ok, I'll wait in there," she replied, though she didn't move as he removed his shirt.

"What for?" Jerome asked, now removing his tank top. "You're about to give me a massage anyway."

Angela gulped. What a fucking body!

Jerome began taking off his jeans.

Angela stopped him. It was too much. If she allowed him to take off his jeans it would be a done deal. She was so wet that she was sure Jerome could hear a squishing sound when she walked.

"I'll have to give you another type of massage," she said, looking at his torso and shaking her head. Jerome was just too sexy. "Come over here...I'm going to give you a 'chair massage'."

Jerome was disappointed but he didn't make it an issue. He followed her over to the specially designed chair and sat down.

Angela got the aromatherapy crème and applied a small amount to her hands. Jerome groaned immediately when she began to massage him.

"God...that feels so relaxing," Jerome murmured, with his eyes closed. "What type of massage did you say it is?"

"A chair massage," Angela responded, loving the feel of his cut, wiry body beneath her fingers. "Its usually done fully clothed so you're one lucky fellow. It promotes better circulation and muscle stimulation. Perfect for you before your try-outs."

"Mmmm," Jerome moaned in agreement. He was impressed. Angela was definitely doing what she was born to do. Her hands felt heavenly.

When Angela was through, Jerome put back on his shirt and they went into her office. They sat down on the small, comfortable couch that was underneath a large a large family portrait. It had been done by a street artist several years ago when the family had vacationed in London. That had been a good time in her life, school was going great, she was in love with Brian and she and her sister were very close.

"Thanks, baby," Jerome told her. "I really appreciate it."

"You're welcome," Angela replied. "Well, I hope you have a safe flight and hurry home...I think I'm going to miss you..."

That pleased Jerome to no end. She really was coming around.

"I'm going to miss you too...we're just getting close and now I have to leave but I shouldn't be gone longer than a week."

Jerome leaned forward and they shared a soft, but passionate kiss. At that moment, Jerome realized with a jolt, that he was really falling in love with Angela. He had liked her a lot from day one but what he was feeling now transcended mere like by far. Jerome broke the kiss and cleared his throat. Angela reached over and wiped her lip gloss off his lips.

"I don't want to leave but I know you have to get back to work," Jerome told her. It was now 2:53 and Angela had an appointment at 3.

"Yeah," she sighed. "I won't be free again until 7. By then you'll be at the airport so I guess this goodbye."

"Yeah, I'll call you before I board the plane though," Jerome told her.

They hugged and Jerome left. He lit a cigarette when he went outside and called Lenky to come and pick him up. Lenky, who was close by in New Kingston at a weed spot, told him that he'd be there shortly.

Angela buzzed Suzzette and told her to send in Mr. Woods. She was really going to miss Jerome. She had to chuckle at how she went from totally resisting him, to finding it hard to go a week without seeing him. Life was so unpredictable.

Jerome hung out with Lenky on the road for a few hours and then went home to relax for a bit before getting ready to go to the airport. Patricia called him just as he was entering the apartment.

"Jerome, why you treat me so bad?" she whined when he came on the line. "Imagine I haven't seen or heard from you and I had to read in the newspaper that you're leaving the Island today."

"Patricia, stop acting like I'm your man," Jerome said to her. "You know I'm a very busy guy so stop tripping."

Patricia started crying.

"You didn't have to say that Jerome," she sobbed. "You know how I feel about you."

Jerome sighed. He didn't have time for this.

"Listen Patricia," he said as he rummaged through his closet, selecting outfits to take with him to London. "We'll talk when I get back in two weeks but I have to go now."

Laura called as soon as he hung up from Patricia. She cursed him out for not answering the phone when she called him last night and told him she was very disappointed that they wouldn't get to spend any time with each other before he left. She wished him all the best and told him to make sure that he called her while he was away. Mercifully, he managed to finish packing before the phone rang again. This time it was Tara. They chatted for a few minutes and he assured her that he had a ride to get to the airport. Jerome checked the time. It was now 5:30. Mrs. Rhoden would most likely be calling him soon to let him know what time she would be picking him up to take him to the airport. He was supposed to be there two hours prior to take off, but he figured 7 would be a good time to get there. He didn't like sitting around in airports too long. He put together an outfit to wear and then went to take a shower.

Mrs. Rhoden sent him a text message when he was about to get dressed: I'll be there at 6:30. He had half an hour to kill. He called Michelle. She was happy to hear from him and he spoke to her for fifteen minutes and then got dressed. Elizabeth arrived at exactly 6:30. She sent the driver up to Jerome's apartment to get his bags. Jerome allowed him to take the bags and wore a bemused expression as he made his way to the vehicle. Elizabeth had gone all out. The vehicle she came to pick him in was a stark white Cadillac limousine.

"Hi there," Jerome said, greeting her with a hug and a kiss. "You sure know how to make a guy feel special..."

Elizabeth waved her hand dismissively. "Life is to be enjoyed my dear fellow and speaking of enjoyment..."

She completed the sentence by taking out Jerome's flaccid dick and dipping it into a glass of ice cold champagne. Jerome sighed contentedly as she skillfully fellated him all the way to the airport. She didn't allow him to climax until they actually reached the airport. She continuously brought him to the edge as Jerome squirmed and moaned loudly on the plush leather seat. He wondered vaguely if the driver could hear him through the partition. She finally allowed him to ejaculate when the car stopped in line at the departure area. Her timing was impeccable.

"Jesus Christ..." Jerome muttered, breathing heavily. He felt like he had just had vaginal sex. "You are something else..."

Elizabeth wiped his semen from off her lips daintily. "Just a little going away present..."

Jerome grinned and shook his head as he exited the vehicle.

"I'll call you," Elizabeth said. Jerome nodded and closed the door. His cell phone would be roaming so getting calls from Jamaica wouldn't be a problem. A porter collected his two bags from the driver and Jerome went inside to check in. He flirted with the pretty agent at the counter and joked with the security personnel at the security check-point much to their delight, then sat down in the departure lounge. The place was crowded. A flight to Miami was delayed and Jerome's flight was full. He called Angela and spoke to her until it was time to board. When they made the boarding call, Jerome hung up from Angela and made his way among the throng of passengers towards the plane. He smiled at the pretty air hostess who was greeting the passengers as they entered the plane. Jerome thought she looked familiar but he couldn't place the face.

"You look familiar," Jerome remarked as she led him to his seat in first class. One of the teams that were interested in him had wanted to pay for his ticket but because that would mean not being able to try out for the other team, he had declined.

Dimples had bought his ticket. He had protested mildly when she insisted on him flying first class. *Yuh might as well get used to it from now*, she had remarked. *After yuh sign yuh big contract that is the only way yuh going to fly.* "Where do I know you from?"

The young lady smiled. "I don't know...maybe you've flown on this airline before? I'm Sara. Sara Charlton."

CHAPTER 19

Jerome landed at Heathrow, the world's busiest airport, 6 a.m. the following morning. He had slept comfortably, thankful that Dimples had indeed bought a first class ticket. He got through customs with ease and Mr. Clarke, Leo Barnes' good friend and an employee of the Jamaican Consulate in London, was outside waiting for him. It was the beginning of summer and the weather was great. Jerome had never met him but he knew Jerome and had no trouble spotting him. They chatted amiably as Jerome placed his luggage into the trunk of Mr. Clarke's VW Passat. He was about to go into the car when he saw the cute air hostess from the flight. He excused himself and walked over to her. She was standing with a co-worker as a van with the airline logo emblazoned on the sides pulled up at the curb to pick them up.

Her co-worker waved hi to Jerome and went into the van.

"Hey," Jerome said. "We meet again."

"So we do...Mr. James," she replied, with a cheeky smile.

Jerome grinned. "You didn't let on that knew me."

She shrugged, magnifying her ample breasts. "I'm a huge football fan. I think I got that from my dad. He used to take me to a lot of football matches when I was growing up."

"So you're staying in London today?" Jerome asked, still pondering where he had seen her before.

"I'll be in London for three days," she replied, throwing her hair back sexily. "I don't go back to work until Sunday."

"Must be great working for a British airline," Jerome remarked. "It has its perks I suppose." She looked over at the van. "I'd love to chat but I have to go...my ride is waiting for me."

"Ok, I'll be in London for a few days...maybe we can get together over the weekend..."

"I'll be staying in at my friend's flat in South London...give me a number where I can reach you and we'll see how it goes."

Jerome gave her his mobile number and she smiled and hurried to the waiting van. She had heard about Jerome's reputation with the ladies as well as talk about the anaconda that he had in his pants masquerading as a penis, and she was definitely open to seeing what he had to offer. The highlight of the weekend was going to be shopping with Deborah, her friend that she'd be staying with, but having a tryst with Jerome James would definitely take center stage.

Jerome called Gunner while on his way to the home where he'd be staying. The JFA President had arranged for Jerome to stay with his nephew, Shane, for the duration of his visit if he so desired. Shane had been cool with it; he was a big fan of the Reggae Boyz and was excited to be housing Jerome during his visit. He had been unable to pick up Jerome at the airport as he had to be at work but he had left the key with his neighbour, a consultant who worked from home, and asked her to listen out for Jerome. Gunner was pleased to hear from him and promised to call him back later as he was tending to some important business at the moment.

They got to the address and Mr. Clarke accompanied Jerome to get the key from the neighbour. Jerome pressed the buzzer and the door opened after a few seconds.

"Yes?" the woman enquired. She seemed to be in her late thirties, rather plain looking but had a very nice, toned body. She obviously worked hard at keeping herself in good shape. She was dressed in short shorts and a tank top. Her hair was pulled back in a bun.

"I'm Jerome," Jerome said, extending his hand. "And this is Mr. Clarke."

She nodded to Mr. Clarke while still holding Jerome's hand.

"So you're the football star, innit?" she said, smiling. "Handsome bloke you are."

Jerome merely smiled, wondering when she was going to release his hand.

She finally unhanded him and went to get the keys.

"Feel free to drop by for a cup of tea when you get settled," she told him as she gave him the keys. "How long will you be here?"

"Only a few days," Jerome replied. He thanked her and went to get his bags from the car.

"Seems like you'll be having your hands full young man," Mr. Clarke teased.

Jerome grinned and thanked him for picking him up at the airport. Mr. Clarke waved off his thanks and told him to contact him if he needed anything.

Jerome then opened the flat and went inside. The flat had two bedrooms and was very neat and clean. Jerome placed his things in what seemed to be the guest bedroom and switched on the TV. It was on a sports channel and they were showing football highlights from the English league. Jerome felt that surge of excitement again. Soon he was going to be a star in the world's most competitive football league. It couldn't get much better than that. He was scheduled to meet with one of the teams at 2 p.m. He checked the time. It was now 8:15 a.m. He decided to relax and make a few phone calls until it was time to leave. He needed to call Angela and let her know that everything was ok and he would try and reach some of his friends in the UK. He retrieved his phonebook from his hand luggage and reclined in the sofa. He didn't think that he would take up Shane's neighbour's offer of tea. At least not today.

"Hi Jerome!" Angela gushed. She had just finished up with a client and was at her desk thinking about him while she cleared her emails when he called. "I was just thinking about you."

"Hi boo," Jerome replied. "Hope they were good, erotic thoughts..."

"No comment..." Angela teased. "How are you?"

"I'm good, everything is ok so far," Jerome told her. "I meet with the team at 2 p.m."

"Ok, I know its going to go well but good luck anyway."

"You miss me?" Jerome asked.

"I do..." Angela said.

"Are you going to show me how much when I return?"

Angela didn't respond immediately. By the time Jerome got back it would be almost two weeks since she had met him. It would still too be early for her to be giving up the goods but...

"Angie?" Jerome prompted when a few seconds passed without a response.

"I'm here honey," Angela assured him. "I most certainly will..."

Jerome smiled at that. They chatted for a few more minutes then Jerome hung up, promising to call her tomorrow.

Shane came home at 1:30, deciding to use his lunch hour to meet Jerome and give him a lift to Old Trafford, where he was scheduled to have his meeting. Jerome was on the phone with Lenky when Shane got there. He wrapped up the phone call and the two men chatted for a few minutes and then they left for the meeting.

"So you met Ms. Campbell?" Shane asked as he navigated his Ford Focus onto Park Lane.

Jerome looked at him quizzically.

"My neighbour," he explained.

"Oh, yeah," Jerome replied. "Nice body."

"Yeah and she loves younger men...surprised she didn't come on to you...offer you a cup of tea..."

Both men laughed.

"I might take her up on the offer before I leave," Jerome told him.

"Trust me...it would be worth it," Shane told him with a smile as he adjusted his spectacles.

Jerome laughed. He tried to imagine nerdy Shane handling the obviously fit and evidently highly-sexed Mrs. Campbell and it just wasn't happening.

They got to the home ground of Manchester FC at 1:58 and Jerome thanked him for the lift and walked over to the security booth. He could see players on the field practicing. There were a few that he recognized instantly. There was Gomez, the left-winger from Mexico who was the captain of his national team; there was Moretti, the central defender from Italy, and he also spotted Bent, the young homegrown upstart – he was only eighteen years old – who also was a starter for England's national team. Jerome felt the excitement flowing through his veins. Playing alongside such world-class players could only elevate his game to the next level. Brimming with confidence, he stated his business to the security guard who directed him where to go.

He went into the room he was directed to and Alex Crouch, the President of Operations, and who had made the offer to Jerome to join the club, stood up and shook his hand warmly. He introduced Jerome to the other three persons seated at the table: Fitzgerald Montecue, the majority owner; Peter Jump, the coach; and Marge Barrett, the public relations officer. Alex did most of the talking, informing Jerome that he had first noticed his talent when Jamaica had played Mexico in a World Cup qualifying group fixture several months ago, when Jerome had scored two memorable goals, leading Jamaica to a tough come from behind win which had set the stage for the big match against the United States which Jamaica had won, again courtesy of Jerome's immense talent. After ten minutes of telling Jerome what would be expected of him on and off the field were he to sign with the club, they all went out to the field where the team was practicing under the supervision of the assistant coach. Jerome changed into football gear and participated in a forty-five minute game with the A side pitted against the B side. He was placed on the B side and led them to a 2-2 draw with the A side. It was the first time that the A side had failed to beat the B side and were it not for some brilliant saves by the goalkeeper – rated as one of the top goalkeepers in English football – the B side would have won the game. They offered Jerome a lucrative contract, which when he saw the figure he would make weekly while signed to the club, he decided he wasn't even going to try out for the other team. He would earn ten thousand pounds weekly and with bonuses and other incentives, the three year contract was worth 2.8 million pounds. He planned to send his savings home and with the exchange rate currently well over a hundred Jamaican dollars to one pound sterling, he would be a millionaire several times over. Jerome accompanied the management team back into the office and after spending a few minutes to read through the surprisingly clear and concise contract, he signed on the dotted line. He shook hands with everyone and they went back out where he was introduced to the other players as an official member of the team. Jerome was now a member of one of the top clubs in English football. He was almost overwhelmed by the feeling of accomplishment. He had come so far. At that moment, he realized that sometimes, dreams really came true.

After getting a lift home by one from one of his new team-mates, Jerome called Angela to give her the good news. She was very happy for him. They spoke for awhile then he called Lenky, Leo Barnes, Dimples, Paul and Michelle, to share the good news. Immediately after speaking with Jerome, Leo made a call to his deputy to inform him to schedule a press conference in the morning. He would inform Jamaica that his star player had struck gold in England.

Gunner came to see Jerome later that evening. Shane came home just as they were leaving. Jerome told him he was going to the pub with his friend to celebrate. Shane looked peeved at not being invited but congratulated him on his contract. Gunner took Jerome to The Spice of Life, one of the most popular pubs in London. They drank a variety of beers and munched on fries as they talked about everything from women to sports. While there with Gunner, his mobile rang. It was Sara, the air hostess.

"Hi there," Jerome said. "What's good?"

"I'm ok," she replied. "Here chilling with my friend. We might go to a club later but I'm not sure."

"Come and hang out with me and my friend," Jerome told her. "We're celebrating tonight."

"Is it...what's the occasion?" Sara asked.

Jerome told her about signing with Manchester FC. She was impressed. She knew it was one of England's most decorated clubs, having won the championship ten times though they hadn't won it in three years. Sara told him to pick them up at 11.

"Which girl that?" Gunner asked, gesturing to the waiter to get them more beer.

"This air hostess I met on the flight here," Jerome told him. "She and her friend look nice. She said to pick them up at 11."

"That sounds good," Gunner agreed.

They stayed at the pub for another hour then they went over to the Park Lane apartments where Gunner kept an apartment. It was his hideout spot. Only his chief Lieutenant knew about it. Sometimes when things got really hot in Brixton, he would hole up there and chill out. The apartment was nice but ridiculously expensive, and very exclusive. Housekeeping was provided and a chef was available as long as he was given three hours notice prior to the meal being needed. The only way Gunner was even able to rent it was because he did it through his lawyer who was one of the top criminal attorneys in London. They watched music videos and sports until 10, and then Gunner freshened up and changed, and took Jerome over to where that he was staying so that he could do likewise. Shane was up playing chess on the internet when they got there. *Damn, on a Friday night? This boy needs a life,* Jerome thought as he went to take a shower. Shane tried to engage Gunner in conversation while he sat on the couch waiting on Jerome but gave up after two curt one word responses. Jerome re-surfaced twenty minutes later, much to Gunner's relief and they left and went to pick up the women.

"Is the friend cute? Does he have money?" Deborah asked Sara as they applied the finishing touches to their make-up. Deborah only dated men with deep pockets, preferably cute.

"I have no idea," Sara replied.

"He better be," Deborah said. "We could've been rolling with Marty tonight."

Marty was a businessman from Atlanta in London on business that she had met a few days ago on a flight. It was as if Deborah had two jobs: air hostess and gold digger. The latter was actually the higher-paying of the two.

A horn blew outside twice.

"Hmmm...sounds promising...that's either a BMW or a Benz," she said.

"How can tell from the just the sound of the horn?" Sara was incredulous. Deborah was a trip but she loved hanging with her. She was a very good friend, almost like a sister. And since she didn't have a good relationship with her real sibling anymore, she welcomed the closeness with Deborah even more.

"What you want to bet?" Deborah challenged as they made their way to the front door.

Sara waved her off and they exited the apartment.

The men watched the women approach the vehicle. They looked hot. Sara was in a short, trendy polka-dot dress with the belt just under her very full breasts, while Deborah was wearing a similarly-styled dress but hers was a dark shade of green which she topped off with matching accessories and sexy Gucci stilettos.

Sara and Jerome made the necessary introductions and they made their way to Orleans night club and wine bar, one of London's hippest night clubs. The girls relaxed and enjoyed the reggae music that was playing at a moderate level through the car's expensive speakers. Deborah gave Sara an 'I-told-you-so' smirk. Gunner's car was a 2007 745 BMW sedan.

The foursome had a really good time at the club. They danced to R&B, reggae, hip hop and garage while consuming three bottles of champagne. Gunner and Deborah really hit it off. She stayed glued to him like white on rice. The fact that he was good looking and obviously had money aside, she liked that he was young and dangerous. He had a hard edge to him that was never too far from the surface even when he was enjoying himself. It excited her. There was no doubt that Gunner was going to get lucky. They left the club at 3 a.m. and Gunner drove over to his Park Lane apartment. Deborah was so impressed that she took her panties off while still in the car. By the time Jerome had used the bathroom and was making his way to the guest room where a naked and horny Sara was waiting, Deborah could be heard screaming Gunner's name. Sara joined her screams two minutes later.

CHAPTER 20

Lenky was in an upbeat mood when he got up on Saturday morning. Preparations for his big party on Sunday were in full swing and he anticipated a very large turnout. It had been an annual event for the past three years, and every year it got bigger and better. It was now truly one of the calendar events for the dancehall crowd. His only regret was that Jerome wouldn't be there. He got out of bed, smacking Laura on her exposed ass as he did so. Half-awake, she threw a pillow at him and pulled the covers over her head. She wasn't ready to get up yet. She had accompanied Lenky to a party that one of his associates had kept the night before, and they hadn't gotten home until the wee hours of the morning. She didn't know how Lenky did it. If only he could transfer some of that energy into sexual staying power, she'd be one happy camper.

"Baby, yuh done know we've been together for awhile now and have three lovely children together," Calvin said to Pat as they sat in the park nearby the hotel. After breakfast, Calvin had suggested that they take a walk and Pat had readily agreed; feeling very rested after sleeping so much since the surgery three days ago.

Pat nodded and Calvin continued, "Is full time now we make it official."

Pat gasped and put her free hand to her mouth as Calvin slipped a ring onto her finger. "Will you marry me?"

Pat cried as she hugged the only man that she had ever loved. She had always considered him her husband but it would be nice to actually get married. "Yes! Oh Calvin!"

A man with a guitar, who was sitting close to them and had observed the proposal, gave an impromptu performance and Calvin and Pat clapped along to the lively but unfamiliar tune. Pat couldn't wait until her eyes were healed so that she could see the ring. Today was one of the happiest days of her life. Only the actual wedding day could eclipse it.

Elizabeth Rhoden fumed as she hung up the phone. She had just tried calling Jerome but his mobile rang without an answer. She was peeved at having had to hear about his contract signing on the news. What, he didn't deem her important enough to call and let her know? She was going to give him an earful when she finally got him on the phone.

Angela yawned as she slowly got out of bed. Jean had casually told her about a party the previous night and to both their surprise, Angela had been enthused to go. Angela realized that since meeting Jerome she was enjoying life a little more – she was beginning to have balance in her life once again. It wasn't all about work anymore. She couldn't wait until he got back so that they could spend some time together. She knew that now that he had signed his contract, he would be going away again in a few months but she would cross that bridge when she got there. She made her way to bathroom to take a shower. She needed to go to the supermarket and then meet her dad for lunch at 12. That was an hour away. She wondered if she should tell him about Jerome. No not yet, she decided. She didn't want to deal with any negativity where Jerome was concerned right now.

Gunner ordered Chinese when the foursome finally emerged from their slumber and met up in the living room. The food arrived in thirty five minutes – the restaurant was only eight minutes away – and they dug into the shrimp fried rice, peppered steak, sweet and sour pork and malah chicken with gusto. The girls were thoroughly enjoying themselves. Hot sex, champagne, good food and a promised shopping spree – Gunner was taking everyone shopping – all equaled one whale of a time. Sara looked at Jerome as she ate. His dick tasted almost as good as the food. She wanted to fuck him for the entire weekend until she had to go back to work. She hoped that he wouldn't mind. The man was addictive.

Jerome had to attend a press conference with his new team in the afternoon so Gunner and the girls accompanied him to Old Trafford. They sat at the very back where they watched the proceedings. The ladies received some curious and lustful glances – they were still in the sexy outfits they had worn the previous night. Jerome got on the podium with the team captain, the coach, the owner and the PR officer, and they announced his signing to the media. It was big news. It was the first time a player from a Third World country had been signed to a premiership club – and one of the top clubs at that. While images of Jerome's exploits for his national team played out on two flat screen TVs on either side of the podium, the press grilled Jerome, eager to hear what the handsome, articulate Jamaican had to say. The press conference lasted forty-five minutes and Jerome handled himself with ease and confidence. When it was over, Gunner took the girls home so that they could change and they then headed to London's West End where Gunner proceeded to spend thirteen thousand pounds on clothes for everyone. Deborah was in Gucci heaven.

On Sunday night, Lenky's party was in full swing. He made his entrance at 2 a.m. with Laura by his side and eight of his soldiers, including Mikey, trailing behind him. He stopped to greet all the other 'dons' he saw on his way up to the VIP section. The party was being held at a large seaside venue in Portmore. There were about 1500 patrons inside and another two hundred outside trying to get in. Lenky was pleased as he stood on the balcony in the VIP section upstairs and looked down at the sea of partygoers having a good time. The four video-men he hired to record the proceedings were kept busy as the girls from different crews tried to outdo each other with their outrageous outfits and risqué dance moves. Lenky sipped champagne and rocked to the music, frowning momentarily when Mikey pulled a firearm and fired two shots skyward. The song that had come on was the hottest song in the streets by a new upcoming artiste from a notorious ghetto. The policemen that Lenky had hired for security didn't bat an eye. It was, after all, a gangster party.

Sara thought about Jerome as she did her part in getting the plane ready for boarding. She couldn't recall the last time she had so much fun. All four of them had ended up spending the weekend together, so she had gotten her wish without even asking. It had just worked out that way. She told Jerome she wanted to see him while she was in Jamaica on leave in two weeks time. He told her that he had a girlfriend but to call him and they would work something out. *Damn right we will*, Sara vowed as she took her position at the top of the steps when the announcer made the boarding call. *Any man I want I can get and Jerome is no exception.*

The rest of Jerome's trip was a blur. Gunner showed him a really good time and before he knew it, it was time to go home. He had a six a.m. flight on Thursday morning so he went home to Shane's at 11:30 p.m. so that he could pack and get some rest. He and

Gunner had gotten really close during his stay. Gunner told him that he was going to come to Jamaica for a week in July. He wanted to attend Reggae Sumfest, the week-long reggae festival that officially kick-started the summer in Jamaica. Jerome was looking forward to that. Gunner felt like the brother he never had. He chatted with Shane as he packed his suitcases. He was going home a lot heavier than he came up. He had had to purchase a large suitcase to accommodate all the stuff he had bought and received. He smiled as he picked up a particular item. He hoped that Angela would like it. Lenky had offered to pick him up from the airport but he told him that Dimples would get him. She had been in Jamaica since Sunday and was anxious to see him. To buy some time, he had told Angela that he would be arriving on the late flight at 12 midnight. He missed her but he couldn't diss Dimples. She had always been there for him. He called Angela again before going to bed. It was 7:45 in the morning her time and they talked until she had to leave for work.

Jerome's cab came to pick him up promptly at 4:15 a.m. Shane had offered to take him but Jerome had told him it was ok. He got to the airport in half an hour and checked in fairly quickly. He took a nap in the departure lounge until it was time to board. The flight departed on time. When Jerome arrived in Jamaica six hours later, he was surprised to be met at the airport by Pearl Saunders, the Minister of Sports, Leo Barnes, President of the Jamaica Football Association, and members of the press. Cameras flashed as she hugged Jerome and congratulated him on his landmark signing. Leo also gave him a hug and fussed around him like a proud father as they made their way to the VIP lounge at the airport, bypassing customs. Jerome managed to exit the airport an hour and a half later. Dimples had been patiently waiting and her chubby face lit up when she saw Jerome sauntering towards her. Jerome grinned and hugged her as people looked on. Whispers of 'Ah 'im name Jerome James' and 'Mi hear say 'im sign contract fi 10 million pound a week' and other remarks filled the air, as Jerome climbed into Dimples' double cab Ford F150.

"Good to see yuh baby," Dimples said as she drove out of the airport. "Yuh enjoy your trip?"

"Yeah man," Jerome told her as he waved to the man who had been selling coconuts at the Harbour View roundabout for over ten years now. Jerome usually stopped because he loved fresh coconut water but not today. "I had a really good time."

"Well, I won't take yuh home until later," Dimples said, giving him a sly glance. "I'm going to feed yuh and then work it back out..."

Jerome grinned. Dimples was very flexible for a forty year old full-figured woman. He remembered the first time he had seen her split. It was amazing. He started getting an erection.

After a heavy lunch of steam fish served with okra and mashed potatoes, and a torrid session with Dimples that included a different position in every room in the house, Jerome poured some fruit juice and checked his phone, finding it strange that he hadn't heard it ring since being back on the island. It was off. He had forgotten to turn it on after he got off the plane. He checked his voicemail. There was a message from Tara, Laura and two cold messages from Elizabeth Rhoden. Jerome remembered seeing several missed calls from her while in London but hadn't bothered to return them. *Elizabeth lucky*, Jerome mused. Why did she have an attitude? He didn't owe her any obligation. He returned Laura's call.

"Hey boo," Jerome cooed when she came on the line.

"Don't hey boo me...how come you're just calling me? What time did you get in?" she fussed. She was getting ready to go on the road. A new plaza was being built in Half-Way-Tree and Lenky had set up a meeting for her with the developer.

"Got in at 12 but had to meet with some government people and the press for awhile," Jerome replied. Dimples came out to the balcony looking for him but went back inside when she saw him on the phone. That was one of the things Jerome loved about Dimples. She always went with the flow; never fussed about anything.

Laura told him that she really wanted to see him today, but doubted she would be able to. That suited Jerome just fine. After leaving Dimples he would go home and relax for awhile before surprising Angela. He planned to go to her office and wait outside by her car when it was near closing time. It was now 4 p.m. and she closed at 6.

When Jerome got home, he unpacked and made a couple of calls. He called Lenky and promised to catch up with him later that day and then he rang Michelle.

"Hi Jerome!" Michelle enthused. She was feeling like her old self again. Her face was pretty much on its way to a full recovery and she was getting used to not being Laura's friend. Khianna, a friend to both but closer to Michelle, had taken Michelle's side when she heard about the incident and had not spoken to Laura since. They were both at the beauty salon when Jerome called. "I was just thinking about you."

"That's good to hear. I have some things to deal with but I'll catch up with you later. Just wanted you to know I got back," Jerome told her.

"Alright, baby," Michelle replied. "Later then."

Khianna put down the magazine she was reading when Michelle got off the phone.

"So that was him huh?" she asked. She wondered why Michelle had gotten caught up with Jerome. Michelle knew that Khianna used to date a popular singer and went through hell with him so why would she get involved with someone like Jerome?

"Yeah, that was my boo," Michelle replied grinning.

"Your boo?" Khianna asked sarcastically, arching her thin eyebrows.

"Yes," Michelle answered emphatically, adding, "I may not be his only boo but he's definitely mine."

"And you're ok with that?"

"It is what it is," Michelle replied. "A piece of Jerome is a hell of a lot more than what most men have to offer."

Khianna scoffed at that. "I'm not into the sharing thing."

"Every man cheats," Michelle asserted. "You best believe that."

The conversation ended on that note as one of the hairdressers indicated for Michelle to come over by the sink to get her hair washed.

Jerome took a cab over to the complex where Angela worked. It was the same security guard on duty from the last time that he had been there and this time he was even more excited at seeing Jerome.

"Mi hear 'bout the big contract man!" he said animatedly. An onlooker would've thought that he was the one who had actually gotten the contract. Jerome indulged him for a few minutes and precisely at six, he hid behind a column that was close to where Angela's car was parked.

Angela exited her office at 6:10 and made her way to her car. She was wondering what she was going to have for dinner when Jerome sneaked up on her, grabbing her from behind.

"Jesus Christ! Jerome! You brute!" she squealed, clutching her heart but smiling now. "You scared me to death honey!"

Jerome laughed at her as they hugged tightly and gave each other a quick kiss. They were aware that other people were in the parking lot.

"You tricked me!" Angela pouted, though it was obvious that she was enjoying the surprise. "I didn't expect to see you until tomorrow."

"I missed you so I came back a day early," Jerome teased.

"Yeah right," Angela replied, as she opened the car and placed her stuff on the back seat.

"You're heading straight home?" Jerome asked, clutching the Gucci shopping bag which had her gifts.

"Yeah..." Angela responded. She was suddenly nervous Seeing him so suddenly and unexpectedly, coupled with the fact that they were about to go to her home together, had her palms sweating, her heart pounding and her body yearning. It was a heady mix of emotions.

"Ok," Jerome said and made his way around to the passenger side. He got into the car and shut the door. That left no room for Angela to maneuver. Home sweet home it was. She took a deep breath and got into the car. She shot him a nervous smile as she drove out of the complex. She knew that today would be a defining moment in their very young relationship one way or another.

CHAPTER 21

Angela got home in ten minutes. Her neighbour, Mrs. Trought, was shocked when she saw the handsome young man exit Angela's car. It was the first time that she had seen Angela bring a man home since the scandalous incident with her ex-boyfriend several months ago. Her fat, wrinkled face was screwed up in concentration as she tried to figure out who he was. She knew his face from somewhere. She picked up the phone to call Sylvia who lived at Apartment C. Miss-I-love-to-act-like-I-can't-mash-ants seems to have gotten herself a new man.

"Long time mi nuh see Michelle," Lenky remarked. He and Laura were having dinner at Georgio's, Kingston's finest Italian restaurant. "Mi not even glimpse her at mi party."

"She has been busy with work and stuff I guess," Laura said, shrugging her shoulders. "I don't even think she's on the island."

"That is strange," Lenky replied, savouring the scrumptious taste of the shrimp scampi. "De two ah oonu not close anymore?"

"Not really," Laura said casually. "You know, people grow apart sometimes."

Lenky's phone rang and he checked the number. He had stopped letting business interfere with his quiet time with his wife but it was an overseas call from one of his customers in Baltimore. He talked for the next ten minutes and when he was through,

Laura deftly changed the topic. It would have been a bit difficult explaining to Lenky how it was possible for two best friends to grow apart in a couple of weeks.

"Six love!" Calvin thundered triumphantly as he slammed the winning domino onto the table. He was playing with Brownie and two other fishermen from the community. Calvin and Pat had returned from Cuba on Tuesday morning. The close knit community had held a fish-fry on the beach to celebrate Pat's successful surgery.

Brownie sucked his teeth in annoyance. His stupid partner had caused them to lose again. He hated losing to Calvin, who would tease him mercilessly when they were out at sea. He wouldn't hear the end of this for weeks. Calvin and his partner had just administered two six loves back to back. Brownie took a swig of his beer and rolled up his sleeves. He'd be damned if he was going to lose for the rest of the night.

Angela and Jerome cuddled in Angela's leather sofa in front the large TV. Angela had taken a quick shower and joined Jeromeon the couch as they waited for the pizza they had ordered to arrive. After her initial nervousness at the prospect of having Jerome in her home, once they had actually gotten inside she was surprised at how comfortable she was at having him there. She sighed contentedly as she snuggled up against him even more. It felt so right.

"I bought you something," Jerome said softly, nuzzling her ear. Angela shivered.

"You did..." she managed. "I was wondering what was in that Gucci bag..."

Jerome laughed and got up to retrieve the bag. It was on the floor next to the coffee-table. Angela sat up excitedly as Jerome handed it to her.

"Thank you baby," she cooed. "Now let's see what we have here..."

Angela took a box out of the bag.

"Oh my God," she whispered when she opened the box: Silver Gucci stilettos. They were fabulous. She tried them on. Perfect fit. Angela hugged Jerome tightly.

"Thank you so much baby," she told him. "They are very nice."

Jerome smiled, pleased at her reaction.

"There's more..." he told her.

Angela dug into the bag and took out a black object. She opened the case: Gucci sunglasses. Large and very diva-like. She tried them on and looked in the mirror. She didn't usually wear sunglasses but she had to admit that they looked incredible on her. Gave her edge.

"Oh baby," Angela said, hugging him again. "I absolutely love my gifts. You have excellent taste."

"You're welcome boo," Jerome replied, their faces inches apart. "Anything for you..."

Jerome was about to kiss her when they heard the unmistakable sound of the pizza delivery guy's small motorbike. Jerome groaned. Angela laughed.

"Saved by the bell," she teased as she went outside to collect the pizza. Jerome smiled to himself as he sat on the sofa. No rush, no fuss. He was confident that he would be getting some tonight.

After dinner, Lenky and Laura went to the Rooftop, a popular sports bar, to hang out. Ever since they had made up, Lenky went out of his way to ensure that he and Laura spent quality time together. They both knew how to play pool and soon settled into a competitive game against each other. Lenky's phone rang while he, and most of the men – and some women – in the bar, he proudly noted, watched Laura bend over to make a shot.

It was Calvin. Lenky wondered what the fisherman wanted. Their business had long been concluded.

"Hello," Lenky said. Shit, Laura made the shot. His wife was busting his ass.

"Lenky, this is Calvin," Clavin replied, slightly nervous. He knew that Lenky must be wondering why he was calling him. "I just wanted to tell you thank you."

"For what?" Lenky asked.

Calvin told him all about his wife's sickness, the successful surgery and his upcoming wedding. Lenky felt good that he had given Calvin the money. It was amazing how what was a small thing to him had so much impact on the well-being of someone else. Lenky thanked him for inviting him to his wedding, and promised to be there. Calvin told him that he would let him know when the date had been set. Laura finally missed a shot and Lenky wrapped up the conversation with Calvin and directed his attention to the table. He needed to remind Laura who was the boss.

"Whew! That was good," Angela commented as she took up the empty pizza box and placed it in the trash. They had eaten off the entire medium pizza. Angela had four slices while Jerome had easily devoured the other eight.

"Yeah," Jerome agreed, patting his full stomach. He needed a drink and a spliff. He wondered if Angela would mind if he smoked weed around her. Well, that wasn't going to change so Jerome figured that she might as well get used to it if they were going to be together. He took a quarter ounce bag from out of his blazer pocket and began crushing up the weed. Angela returned from the kitchen. To Jerome's surprise she didn't comment or bat an eyelid. She told him that she was going to the bathroom and would be right back. A few seconds later he could hear her brushing her teeth. Jerome chuckled to himself. Maybe Angela wasn't as prissy as she seemed.

When Angela returned to the living room, Jerome had lit up and was puffing away.

"Would you like something to drink?" Angela asked. "I don't drink much but I have liquor. Jack Daniels and Pepsi?"

Jerome laughed. "Sure sweetheart."

"Don't laugh at me," Angela said smiling as she playfully punched his shoulder. She made him the drink and sat between his legs on the couch.

"Give me a drag," she said to Jerome, holding her hand out to take the joint from him.

Jerome coughed. "What?"

Angela smirked as she took the joint and took a drag.

"Surprised huh?" Angela said to him smiling. "My exboyfriend was a Rastafarian and he used to smoke weed a lot. Occasionally I would have a little."

Jerome was amused. Then amazed. The weed was very potent and Angela took four strong drags and didn't even cough once. Not bad for someone who didn't smoke regularly.

"I know you think I'm this sheltered, little innocent thing... and I am, admittedly, in many ways, but I'm also cool...you know."

Jerome smiled. That she was. Angela wasn't nerdy or uptight in the least. There was an air of expectancy between them as they lay together on the couch watching TV. Jerome finished his joint and leaned over to drop the tail in his now empty glass. His erection poked Angela in her side when he moved. Angela swallowed nervously. That could not have been his dick, Angela thought. It felt so big and hard. But it was. There was no mistake about it as Jerome pulled her directly on top of him and devoured her lips. Angela moaned in his mouth. His kisses always ignited a blazing fire that consumed every fiber of her being. Jerome's kisses were deep and probing, unpredictably alternating between gentle and rough, sometimes nibbling and sucking on her lips, sometimes wrapping his tongue around hers. He then explored her neck and collarbone, biting and sucking until she was writhing in his arms and whispering his name.

Jerome sat up and placed her to straddle him. He pushed her baby T above her breasts and she groaned loudly when she felt his hot mouth on her painfully erect nipples. Angela didn't think she had ever been this horny in her life. She was literally soaked. Jerome took his time as he kissed, licked and sucked her full, firm breasts. After a few minutes, Jerome got up with her in his arms and moved them to the bedroom. He gently lowered her onto the bed and raised her legs, snatching off her shorts and underwear in one fluid motion. Angela gasped and her heart pounded. She was sure that Jerome could hear it. She was about to have sex with only the second man in her life. Shyly, she kept her legs slightly closed though the room was not brightly illuminated. The only light was the little that was filtering in from the living room. Jerome then took off her top and stood.

Angela laid there and watched transfixed as Jerome slowly discarded his clothing. She gasped audibly when his rigid dick sprang free. Certainly Jerome didn't really think that thing could fit inside her. It was ridiculously large. A double-edged sword of excessive length and girth. Unconsciously, she tightly closed her legs.

Jerome climbed on top of her and kissed her softly.

"I've dreamt of this moment many times," he whispered as he nibbled her ear. "I want you so bad my dick hurts."

Angela didn't think that she could get any wetter as Jerome kissed his way down her body. Her clit was throbbing. Jerome's face hovered over her cleanly shaven sex, breathing in her essence. His breath tickled her clit unbearably.

"Oh god Jerome," Angela moaned.

Jerome then kissed her thighs, lifting her legs in the air as he kissed the entire length of her frame. He worked his way back up to her groin and did something that he had never done before. He covered her vulva with his mouth and kissed her pussy like he was kissing her mouth. Angela made an unintelligible sound and clutched the sheet tightly as she spread her legs even wider. Jerome took his time exploring Angela's essence. He licked and nibbled on her vulva in languid fashion, and when he started sucking on her protruding clit, Angela went berserk. She clamped his head with her thighs and begged him not to stop. Her orgasm felt as though it was rushing from every section of her body to meet in one gigantic explosion at the intersection between her legs. When it arrived, it was unlike anything that she had ever experienced. She squirted long and hard as she convulsed and shook like a woman possessed. Long after Jerome had removed his mouth and got up to put on a condom, Angela was still shaking.

"Mmmm...mmmm...mmmm..." Angela kept moaning with her eyes closed. She was still waiting to come back down to earth. She had always thought that cloud nine was a figure of speech.

Jerome climbed back on top of her and Angela opened her eyes. They maintained eye contact as Jerome guided his turgid shaft inside her pulsating wetness. Angela groaned as he went deeper and deeper ever so slowly.

"Don't hurt me Jerome," Angela whispered, still looking into his eyes.

Buried to the hilt but not yet moving, Jerome knew that she didn't mean sexually.

"Your heart is safe with me baby," he replied as he started to move.

Angela kissed him passionately as she moved with him, acclimatizing herself to his massive tool. They clutched each other tightly and continued kissing as they moved in unison. Jerome felt like he was soaring. He broke the kiss and increased his tempo as he readied to climax, unable to hold back his insistent orgasm.

"Jerome...oh...Jesus Christ...oh god baby...I feel it in my belly..." Angela breathed as Jerome thrust in and out of her with hard, fast, precise strokes. Angela's tight wetness squeezed his dick with each thrust.

"Fuck...Angie...you... feel... so... good... baby...so...good... boo...its coming baby...oh shit..." Jerome grunted as he ejaculated.

Angela caressed his wiry frame as he shook in her arms.

"Damn baby, I really enjoyed making love to you," Jerome told her as he got up to discard the condom. "You were definitely designed for me."

Angela smiled as she watched him go into the bathroom. She had done the deed and there was no turning back now. She could only trust that her handsome, well endowed man would be true to his word and wouldn't break her heart. When she loved she gave her all and something told her that she was on the road to loving Jerome with all her heart and then some. She winced slightly as she got up and went into the walk-in closet to slip into her silky bathrobe. She was very sore. She figured that it would take a little while to get used to Jerome's size. The more they had sex the quicker she would, she reasoned. Angela smiled as she went into the kitchen to get some juice. It would be good to be having regular sex again. Jerome was phenomenal.

Laura was pensive as she sipped champagne by the poolside. The meeting with the developer had gone well and she had secured space for her boutique when construction was completed in five weeks. But her excitement was tempered by the fact that her period was late. It had been late for damn near ten days. She knew she should take a pregnancy test as soon as possible but she was scared. She wasn't ready to have a baby. And, if she was pregnant, the father could very well be Jerome. Naturally, everyone ould assume the baby was Lenky's but what if the child looked just like Jerome? Then what? She wished she had some-one she could talk to. This was too private to share with Bigga. For the first time since the fight, she missed Michelle.

"Ok baby, I'll talk to you tomorrow," Jerome said as he kissed Angela by her living room door. "Sleep tight."

"I'm sure I will," Angela replied, with a big yawn. "I'm so tired...you wore me out honey."

Jerome laughed. "It's all your fault...your pussy is too sweet."

"Jerome!" Angela blushed furiously. She kissed him and pushed him out.

Jerome laughed and hopped into Lenky's waiting vehicle. He had called Lenky to pick him up twenty minutes ago.

Angela walked gingerly to her bed and got in. She was extremely tired and sore. Jerome had gone into the kitchen while she was bent over putting the juice back into the fridge. He had eaten her out from behind, not even allowing her to close the fridge door. She came three times in Jerome's mouth while the cold air blasted her face. Then he had fucked her from behind mercilessly against the kitchen counter without using a condom. She had asked him to put one on but his answer had been to throw her against the counter and ram his dick inside her while telling her that he would never again fuck his future wife with a condom. The roughness had excited her to no end and it had felt so good when he came inside her. She definitely preferred it bareback so she would just have to trust Jerome not to give her anything. She would have to start taking birth control until they decided they were ready to start a family. She fell asleep with Jerome on her mind.

"So big balla," Lenky began as they headed to New Kingston. "Enjoy yuhself in England?"

"Yeah man," Jerome replied. "Me and Gunner was doing it up real big."

Jerome filled him in on some of his escapades in London and was amused when Lenky seemed a little peeved that he and Gunner had gotten so tight. When Jerome told him about the two hour thirteen thousand pound shopping spree, Lenky commented that "ah show off Gunner ah show-off" and "thirteen thousand pound ah nuh nuff money". Jerome merely laughed. Lenky had money but from what Jerome saw, Gunner was seriously paid, and with the exchange rate being what it was, he'd definitely give the nod to Gunner. They hung out for awhile at Togetherness Thursdays, a weekly Thursday night party that ended precisely at 2 a.m., and then they went up to Lenky's home so that Jerome could pick up the Lexus truck. Lenky had told Jerome that he could use it as he wished until it was time for him to report to training camp in England in eight weeks time.

CHAPTER 22

Jerome was at Angela's having Sunday dinner when his phone rang. Jean, Angela's best friend, was also there. He didn't recognize the number when he checked the caller ID.

"Hello."

"Jerome?"

"Yeah..."

"Hi, this is Sara."

"Hey you, what's up?" Jerome replied. Freaky Sara. She was the only woman he had ever met who genuinely liked the taste of semen. She got off on swallowing.

"Nothing much," she replied. "I told you I would've called when my vacation started. I got in midday today."

"Ok...I'm at my girlfriend's having dinner," Jerome told her. Jean, still extremely excited about Jerome and Angela hooking up, shot Angela a wide you-go-girl smile. "I'll catch up with you later. Is this your mobile number?"

"Yeah," Sara replied. "Make sure you call me later."

"I will. Bye."

Sara smiled as she hung up the phone. It was good to hear his voice. She hoped that he would be able to see her later that night. She had thought of very little else in the two weeks since she'd seen him in England. It didn't help that Deborah and Gunner were now an item. She wondered what his girlfriend was like. Sara picked up the phone and dialed the number for her parents' home. She wanted to let her mom know that she would be in the island for a week. Sara hoped her dad didn't answer the phone; he was always so cold to her and refused to let bygones be bygones. She thought of her sister as she made the call. She was amazed that Angela still refused to speak to her. Yes, it was terrible what she did, she'd be the first to admit that, but people make mistakes. You forgive and you move on. Oh well, Sara thought breathing a sigh of relief when her mom picked up the phone. She was done trying to mend the relationship. Her last attempt had been a month ago when she had a stopover in Kingston and she had gone by Angela's office to say hi. Angela had called the security guard to escort her from the premises. Sara had been very embarrassed and humiliated.

"Hello," Mrs. Charlton said when she answered the phone.

"Hi mommy," Sara said. "How are you?"

"Hi Sara, I'm good sweetheart," her mom replied as David looked up from the newspaper he was reading with a frown upon hearing his daughter's name. His wife ignored him.

"I'm in Jamaica for a week," Sara told her. She was staying in the one bedroom apartment in Waterloo Close that was one of several properties owned by her parents. "I'm longing to see you mommy. When will you have time for us to link up?"

"I'll come and see you tomorrow at about 10 a.m. We can go have lunch and do some window shopping."

Sara liked the sound of that. Her mom's idea of window shopping was to buy anything she saw in a store window that she liked. They spoke for a few more minutes and then Mrs. Charlton terminated the call so that she could get back to C.S.I Miami. Aside from the news and the various shopping channels, it was the only thing that she watched on television.

Jerome went by Michelle's apartment after leaving Lenky. It was 3 a.m. but Michelle didn't mind. She had never been to his place so she pulled on a pair of shorts and a tank top, and they went to Jerome's apartment. Jerome gave her the gift he had purchased – a very trendy antique-white Chloe satchel leather handbag which she absolutely went bananas over, and they made love on the thick rug in front of the TV. They fell asleep right there until Jerome woke up to pee at 5:30, after which they went into the bedroom.

Laura sobbed as she sat on the closed toilet seat in the bathroom. Her worst fears had just been confirmed. She was pregnant. Wondering had become an unbearable burden so she had gotten up early and made her way to the pharmacy and purchased two home pregnancy tests – different brands – so that she could know her status. It's a good thing Lenky wasn't home when she had gotten back to the house. She had been unable to hold back the tears when both tests were positive. Her gut told her it was Jerome's baby. If that was the case, all hell would break loose when she gave birth. She had to have an abortion. She couldn't take the chance.

"Hi mommy!" Sara gushed as she let her mother into the apartment. "It's so good to see you."

"Good to see you too honey," Dahlia Charlton said as she hugged her youngest daughter. Sara was two years younger than Angela. The whole family had always been close but since the incident between Sara and her sister, Dahlia and Sara had definitely gotten noticeably closer.

They went into the kitchen and Sara made coffee as they played catch up. They had hardly spoken over the last few weeks because of time differences and conflicting schedules.

"I met this guy the other day," Sara said to her mom as they sipped coffee at the kitchen counter. "He's very hot."

Dahlia laughed. Her youngest daughter was a trip when it came to men. She was happy though that her daughter confided in her about her personal life. It gave her a chance to know what was going on and to offer advice accordingly. And Lord knows, there were times when Sara badly needed someone to talk some sense into her.

"Ok, where did you meet him?"

"In England," she replied. "He's a star footballer. Plays for Jamaica's national team."

"I see...be careful honey. If he's as hot as you say and a star athlete...well you know how that goes."

"Yeah...he has a girlfriend and stuff but I think he really likes me too."

"Ok baby, just take things slow and if he really wants you let him come to you. Don't get caught up ok?"

"Ok, mom."

It's a little late for that Sara checked the time and placed her cup in the sink.

"I'm going to take a shower and then we hit the road," she told her mother as she made her way to the bathroom.

Dahlia nodded and went into the living room to turn the TV on. She settled on a news channel. Another suicide bombing in Iraq. That country was much better off before the invasion, she thought as she looked at the devastation. She was sure that many people would disagree with that point of view but as far as she was concerned the war in Iraq was one of this century's biggest blunders thus far.

"Hi baby," Jerome said as he went into the kitchen to take the call. It was Angela. Michelle was still in his bed fast asleep. "How is the love of my life?"

Angela smiled. "I'm ok. Tried calling you earlier."

"Yeah, I saw the missed call when I got up not too long ago," Jerome replied with a yawn. "I was tired. We were on the road until the wee hours of the morning."

"Ok...you and that guy that came by the house to pick you up?"

"Yeah...that's Lenky, very good friend of mine. You'll meet him soon," Jerome told her.

"Ok, cool. Alright baby, I'll talk to you later. My next patient is here," Angela said.

"Later babes."

Jerome ended the call and padded back into the bedroom.

He got back into bed and snuggled up with Michelle. Just as he did that he heard his cell phone ringing in the kitchen. He didn't bother to get up and answer it.

Elizabeth cursed as she threw the phone down onto the bed. Every time she called Jerome she wasn't able to reach him. She hadn't spoken to him since that day she gave him a ride to the airport and despite the fact that she left several messages on his voicemail; he had yet to return her call. Who the hell did he think he was playing with? She was not some cheap floozy that he could just cast aside. He had some nerve. Just wait until she got a chance to confront him.

"Yuh not even pay mi nuh mind at yuh dance," Jada pouted. Lenky had stopped by for breakfast on his way back from an early morning meeting with a gang leader over in Jones Town. The man wanted some guns to buy as he had an escalating feud with a rival gang from the community. Lenky could have sent Braveheart, who usually handled the distribution of the guns Lenky bought into the island, but because he was Jada's brother, Lenky saw him personally.

"I was busy," Lenky replied as he lit a spliff. He had just eaten a meal of roast breadfruit and salt mackerel. "Plus yuh nuh see say ah mi an' mi wife did inna de place."

Jada was pissed. Since the last time he was there, the way he treated her had given her renewed hope that they could really get back together. But lately he seemed to have regressed to his old ways.

"Why yuh treat mi so bad Lenky?" Jada complained, tears welling up in her eyes. "It betta mi jus' give up and find a man. Nuh tree nah grow inna mi face. Nuff man out deh want a good woman like mi."

"Ah nuh who want yuh...ah who yuh want," Lenky replied smugly. "An' who yuh want is me."

With that he pulled Jada to him. She resisted half-heartedly.

"Jus' cool baby," Lenky said in a gentle tone. "Yuh know mi check fi yuh certain way. Yuh give mi a child and yuh is a good mother an' good woman. Mi tek good care ah yuh...give yuh anything what yuh want..."

"Not everyt'ing," Jada interjected.

That got Lenky upset. He shoved Jada away from him.

"Cho bloodclaat man," Lenky said, exasperated. "Mi jus' caan badda wid yuh sometime enuh. Wey de rass yuh want mi fi do? Lef mi wife?"

"Yes!" Jada shouted. "Nuh lef yuh did lef mi fi har? Nutten nuh wrong if yuh lef har an' come back to me."

Lenky sucked his teeth and grabbed his keys.

"Mi nuh know why mi did badda come over yah," he said shaking his head as he walked away, slamming the front door behind him. He got into his truck as he heard something smash inside the house. Jada was royally pissed. Lenky sucked his teeth again as he drove off. *Damn unreasonable*, he thought irritably as he exited Nannyville and turned on to Mountain View Road. *She lucky mi neva box har dung.*

"Damn, sleepy head...about time you woke up," Jerome remarked. He was standing in the bedroom applying lotion to his nude body when Michelle opened her eyes. He had just gotten out of the shower. It was now 1 p.m.

"Mmmm...what a sight for sore eyes," Michelle said, sitting up as she admired Jerome's body. The sheet fell away exposing her full breasts.

Jerome grinned.

"I'm starving," he announced as he retrieved a pair of boxers from a top dresser drawer and slipped them on.

Michelle yawned. She still felt tired. Sometimes she forgot how Jerome could wear the body out. Anyone who fucked Jerome on a regular basis did not need to exercise. She smiled at the thought.

"What are you smiling at?" Jerome asked, fixing Michelle with a quizzical look.

"None of your business," she replied, childishly sticking out her tongue. She then got out of the bed and stretched her petite but curvy frame. "Drop me home and go do your thing."

Jerome dropped Michelle off at her apartment ten minutes later and made a spur of the moment call to Tara, who readily agreed to meet him for lunch at the new Chinese restaurant on Dumfries road.

Tara hugged him tightly when they met up at the restaurant. The place was packed with some of the more affluent New Kingston lunch crowd - the restaurant was very expensive - but they managed to secure a table for two close to the small bar area.

"It's so good to see you," Tara said as she continued to hold him in a tight embrace.

"Yeah," Jerome replied. "Good to see you too, T."

They sat and a waiter, a voluptuous young lady who was at least 6 feet tall, came over to take their order. They ordered Beijing Duck, Guangdong dumplings and Sichuan soup.

"I don't have on any panties," Tara announced when the waiter left, eyeing Jerome mischievously.

◆

Jerome smiled and was about to respond when he saw a familiar face come into the restaurant.

Mikey, Blacka and Ping Pong went up by the house in the afternoon. They had just finished making some collections from the various illegal activities that Lenky had going on in several ghettoes. This was done every Friday like clockwork. The trio headed straight for the kitchen. They were famished.

"What the fuck?" Mikey exclaimed. The kitchen was spotless. No food had been prepared. Bigga was supposed to cook three times a day and leave the food in the kitchen so that anyone who came to the house could have a cooked meal if they so desired. "De bwoy Bigga want a man lick him inna him face. What him t'ink say mi bredda ah pay 'im big money fah?"

Mikey started to shout Bigga's name as he walked out to the pool area with Blacka and Ping Pong in tow. There was no sign of Bigga. Mikey went up to the apartment on the rear of the property where Bigga lived rent free. He had seen Bigga's CBR motorbike parked out front when he had driven in, so he must be home. They could hear the sound of the TV as they neared the apartment. Mikey knocked on the door but there was no answer.

"Him mussi lock dung wid a gal," Blacka remarked.

"Mi neva si Bigga carry a woman come up yah yet," Mikey scoffed.

"Rassclaat!" Ping Pong exclaimed. He was looking through the side window. The others ran over to see. The window was closed but the curtain was slightly parted, allowing the men a partial view of the living room. Bigga was sitting in the couch with his back to the window. It was obvious that he was masturbating. The disturbing part to the three men, who looked on in disbelief, was what Bigga was watching on the screen. Two men in cowboy attire were kissing each other. Outraged, Mikey pulled his firearm and went back to the front door where he proceeded to shoot off the lock and kick in the door. Paralyzed with fear and surprise after suddenly hearing two quick shots at his front door, Bigga jumped up quickly as the men barged in, kicking over the open bottle of baby oil that was on the floor next to his feet. His pants were at his ankles and his T-shirt had been pushed up, exposing his extremely flabby stomach.

Laura heard the bullets but thought she was dreaming. After crying for a long time in the bathroom, she had gone back to bed, thinking that some sleep would help her to escape from the nightmare that was unfolding. It had taken her an hour of staring at the ceiling, but eventually she had fallen asleep.

"Jesus Christ!" Bigga exclaimed as he clumsily tried to pull up his pants. "Mikey! What yuh doing?"

"What am I doing?" Mikey asked, mimicking Bigga's high-pitched voice, which was higher than usual due to his fear. "De question is fat man, what de fuck are you doing watching homo movie and ah jerk off? Eeeh batty bwoy?"

"Ah...nuh..."Bigga stammered, fearing for his life. He knew how much the three gun wielding men in front of him hated homosexuals.

"Ah nuh what? Eeeh?" Mikey shouted. "How yuh t'ink mi feel fi know say mi ah eat from battyman all dese years?"

He didn't wait for Bigga to respond. He squeezed off four shots in quick succession. The first shot was all that was necessary. Bigga was dead before the following three hit his body.

Laura jumped out of her sleep. It wasn't a dream. Shots had been fired on the property. She pulled on a pair of sweats and hurried downstairs. She called Lenky's cell as she looked around.

"Baby I heard just heard shots fired on the property," Laura told him breathlessly as she cautiously looked out by the pool.

"Wha'! Who else is there? Wey Bigga deh?" Lenky asked. Good thing he was on his way home. He'd be there in five minutes.

"I don't know," Laura replied, "I'm not seeing anybody."

"Mi soon reach home," Lenky told her. "Go back upstairs and close the door."

"Ok, baby." Laura terminated the call and was about to do just that when she heard voices. One sounded like it belonged to Mikey. She went out by the pool and looked up at Bigga's apartment. Someone was standing in the doorway. That must be Blacka, Laura thought, her eyes squinted. Even in the daylight it was hard to see anything but his clothes. She made her way up there.

Jerome watched surprised as Sara and an older woman who bore a slight resemblance to her looked around for somewhere to sit. They made eye contact when she looked over where he was sitting. She covered her mouth in surprise and said something to the woman. Jerome smiled and waved her over.

"Oh my God...that's him mommy," Sara said. "The guy I was telling you about."

"Oh," Mrs. Charlton said. "He really is a handsome fellow. Is that the girlfriend?"

"I don't know but he's waving us over. Come let me introduce you," Sara said as she walked over with her mother in tow.

Jerome stood when they got to the table.

He hugged Sara.

"Sara this is my friend Tara, Tara meet Sara."

The girls flashed fake smiles at each other and Sara introduced Jerome to her mom.

"A pleasure to meet you young man," Mrs. Charlton told him pleasantly. She instantly liked him but she was going to advise Sara to leave this one alone. He would break her heart.

"Anyway, just saying hi," Sara said. "I won't disturb you any longer. I'll call you later. Bye...Tina is it?"

"It's Tara," Tara told her. Bitch!

Sara smiled and walked off. Mrs. Charlton waved bye to Jerome and his companion.

"That was not nice," she chided gently, as they walked beside each other towards a table that three people had just left.

Sara just laughed. "Please...I know her. Tara Reid, the Minister of National Security's daughter. She's such a snob."

"She seems nice enough...maybe you're just jealous," Mrs. Charlton teased.

"Mommy...who's side are you on?" Sara asked, pouting comically.

Mrs. Charlton laughed. "Yours of course darling."

Sara laughed and stole a look at Jerome as she took up the menu. He was too fine.

"Yo, Laura ah come," Blacka murmured to Mikey. Mikey had switched off the television and was sitting on the arm of the couch, looking at Bigga's dead body with disgust. He didn't respond.

"Blacka? What the hell is going on here?" Laura asked as she reached the door and pushed past him inside.

"Oh Lord!" she exclaimed when she saw Bigga's bloody, bullet-riddled body on the floor. "Why the fuck would you guys kill Bigga?"

She slapped Mikey's face hard. "I'm sure you were the ring-leader. What did he do to deserve this?"

Mikey rubbed his jaw. "Mi come here an' see the batty bwoy ah jerk off while watching gay movie. So mi shot him. We nuh play dem game deh roun' here."

Laura shook her head. The stupid pig. "Are you high? How can you shoot a man for what he does in the privacy of his home? You ignorant fool!"

Mikey bristled at the insult but he knew better than to go against Laura. "Just cool Laura, yuh nuh understand how de t'ing set up. Batty bwoy fi dead! It inna de Bible!"

"You just wait until Lenky gets here," Laura warned. Surely Lenky would disapprove of his brother killing Bigga in cold blood.

She dialed Lenky's number. "How far are you baby?"

"Just around the corner," Lenky replied. "Yuh hear any more shots?"

"No, you are not going to believe what happened," Laura told him, scowling at Mikey. Damn psychopath. "When you get here come up by Bigga's apartment."

"Alright," Lenky replied as he entered the driveway. He quickly got out and hurried around to the back of the property.

"What is going on?" Lenky asked when he got within earshot of Laura, who was standing in the doorway. She moved and allowed him to enter by way of response.

"Rassclaat!" Lenky exclaimed when he saw Bigga's body lying in a pool of blood. "Ah who do dis?"

"Ah me shot de batty bwoy," Mikey proclaimed as he rolled up a spliff, dumping the seeds on Bigga's body.

He went on to tell Lenky what he and the other two men had seen when they came to the apartment looking for Bigga. Lenky shook his head. What was the world coming to? He called two of the policemen on his payroll, Officer Cuthbert and Officer Radcliffe, to come and dispose of the body. He was unable to reach Radcliffe but he got Cuthbert and told him to come and take care of the situation. He would know what to do.

Laura was very disappointed at Lenky's nonchalant response to his childhood friend's murder but she refrained from getting in an argument with him in front of the men. That wouldn't do any good. She decided to discuss it with him later when they were alone.

Mrs. Charlton got home at six. Her husband was in the den watching a repeat showing of Jamaica's historical World Cup berth clinching victory over the United States a few weeks ago.

"Hi honey," she said, kissing him on the cheek. "Have you eaten?"

"Not really," David replied. "Did you bring back anything?"

"Yeah, some Chinese," she responded as she looked on the 72 inch plasma screen. She smiled when she saw Jerome collect a pass on the right wing and blew by two defenders like they weren't there. Poetry in motion. He was so skilled and talented.

Dahlia shared her husband's passion for football. It was actually at an inter-collegiate football game that they first met thirty years ago. "I met him today."

"Who?"

"Jerome James," Dahlia replied. "Someone introduced us."

She didn't want to tell him that it was Sara. He would only have something negative to say. His reluctance to forgive his youngest daughter for her past mistakes was a bone of contention between them.

"Ok, that's cool," David said. "I can't wait to see how he does in the English league."

"Yeah," Dahlia agreed. "That will be interesting to watch. I'm sure he'll excel though."

She then went into the kitchen to give her husband some of the hazelnut chicken mandarin that she had brought back for him.

"Yuh want to go out fi dinna or yuh want fi order in?" Lenky asked. Laura was sitting on the love seat next to bed channel surfing while Lenky, who had just gotten out of the shower, was drying himself with a towel.

"No, I'm not hungry," Laura snapped.

He and Laura had just finished arguing about what Mikey had done. He had refused to discuss it, telling Laura that she just didn't understand the code of the streets and that it didn't concern her in any event. All she needed to do was to go hire a competent cook to replace Bigga.

His reasoning had upset Laura but she had dropped it. No use stressing herself over something that couldn't be undone when she had her own problems to deal with. Lenky told her to suit her-self and he got dressed and left the house. He called Jada and told her to cook him dinner. Though she had been furious with him when he left the house that morning, she told him ok. It was difficult for her to stay mad at Lenky for long. After getting the call, she started a quick meal of dumplings, boiled bananas and corned beef and cabbage. It didn't matter what she prepared, she knew that Lenky would enjoy it.

After Lenky had left, Laura called Jerome. She had decided that she was going to have an abortion rather than risk humiliating Lenky, who would surely kill her, by giving birth to Jerome's child. She started crying again. As much as she had always said that she wasn't ready to have a child, she did not believe in abortion. It was a very difficult decision but one her sense of self-preservation con-vinced her that she had to make.

"Hi babes," Jerome said. Seeing her name when he checked the caller ID had reminded him that they were yet to spend any time together since he got back.

"Hey...are you alone?" Laura asked, sobbing.

"Yeah...I'm on my way home," Jerome replied. He was going home to shower and change, and then swing by Angela's apartment. Angela said she wasn't sure what she wanted to do but that he should come by before 8 p.m. so that they could still catch the 8:30 movie if that's what she decided on. "Why are you crying baby? What's wrong?"

"I'm pregnant Jerome!" Laura blurted out as the tears increased.

Mikey was about to knock on Laura's bedroom door when he heard Laura's proclamation. Mikey froze in his tracks, convinced that his ears must be deceiving him. Did Laura really say what he thought she said? He pressed his ear against the door.

"I have to abort it Jerome," Laura was saying. "Lenky would kill me, you and the baby."

Bloodclaat! Mikey exclaimed inwardly. He couldn't believe that Jerome would do that to Lenky. Eat his food, sleep at his house, drive his vehicle, hang out with him and then turn around and fuck his wife. As to Laura, damn whore. His heart racing and his adrenaline pumping like it always did when he was getting ready to kill someone, Mikey listened some more.

"I'm going to do it as soon as I get a chance...maybe tomorrow" he heard her say.

She was silent for awhile then he heard her say "ok".

There was silence then he heard the shower running. Mikey took a deep breath and went back down the stairs. He had gone up there to put some money into the safe that Lenky had behind the large portrait of his son Nathaniel. It was a large sum of money – nine hundred thousand dollars in cash – and he didn't want to just leave it lying around in the house. He placed the bag of money in one of the guest rooms downstairs and locked the door. He then called Jerome. He tried to control his anger so that he wouldn't alarm him.

"Hello," Jerome said as he parked in front of his apartment.

"Yes, Jerome, ah Mikey dis," Mikey told him. "Yuh deh home? Mi need fi show yuh something."

"Yeah, I'm home," Jerome replied. What could Mikey possibly have to show him that couldn't wait? "What you have to show me? I'm kinda in a rush rude boy...that might have to wait until another time."

"It nah tek long man but mi trust yuh judgement so mi just want yuh fi tek a quick look and mek mi know if it alright,"

Mikey said, already rushing out the house so that even if Jerome said no he would still be able to catch him at his house before he left. He hopped into the Toyota Tundra and gunned the engine.

Jerome sighed. "Ok, check me but if you don't get here by the time I'm dressed I won't be waiting on you."

"Alright, mi soon forward," Mikey said as he quickly exited the driveway and drove onto the main road.

Jerome terminated the call and went inside. His head was spinning. He couldn't that believe that Laura was pregnant with his baby. He was sure that it was a boy. He wanted to talk to her before she did the abortion. He understood where she was coming from but he felt they still needed to at least discuss it. She had agreed to come and see him in the morning. Her revelation had rattled him. He went into the kitchen for his marijuana stash and proceeded to roll a spliff. He wondered what the hell crazy Mikey wanted to show him.

The more Mikey thought about it, the more enraged he got. If word of this ever got out, it would make Lenky look like a fool. People would talk behind his back, business associates would think he was getting soft...the consequences would be dire on a lot of levels. Mikey would not allow that to happen. He was going to kill Jerome. It was unfortunate but it had to be done. The reputation of Lenky and the organization was riding on it. He wanted to call Blacka and Ping Pong to assist him but he would have to explain why he was killing one of his brother's best friends and Jamaica's star footballer. No, he had to do it alone. He would blow Jerome's head off, ransack the apartment and remove a few items. Make it look like a robbery. Everyone knew that he had just signed a huge contract so it wouldn't be farfetched for him to be a target. He stepped on the gas.

Laura felt better as she stepped out of the shower. She was glad that she told Jerome. Now that she had told someone, it felt like less of a burden. She dried herself and took up her Victoria Secret moisturizer. Tomorrow morning she would tell Lenky that she was going to the gym and go see Jerome for a couple of hours.

"Cho bloodclaat!" Mikey cursed. The two cars in front of him were moving much too slowly for his liking. He swung impatiently and drove as fast as he could, planning to overtake the two vehicles and swing back into his lane before reaching the corner. A trailer coming around the corner hit the right side of Mikey's vehicle as he attempted to get out of the way and Mikey lost control of the vehicle as it swerved and spun, then careened into the large bus that was desperately trying to slow down. Mikey, who was not wearing his seat belt, screamed just before his neck broke upon impact. He died instantly.

CHAPTER 23

Lenky received the call from one of the policemen on his payroll. He was still at Jada's, having eaten and was relaxing before going back on the road. He jumped up in shock.

"Ah weh de bloodclaat yuh ah say to mi?" Lenky shouted. "Mi bredda dead?"

Jada was in the bathroom peeing when she heard Lenky shouting. She wiped and rushed into the room.

"Is what happen baby?" she asked worriedly. Tears were in Lenky's eyes as he spoke on the phone. The last time Jada had seen Lenky cry was at his mother's funeral many years ago. This must be serious.

Lenky did not seem to hear her.

"Jesus Christ! Dead pon de spot?" Lenky was saying, tears flowing freely now. "Alright, mi deh pon mi way."

"Baby Mikey dead," Lenky said as Jada rushed to hug him.

"Lawd 'ave mercy," Jada said, crying too. Mikey was crazy but Jada always liked him because he was nice to her and always told her that he thought she was a better woman for his brother than Laura.

"Dem say..." he broke down and continued, "...say him crash roun' a deep corner in Barbican. Crash inna one bus."

"Oh baby," Jada said hugging him tightly. "Mi so sorry fi hear."

"Mi ah go out ah de scene," Lenky told her as he pulled away and grabbed his keys. He went into the bathroom and splashed his face with water before he ran out the door. Jada called Ping Pong and Blacka and told them what happened. She told them to meet Lenky at the accident scene and make sure that he was ok. Jada wanted to be there for Lenky but she knew that Laura would be on the scene as soon as she got word. She decided to stay in the background and let Lenky come to her if he needed her.

Laura was shocked when Lenky called with the news of Mikey's demise. She guessed she was more shocked at the fact that Mikey died from a car accident than the fact that he was dead. She always knew Mikey was too wicked to have a long life but she figured he would've died by the gun. Anyway, her husband needed her so she got dressed quickly and drove to the scene of the accident.

Jerome was on his way to Angela's when Lenky called him and gave him the news. After he had gotten dressed, he had been mildly surprised but pleased that Mikey hadn't turned up seeing as he had stayed in the house a bit longer than planned. Jerome was shocked to hear about Mikey's death but not too surprised at the way he died. Mikey was the worst driver he had ever seen. He told Lenky that he would be there soon and turned to go back onto Trafalgar road instead of heading onto Lady Musgrave road where Angela lived. He called Angela and apprised her of the situation and that he would see her later if possible.

Angela was disappointed but she understood that his friend needed him right now. She said a quick prayer for Mikey's soul though she never knew him. She wondered what to do with her evening now that Jerome wasn't available. Angela called Jean but she was all the way over in Spanish Town with a friend. She called her dad to see what he was doing.

"Hi pumpkin!" David said, pleased to hear from his princess.

"What are you up to daddy?" Angela asked.

"Nothing much," he replied. "Your mom and I are just here watching TV."

"Ok, I'm going to pop by," Angela told him. She would go there for a few hours and hopefully Jerome would be available by the time she left.

"Great," her daddy said. "I'll beat you up on the chess board."

"In your dreams old man," Angela scoffed. Her father was an avid chess player and had taught Angela how to play from an early age. Though they didn't play as frequently as they did when she was younger, any time they did, the games were ultra competitive affairs as they both hated to lose.

David laughed and hung up the phone.

"Angie's coming over," he said to Dahlia as he got up to get a beer. He knew better than to disturb his wife when she was watching C.S.I. Miami.

Dahlia nodded, not taking her eyes off the screen.

Jerome arrived at the crowded accident scene and found Lenky surrounded by some of his employees, several cops and Laura. The accident had caused a severe back-up of traffic and the cops were in the process of clearing the road of the wreckage.

He patted Lenky on the back and nodded at Laura. Lenky spoke quietly with the senior cop on the scene and then he gestured for Jerome to follow him. They went over to where Lenky's truck was parked so they could talk privately.

"Bwoy, 'Rome, mi caan believe mi bredda just dead so," Lenky said as Jerome rolled him a spliff. Lenky was in bad shape. A good joint would help to ease the pain.

Lenky's phone rang but he ignored it and when it kept ringing he shouted for Laura to come and take it from him.

"Mikey was a knucklehead but 'im did 'ave a good heart and was fiercely loyal to mi an' de organization," Lenky continued, when Laura took the phone and went back across the street. "Mi ah go miss 'im 'Rome...Jah know."

Jerome nodded and lit the joint and handed it to Lenky.

"He had called me saying that he had something to show me," Jerome said. "I think he might have been on his way to my apartment when it happened."

"Something to show yuh?" Lenky found that strange. What could Mikey possibly have to show Jerome?

"Yeah," Jerome continued. "He didn't say what... just asked if I was home and said he was coming by to show me."

The two men chatted a while longer and they went back over to the others when Lenky finished smoking the joint. Mikey's body was now on its way to the morgue and a wrecker had removed his vehicle, allowing traffic to flow once again. A reporter from one of the local TV stations came up to Lenky while he was wrapping up a conversation with the senior cop on the scene. They were discussing the sensitive matter of the two illegal guns found in the vehicle that Mikey was driving. The two cops who had found the two powerful handguns had turned them over to the senior cop, who, though not on Lenky's payroll, figured something was in it for him if he kept the find out of the official report and returned the guns to Lenky.

"Excuse me sir," the young reporter said, cameraman in tow. "I heard you are the victim's brother. What do you..."

Lenky punched the man in his face and told his soldiers to grab the cameraman. Ping Pong and Blacka held him while Braveheart took away the camera and placed it in his vehicle. The reporter, who was bleeding profusely from the nostrils, wondered who the hell this man was that he could assault a news team in front of the law and they look the other way. Lenky conferred with the senior cop who then told the reporter and the cameraman to accompany him to his vehicle. Lenky gave some instructions to

Ping Pong and then he and Laura drove off with Jerome following in the Lexus truck.

"Shut up yuh mouth," the senior cop snarled at the reporter, who was voicing his disgust at what just took place. "Yuh just hold this and keep yuh rass mouth quiet. Not a word about what happened to anybody or else..."

The cop gave the reporter the pouch that Ping Pong had handed to him.

"This will cover yuh doctor bill fi yuh nose and replace de camera," he told him. He then ordered the reporter and the cameramen to leave the scene as he couldn't guarantee their safety.

They hurried to their news vehicle and drove away in a daze. Jamaica had gone to the dogs. Lawlessness and corruption seemed to be the order of the day.

Angela greeted her parents warmly when she got there. She sat with them and watched the remainder of C.S.I. Miami. All three went out to the patio when the program ended.

"How is work mom?" Angela asked, as she munched on crispy banana chips.

"It's great," Dahlia replied. "I have to attend a conference in Atlanta next week. How are things at the office?"

"Pretty good," Angela replied, then took a deep breath and added, "I'm dating again."

David's ears perked up.

"Really! That's good honey," David said smiling. It must be that nice Christian young man that he had introduced her to. "So, you decided to give that chap Steven a chance. That's just great. A pretty and smart woman like you should not be alone. It's unnatural."

"A woman does not need a man to validate her daddy," Angela retorted, and then added laughing, "but you're right, I'm way too hot to be by myself."

Her parents chuckled.

"Anyhoo...it's not Steven," she announced. "Sorry daddy but Steven is a dork. I don't know how on earth you thought I would've been interested in him."

"So who is it?" her father asked anxiously.

"Daddy I know you're going to be surprised but he's very nice and I really like him and..."

"Jesus Christ Angie! Just tell us man!" David said exasperated.

"David, don't swear," his wife chided, though her interest was just as piqued.

"Ok, ok," Angela said. "It's Jerome James. The football star."

"Oh Lord!" her parents uttered in unison, though for different reasons.

"Angie! Jerome James?" her father asked, his face etched with an equal mixture of concern and disappointment. "He's a playboy... that's not the kind of man I want for my princess. How long have you been seeing him?"

"Daddy, I'm not a little girl," Angela said gently but firmly. She wanted his blessing due to the close relationship they shared but under no circumstances would she allow his opinion to interfere with her happiness, and she was very happy being with Jerome. "I've been dating him for a couple of weeks now and I really like him a lot. Please don't be negative. Just be happy for me."

Dahlia excused herself and went into the bathroom. *Sweet gentle Jesus!* She thought. This can't be happening. Sara was once again entangled in her sister's love life, though unwittingly this time. She had to talk to Sara as soon as possible and let her know that the girlfriend that Jerome mentioned was none other than her sister, Angela.

David sighed. The stories he had heard about that fellow. He was one of Jerome's biggest fans but he didn't want his daughter to get hurt. Despite her assertion that she was a grown woman, she would always be his little girl. "But Angie..."

He saw the determined look on her face that he knew so well; the one that indicated she would not be deterred. "Ok, sweetheart, I have my concerns because he has a certain reputation but if you're happy, I'm happy."

"Thank you daddy!" Angela hugged him tightly as she grinned. "I'll invite him over for dinner tomorrow so that he can meet you and mommy."

"Ok princess," David replied. He considered the upside in his beloved daughter dating the football star. It was actually kind of cool, Jerome seeing his daughter. He would have bragging rights amongst his group of football-loving friends. But God help him if he ever hurt his baby.

Dahlia composed herself and went back out to the patio. She wasn't surprised to see that David had changed his tune. Angela had always been able to wrap her doting dad around her little finger. She sat and watched them play chess, their faces a study of concentration. After a few minutes she got up to call Sara from the bedroom so that she could talk privately.

After they left the accident scene, Jerome was driving behind Laura and Lenky, heading up to their house when he decided to let them be by themselves. There was nothing more that he could do to comfort Lenky right now. He called Lenky on his cell and told him that he would swing by to see him tomorrow. Jerome ended the call and was about to place one to Angela when the phone rang in his hand. It was Sara.

"Hey you," Jerome said.

"Hi...you sound a little down...everything ok?" Sara asked.

"Yeah...I'm good."

"Ok. Am I seeing you tonight? Please don't say no. My pussy has been playing hopscotch all day in anticipation of your visit."

When she put it like that how could he say no? He whipped the truck around at the first opportunity and headed in her direction as they spoke. He asked for her exact address and coyly told her that he would try his best to see her later. While at the stoplight at the intersection of Old Hope Road and Trafalgar Road, his phone rang. Jerome sighed. It was Elizabeth Rhoden. She was really becoming a nuisance.

"Hello," Jerome said, allowing his annoyance to seep into his voice.

"Aren't you happy to hear from me," Elizabeth said, her tone laced with sarcasm. "I've been trying to reach you since the day you left for England. Apparently the contract has boosted an already inflated ego to the point where you think you can just brush the likes of me aside on a whim."

"Elizabeth, what is it you want from me?" Jerome asked as he turned onto Waterloo Close where Sara's apartment was located.

"I just don't appreciate the way you have dealt with me Jerome. I'm Elizabeth Rhoden!"

Jerome chuckled. *You snobby slut*, he mused as he parked in front of Sara's apartment. He blew the horn twice and saw Sara look through the living room window. She grinned from ear to ear when she realized that it was Jerome and hurriedly opened the door. Jerome activated the alarm and leaned against the vehicle.

"Elizabeth, you came on to me, I obliged and we had a couple of fun experiences. Now it's a wrap...surely we can move on without there being any drama," Jerome told her calmly. He looked at Sara waiting by the door and signaled that he would be there in a minute.

Elizabeth was miffed. How dare he? She was angry but at a loss for words. It was really not a good time for this to happen.

"But why...I thought..." Elizabeth said as she struggled to articulate her feelings.

"Don't make a big deal, Elizabeth," Jerome interjected. "It was fun but let's not act like it was more than that. Take care of yourself."

Jerome terminated the call and went inside where Sara was perched on the arm of the sofa waiting on him. He stepped in and closed the door behind him. She stood up and kissed him passionately.

"Mmmm...I missed you Jerome...feel how hot my body is," she said as she rubbed up against him sensuously. Jerome cupped her small but shapely ass and nuzzled her neck. Her body was indeed on fire. "I couldn't stop thinking about how good you taste...how you stretch my tight pussy and make me explode over and over again..."

Jerome made an unintelligible sound and literally ripped Sara's skimpy top and shorts from her body. Sara knew just how to push his buttons. During that fun-filled weekend in London she had figured out all the things that got Jerome to unleash the tiger in him. She loved when he was like this: rough, passionate, primal. She enthusiastically threw her long legs atop his shoulders and balanced precariously on the arm of the sofa as Jerome plunged into her welcoming wetness with wild abandon. Sara threw her head back as she savoured the I-can-never-get-enough feeling of Jerome's massive tool stroking her insides. The house phone rang as she screamed her way to her first orgasm of the evening. She ignored it. Nothing could get her from off of Jerome's dick right now. Not even fire.

Mrs. Charlton threw the phone down disappointedly. Sara's land line and cell phone had both rung without an answer. She really needed to talk to Sara and nip this thing between her and Jerome in the bud. If Angela and or David found out, and knew that she was aware of the situation, it would tear the family apart. She picked up the phone and dialed Sara's number again.

"Come to bed honey," Laura said to Lenky as she hugged him and led him into the bedroom. Since they got home they had been on the bedroom balcony. Laura had dutifully listened to Lenky as he reminisced about growing up with Mikey. He was close to finishing a bottle of Hennessey and had started slurring his words. Laura felt really sorry for him. She had never seen her husband like this. He was really taking his brother's death hard.

She undressed him down to his boxers and placed him under the comforter. She then took a quick shower and joined him in the bed. She cuddled with her already snoring husband and thought about her situation. It would've been the perfect news to cheer up Lenky but she really couldn't take the chance. Laura sighed.

One would think in this technological day and age that a paternity test would be possible long before the child was born. She wondered if she would be able to go and see Jerome in the morning as planned. Lenky was in really bad shape.

Elizabeth Rhoden stood naked in front of the full length mirror in her lavish bedroom. Jerome's casual dismissal had really taken a toll on her already fragile self-esteem. A week after that day when her husband had told her he knew about her and Jerome, he had turned up at the house with one of his business associates from the States. After dinner, they had retired to the den for cocktails and her husband nonchalantly told her that they would be having a threesome. She hadn't wanted to and her husband had calmly popped in a DVD. A few seconds later, images of her and Jerome having sex at the Prometheus played on the large flat screen TV. Elizabeth had been shocked and humiliated while her husband reveled in her shame and discomfort. Her husband and his friend then had sex with her one at a time and together. It had happened every other night last week, each time a different man accompanying her husband, and two nights ago, it had been four of them. The more vile and degrading the act, the more excited her husband seemed to get. Thank God he had left earlier that day for a four day business trip in Venezuela. What kind of man gets off on degrading and abusing his wife? As she stared at herself in the mirror, she wondered what kind of woman would stay in such a marriage. She didn't want to face the answer.

"Good god...Jerome...unbelievably it just keeps getting better each time," Sara remarked contentedly as they relaxed on her large, comfortable bed. "I came so many times I lost count."

Jerome chuckled. She was right though. The sex between them was the bomb.

"What's the craziest thing you ever did sexually?" Jerome asked as he idly stroked her right breast.

"Hmmm...that's a tough one...I've done it all," Sara replied. Then she frowned. "Actually, that might be sleeping with my sister's boyfriend."

Jerome laughed. "Damn...that's cold."

"Well...I'm not proud of it but it happened. She hasn't spoken to me since."

"How long ago did it happen?"

"About a year now," Sara replied, breathing a little heavier as her nipple responded to Jerome's absent caressing. "I've tried countless times to reach out to her but to no avail."

"Hmmm...she's not the forgiving type huh?"

"Nope," Sara concurred as she rolled over and started giving him a leisurely blow job. The phone rang and she sighed as she released his scrotum from her mouth and reached over to answer it. It had rung quite a few times in the past hour and a half while she had been having sex. Someone was really trying to reach her.

"Hello," Sara said, spreading her legs as Jerome playfully slid his index finger inside her.

"Sara! You know how long I've been trying to reach you!" Dahlia said, relieved that she finally got her.

"Ok, I was busy...what's the matter mom?" Sara asked as she sat up. Jerome had ceased playing with her when he realized that she was talking to her mother.

"Sara, Angela came by the house tonight...she just went home... we were on the patio talking...and she told me and David about her new boyfriend..."

"Get to the point, please, mother," Sara said. She had a bad feeling where this was heading. Her heart raced.

"Watch your tone young lady," Dahlia said sternly. "Anyway, your sister's new man is Jerome James."

Sara remained silent. She was right, that's where it was heading.

"I don't know how far things have gone between you and Jerome but you must stop communicating with him immediately," her mother was saying.

Why does my sister always have to get what she wants, Sara thought. *Jerome and I are so good together...and it's not like I knew...*

"Sara!" her mother said sharply. "Are you listening to me?"

Jerome realized that something was amiss. Whatever Sara's mom had said to her had drastically changed her mood. Sara looked angry and sad at the same time.

"Yes. I'm listening," Sara responded coldly.

"You had better...there's no way we can allow Angela and her father to find out. It stops now and that's the end of it. Do you understand me?"

"I have to go mother." Sara hung up the phone and cradled her head in her hands.

Dahlia couldn't believe that Sara had hung up on her. Furious, she called back but got a busy signal and when she called Sara's mobile it went straight to voicemail. She just hoped that Sara would do the right thing. Lord knows her youngest daughter could be a real pain in the ass when she wanted to be. But the stakes were too high in this one. Sara had to let go and do what's best for the family. Angela could find out on her own time the kind of man that she was in love with. But not like this and damn well not with Sara at the thick of it yet again.

Angela wanted to call Jerome but didn't want him to think that she was too clingy. She had gone straight home after leaving her parents. She was in a good mood having beaten her dad 4-2 in six games of chess and having finally told him about Jerome. She couldn't wait for them to meet. She just knew they would get along well. She was a little puzzled at her mother's behaviour though. Her mom had been very quiet after she told them about Jerome. Come to think of it, after her original utterance of 'Oh Lord', she hadn't said anything. She had even left the patio a few times which was unusual as she loved to watch them play chess. Angela decided that she would raise it with her tomorrow. She checked the time. It was now 10:30. She curled up in bed with the TV on and kept her mobile close by just in case Jerome called and she'd fallen asleep.

"Sara, what happened?" Jerome asked, concerned as he sat up beside her. The first thing that crossed his mind was that someone had died. Sara didn't respond. She just kept on shaking her head and sobbing.

"Sara. Sara. Talk to me," Jerome implored. Sara got up abruptly and locked herself into the bathroom. Jerome got dressed and waited for her to come out. Several minutes later he heard water flowing. She came back into the bedroom in a much more composed state.

"Jerome...we can't see each other anymore." She paced the room with her arms folded as she spoke. "I'm really feeling you but I have to leave you alone."

Jerome waited for her to elaborate. Sara was a really good fuck and was fun to be around but he would not lose a night's sleep if he never saw her again. He was curious as to the reason though. Sara looked at him and was disappointed by his lack of emotion at her statement. Didn't he care about her at all?

She started to cry again as she continued. "Your girlfriend, Angela, is my sister."

Jerome shook his head in disbelief. It was such a small world. She was right; it damn well had to end now. There was now way he could risk losing Angela by playing around so close to home.

"Damn...this is crazy...how much does your mother know?" Jerome asked. He didn't want Mrs. Charlton to think that he was playing Angela.

"She knows I like you a lot and that we met in London but I didn't tell her we were sleeping together or anything." Sara was hurt by Jerome's business-like attitude. It was as if her feelings didn't count and it was all about making sure precious Angela didn't find out. Her mother had acted the same way.

Jerome was relieved. He would charm Mrs. Charlton and do some damage control. Everything would work out. He got up and grabbed his keys.

"Guess this is goodbye then," he said, brushing her cheek lightly with the back of his hand. She swatted it away.

Jerome exited the apartment quickly, leaving Sara standing in the middle of the bedroom crying her heart out.

CHAPTER 24

Jerome dialed Angela's number as he drove out of Sara's apartment complex. The phone rang several times before Angela picked up. She had fallen asleep watching a movie on Lifetime.

"Hi baby," she murmured sleepily. "Are you ok?"

"Yeah...a bit tired though. Helping Lenky deal with his grief is no easy feat. He's in pretty bad shape. I'm just now leaving his house."

"Ok, honey." Angela yawned. "Just call it a day and go home and get some sleep. I'll see you tomorrow."

"Alright boo...sleep tight."

Jerome sighed as he hung up the phone. He really loved this girl. The Sara incident had reconfirmed how strong his feelings were for Angela. He had almost wet his pants with relief when Sara told him definitively that the mother didn't know that anything had really transpired between them. He wondered if one day he would be able to leave women alone and just focus on Angela. Only time would tell. Jerome decided to drive through New Kingston's hip strip. It had been such a weird day that he had forgotten it was Friday. The strip was teeming with people but Jerome was in a pensive mood and did not feel like partying. He saw several people that he knew as he cruised pass the various hot spots but didn't stop and no one knew it was him anyway as the tinted windows were up. He decided to take Angela's advice and go home.

It was not a good time for Lenky. He woke up with a bad hangover the following morning and Laura greeted him with the news that the plaza he owned on Molynes Road had been razed by fire early that morning. The fire department had yet to ascertain the cause of the blaze. It was one of his most profitable ventures. Apart from owning the plaza, he had operated three businesses there as well: a bar, an auto parts supply store and a liquor wholesale. He wondered how Missy was coping. She was from the ghetto where he hailed and had gotten some insurance money from a car accident which she had used to open a restaurant on his plaza three months ago. The fire would be a crushing blow for her. Lenky went into the bathroom to take a shower. He was about to shout for Laura to get Bigga to whip up a concoction to get rid of his hangover when he remembered that Bigga was dead. He sighed as he lathered himself. He had always heard that bad things came in threes. What was next?

"Hi baby," Angela said when Jerome finally answered the phone. She had called twice. "I'm sorry...did I wake you?"

"Yeah...took me awhile to fall asleep last night," Jerome told her, glancing over at the clock. It was 9 a.m. He had tossed and turned for most of the night and hadn't really fallen asleep until the wee hours of the morning.

"Ok, go back to sleep baby. Call me later."

Jerome turned off his phone and threw the comforter over his head. He didn't plan to get up before one in the afternoon.

After talking to Jerome, Angela got dressed, had a quick breakfast and went to the Headley Children's Home where she volunteered at least twice a month. The kids loved her and looked forward to her visits. She had been volunteering there for a little over a year now. Her last visit had been when Jerome was in England and she had been surprised to find herself wistfully thinking that it would be nice to have a child. Since her freshman year in college, she had always planned to get married and start a family at twenty-eight. That was still four years away. Maybe the sudden yearning had something to do with Jerome being in her life. Maybe that's why she hadn't yet gotten back on the pill. She would discuss it with Jerome seeing as he refused to use a condom. If she got pregnant her dad would raise hell if he didn't marry her, and truth be told, so would she.

Sara was pensive as she sipped coffee at the kitchen table. She had cried for what seemed like an eternity last night. Emotionally spent, she had slept soundly. Sara analyzed her life and was unhappy with the way things were. She was estranged from her father and sister, and now, her mother, the only person who she was close to in her immediate family, had chosen Angela's feelings over hers. Protect precious Angela at all costs. It wasn't right. She didn't know that Jerome and Angela were an item when she met him. The past was the past yet her family would always hold what happened with Brian over her head. Well, she had news for them. She didn't care anymore. She didn't give a fuck about being left off her daddy's will, she didn't care about what they thought of her and she definitely didn't give a shit about reconciling with Angela. Matter of fact, she was going to apply for permanent residence in the UK. Her job with the number one British airline and her family background would make the process a shoo-in. She had nothing in Jamaica anymore.

No man, no family – at least not after what she planned to do, no real friends to speak of – they had drifted apart due to her job and she loved London. Sara smiled for the first time since getting that phone call from her mom yesterday. She felt liberated.

Lenky shook his head as he looked at the devastation. Millions of dollars in damage. The building was not insured. Lenky did not believe in insurance. The only thing that he insured was his vehicles and that was only because it eliminated the hassle with the cops when they stopped him on the road. Lenky considered insurance companies a rip-off. You pay them all this money in case something happens and when nothing happens you don't get your money back. But now something had happened. Lenky sighed and went to his vehicle, nodding at some of his employees who were still in shock that they were suddenly out of a job. He had held a quick meeting with the staff and managers of each of the three businesses under the large shade tree that was across the street by the Pentecostal church, and let them know that he would try and see if he could re-assign them to some of his other operations until he rebuilt. He hopped into his Lincoln Navigator and headed towards Nannyville. He could use some of Jada's cooking right about now.

Laura called Lenky to see if he would need her anytime soon and when he told her no, she told him that she was going to go to the gym and run a few errands. She then called Jerome but his phone went straight to voicemail. She went into the bathroom to take a shower and decided that she would still swing by his apartment even if she didn't get him on the phone as she had to go to New Kingston anyway. Lenky had asked her to get the suit that Mikey was to be buried in and to get the funeral program to a printer. Lenky wanted his brother to be buried quickly. The funeral would be in eight days time. Lenky had also remembered that Michelle was a good singer, and instructed Laura to ask her to sing a song at the graveside. Laura didn't know how she was going to accomplish that one.

Jerome got up an hour earlier than planned and immediately took a shower. He then went into the kitchen to make a protein shake. He quickly whipped it up and was taking a sip of the frothy drink when he heard the doorbell. Surprised, as he wasn't expecting any visitors and hated when people came by unannounced, he went to the door and looked through the peephole. Laura. He forgot that he had asked her to come by that morning. He wondered why she hadn't called ahead to let him know that she was definitely coming. Then it suddenly dawned on him that he had turned his phone off after Angela had woken him up earlier that morning. He opened the door and let her in. She looked ravishing as usual. Laura was wearing a white Christian Dior sweat suit with matching shades and pocketbook. She hugged him and went to sit on the couch.

"How are you doing?" she asked Jerome as she slipped off her trendy black and white Jimmy Choo sandals and removed her sunglasses. "I'm so fucking stressed Jerome."

Jerome sat beside her and draped his arm around her shoulder.

"Hush baby, everything is going to be ok," he said. "Just take it one problem at a time."

"Easy for you to say...everything is just happening at the same time." She took a cigarette out of her pocketbook and Jerome fetched a lighter and lit it. Laura took a deep drag and continued. "I have to be making the arrangements for Mikey's funeral, and get this, Lenky asked me to get Michelle to sing at the graveside."

Jerome laughed.

"You called her yet?"

"Hell no! There's no way I'm calling that bitch!" Laura stated vehemently. "I'm going to tell Lenky that I couldn't reach her...that she's probably overseas."

"Suppose she shows up at the funeral?"

"My story would still stand...but I doubt she'll come anyway," Laura said dismissively.

She snuggled up even closer to Jerome and peered up at him.

"I can't believe I'm pregnant with your child," she said softly. "I always said I wouldn't want a baby anytime soon but I swear having your seed alive inside of me is an incredible feeling. It's a pity that we can't keep it..."

Jerome was silent as he contemplated the situation. He understood where she was coming from. It didn't make sense on any level for her to keep it. It saddened him though. His first child would have to be aborted. Like Laura, he was just sure the baby was his. He wasn't sure who made the first move but they started kissing and Jerome made love to her right there on the couch. He surprised Laura by being tender and gentle all the way through. When she climaxed it was different this time. She didn't scream. She cried.

"Yuh ok baby?" Jada queried. "Want anything else?"

Lenky had just eaten a meal fit for a king. Jada had prepared conch, fried chicken, mashed potatoes and yam salad. Though Lenky had protested that she was giving him too much food when she placed his plate in front of him, he not only had eaten it all, but had asked for seconds. Now he was so full that he could barely move. He was sitting on the couch with his feet up on the coffee-table, rolling a spliff.

"Not a t'ing more baby," Lenky replied. "Mi good man. Just need fi blaze up some weed and settle the stomach."

Jada smiled, pleased that he had come to see her today. She loved him so much and her heart really went out to him for his loss. She knew that he would miss his brother dearly. She sat beside him and switched on the TV. An action flick was just beginning on Showtime. They watched the movie in comfortable silence.

Jerome called Angela half an hour after Laura left his apartment.

"Hi sweetheart," Angela said. "I was just thinking about you."

"That's good to hear." Jerome pulled a Ed Hardy T-shirt and a pair of Evisu jeans out of the closet to put on. He was about to go on the road and wanted to know where Angela was. He was thinking they could have lunch together. He was famished. "Had lunch yet?"

"Actually no...I did volunteer work today and I'm just getting ready to leave," Angela replied, still hugging Celia, an adorable nine year old who suffered from respiratory problems.

"Taking me to lunch?"

"Yep. What you feel like having?"

"You..."

Jerome laughed. "Mmmm...rude...you deserve a spanking..."

"I'm counting on it..."

"That will definitely be arranged...anyways baby, meet me at Mr. Wong's in thirty minutes. I feel for chicken in black bean sauce."

"Ok baby, see you in a bit."

Angela smiled as she ended the call. It was so easy for her to talk to Jerome. To be silly, naughty...anything really, without feeling like he was judging her. She was so happy that they met. He must really be her soul mate.

Jerome thought about Laura as he finished getting dressed. She was definitely going to have an abortion. She planned to do it the day after Mikey's funeral. She was going to just pick a random doctor from the yellow pages and make an appointment. Laura getting pregnant had him thinking that maybe it was time to start a family. It was early days yet with him and Angela, but he planned to discuss it with her anyway. If she wasn't ready, then perhaps they could set a target date for the near future. He finished dressing and headed out the door. He planned to stop at his weed supplier on his way to meeting Angela at the restaurant. His stash at home was getting low.

Laura sighed after she put the phone down. She had just spoken to a Dr. Ramsey, her second random pick from the yellow pages. The two numbers listed for the first place that she had called were busy. The office she called had actually been closed but the doctor, because he had closed up two hours earlier than usual, had forwarded the office number to his blackberry and had spoken to her directly. He just hated to lose potential income. Only the prospect of money and social status had motivated him through the eight years of medical school. She felt nervous now that she had actually made the appointment. The doctor had assured her that the procedure was routine and low risk but Laura couldn't help but wonder what if something went wrong and she couldn't have kids. Or worse, something going wrong during the procedure and she had to be hospitalized. Then Lenky would know and all hell would break loose. She retrieved a cigarette from her pocketbook and lit it. She had smoked more in the past two days than she had in the past ten years. She couldn't wait for everything to be over. The 'what ifs' were making her a nervous wreck.

Dr. Ramsey was thoughtful as he idly rocked his large, well worn, comfortable chair side to side. What were the odds of Lenky's wife calling him randomly from the yellow pages to schedule an abortion that her husband didn't know about? Perhaps a million to one. He had just stepped into his house when his mobile vibrated on his waist. He had been surprised to see that it was Lenky's home number. He hadn't heard from him in awhile. He was even more surprised when it was a woman who gave her name as 'Mrs. Phillips'. He had listened to the woman's story of how she had been raped by a close friend and had gotten pregnant and needed to have an abortion as her husband would kill the man, and their marriage would be ruined if he found out. Dr. Ramsey had never met her but he knew that Lenky had married a young woman who had been living in the States for quite some time. This 'Mrs. Phillips' definitely had an American accent. It had to be her.

Dr. Ramsey and Lenky had met three years ago when Lenky and four of his men had saved his life. He had been carjacked one night at a stoplight while returning from a colleague's cocktail party and Lenky, having arrived at the light just as the two men were forcing him out of the vehicle at gunpoint, had thwarted the robbery. It had resulted in the unreported deaths of the two would-be robbers. Dr. Ramsey was forever in his debt. Lenky had requested a few favours from him over the years. He had treated three of Lenky's men for gunshot wounds when they couldn't go to the hospital and the biggest favour of all – though he had been well compensated – was when he had performed surgery on one of Jamaica's most wanted man who was badly wounded by the police in a shootout. Lenky and the man had grown up together and when he turned to Lenky for help, Lenky had personally taken him to Dr. Ramsey. Dr. Ramsey sighed and picked up the phone. He had to notify Lenky of his wife's intentions. If he did it and somehow Lenky found out that he was the one who had performed the procedure, he would be a dead man. He decided not to call back the house so he looked in his address book for Lenky's mobile number.

"Are you ok Sara?" Dahlia did not like the way the conversation had ended between them the night before. There was no other way to deal with the situation but at the same time she didn't want Sara to think that she didn't care about her feelings.

"I'm ok mother," Sara responded. "How are you?"

Dahlia winced at the coldness of her daughter's voice.

"Not bad...I'm cooking," she replied, as she bustled about the kitchen putting the finishing touches to dinner. "I was worried when I kept calling back last night and couldn't get you."

"You are cooking? On a Saturday?" Her mother never cooked on a Friday or Saturday.

"Umm...yes...we are having guests for dinner," her mother replied ambiguously.

"Who?" Sara pressed.

Dahlia didn't answer.

"It's my *darling* sister and her new-found love isn't it?" Sara asked.

Dahlia hadn't thought it possible that Sara's tone could have sounded any colder but it did.

"Sara...it's..."

"Isn't that sweet," Sara said, her voice dripping with sarcasm. "Have fun."

"Sara..." Dahlia began but trailed off when she realized that her daughter had hung up. Dahlia sighed. She resolved to make up with Sara before she went back to London in a few days time. She didn't want her to feel totally isolated from the family. It was bad enough that David and Angela refused to even speak to her. She tasted the sauce for the barbecue chicken. Perfect.

It hit Sara as soon as she hung up the phone and she laughed out loud. She would be able to carry out her plan much sooner than expected and in a much more dramatic fashion as they would all be together. She had decided that since no one cared about her happiness, she wouldn't care about anyone's either. She had planned to pay Angela and her parents separate surprise visits before leaving for London but today was perfect. Jerome being present would be the icing on the cake. She would leave everyone in an uproar and then calmly make her exit. Her mother was still cooking so everyone should be present at the house in at least another two hours. Giddy with excitement, she went inside the bedroom to find something sexy to wear.

"Dr. Ramsey," Lenky said, surprised to be hearing from the doctor. "How yuh doin' man?"

"I am fine Lenky," Dr. Ramsey replied. "Let me get straight to the point. I know you are a man who doesn't like to beat around the bush."

"I'm listening," Lenky said, sitting up. Something told him that this wouldn't be good. Was this number three?

Dr. Ramsey cleared his throat and told him about Laura's phone call. Lenky was silent for several seconds and then he demanded that Dr. Ramsey repeat what he just told him. He then asked him over and over again if he was absolutely certain that the call had come from his house phone. Dr. Ramsey assured him that he could show him proof of the call on his Blackberry if he so desired. Lenky thanked him for calling and hung up the phone. He was so angry, hurt and disappointed that he was eerily calm. Jada came back into the living room to find Lenky putting on his shoes. She had gone into the kitchen to do the dishes after the movie had ended.

"Yuh leaving now baby?" she asked, noticing that he had a strange look on his face. Well, it was actually his eyes that looked strange. His face was calm but his eyes were wild and his body was taut with tension. "Yuh ok baby?"

Lenky nodded and left without a word, leaving Jada to ponder what that was all about. She resolved to start turning Lenky's phone off whenever he came by. It was the second time in as many visits that he had received bad news over the phone. She didn't want to give him any excuse for not coming there. Lenky was a superstitious man.

CHAPTER 25

"Damn! Its getting late honey," Angela said as she scampered off the bed. After lunch, she and Jerome had gone to his apartment to chill and they had talked about having children. Both were pleased that the other was thinking along the same lines. Jerome had even agreed to getting married if Angela got pregnant any time soon. But even though he had said that he would without any hesitation, inwardly he wondered if he could really handle marriage. He could see Angela being in his life for a very long time but marriage...that was a whole different ballgame. He figured that he would cross that bridge when he got there. They had spent the afternoon in bed and it was now 4:30. Angela had promised her mom they would be there at 5.

Jerome followed her into the shower and despite Angela's protestations that they didn't have time, braced her against the shower wall and had his way with her. Angela called home and told her mom that she was running a bit late and would get there about 6. Jerome got dressed and they went to Angela's home in the SUV leaving Angela's car parked at his apartment. She changed quickly and they made their way to her parents' palatial spread in Norbrook.

Lenky did not call ahead to see if Laura was still at home as he quickly but carefully made his way there – Mikey's fatal accident was still fresh in his mind. If she wasn't home, he would simply wait. He didn't want to speak with her until they were face to face. He wondered what her explanation would be for wanting to abort his child. She knew how badly he wanted them to have a child. He didn't believe the story she gave the Dr. Ramsey. There was no way Laura could've gotten raped by a close friend. He didn't know of her having any close male friends and who would've dared to rape his wife? No, he wasn't buying that for fifty cents.

Jerome wasn't nervous when they arrived at Angela's parents' home. He knew that he could charm anyone. Angela rang the doorbell and Mr. Charlton, dressed in a replica of Jerome's number 10 jersey – mostly to prove to his daughter that he was serious about accepting Jerome – greeted them at the door.

"Hi daddy," Angela said as they hugged. "Daddy meet my love, Jerome. Jerome, meet the other man in my life."

The two men shook hands firmly and David gave him a warm smile.

"Welcome to my home, young man, it's really a pleasure having you here," he enthused.

"Thank you, Mr. Charlton," Jerome replied.

"Please, call me David," he said as he ushered them inside. Angela grinned from ear to ear as her mother, who had been in the bedroom, came out to meet them.

Lenky sat in his SUV for a full five minutes before he got out and went inside the house. The closer he had gotten to home, the more his emotions had gotten the better of him. He composed himself and slowly got out of the vehicle. He took his handgun from the glove compartment and tucked it in his waist. Then he went inside.

Laura was startled when Lenky entered the bedroom. She had been lying on her back, staring at the ceiling deep in thought when she suddenly realized that he was inside the room. She sat up on the bed and forced a smile.

"Hi baby," she said. "I didn't hear you come in."

Lenky looked at his wife without speaking. Even now, with all the anger and disappointment he was feeling towards her, he couldn't help but admire her beauty. A gorgeous devil.

"Baby?" Laura said when she realized that something was amiss. Her husband had a look on his face that she could not read and his body was taut with tension. "Is there something wrong?"

Lenky finally spoke.

"Mi ah go ask yuh some questions an' Laura, ah swear to God, yuh betta nuh lie to mi."

Laura was taken aback by his low, vicious tone. Not even the other day when he had hit her, had he sounded so scary. She racked her brain as to what could possibly be the source of his anger. No it couldn't be...how would he have known? It must be something else.

"I wouldn't lie to you baby," Laura said softly.

Lenky gave her a look that suggested he doubted that very much.

"Yuh pregnant?"

Laura gasped in shock. Why would he ask her that? How did he know? Or was he just guessing?

The lie was right at the tip of her tongue but when she looked into his eyes fear made her speak the truth.

"Yes..." she whispered, feeling a sudden urge to use the bathroom.

"Why yuh didn't tell me?"

Laura started crying.

"I wanted it to be a surprise honey –"

Lenky moved so fast that his hand was a blur. He gave Laura a vicious slap to her right cheek, cutting her off in mid-sentence.

"Is dat why yuh ah plan fi 'ave abortion?" Lenky thundered. "Eh? Yuh fucking liad!"

Laura started to really cry now, holding her head in her hands. How did he know? Her worst fears were being realized and she started to think that she would not live to see another day. Her husband was going to kill her.

Sara hummed as she drove towards her parents' home. She couldn't wait to see their faces when she showed up unannounced and unwelcome. *Every dog has their day and today belongs to this pretty bitch* Sara mused, smiling as she glanced at her Burberry sunglasses framed reflection in the rearview mirror. How could Jerome want Angela over her? Admittedly, Angela was very pretty, but pretty in a Barbie dollish kind of way. Sara was pretty in a sensual womanly kind of way even though she was a couple of years younger. To her it was a no-brainer. Men. Stupid creatures. A sudden thud pulled Sara from her reverie and she frowned then pulled over to the side of the road. It felt like she had a puncture.

"I never knew I would ever meet anyone to top my grandmother's cooking but Mrs. Charlton, I tip my hat to you. Dinner is fabulous," Jerome said, flashing his trademark smile at Mrs. Charlton, who though she had her reservations about his intentions where her daughter was concerned, was very pleased with his comment.

"Why, thank you Jerome," she said. "Your grandmother and I should trade recipes one of these days."

Jerome became somber.

"Unfortunately she died in a fire many years ago," he responded quietly.

"Oh, I'm very sorry to hear that," Mrs. Charlton said, thinking that being burnt to death had to be the cruelest way to meet one's maker. David changed the subject to football and that started an animated discussion on Jamaica's chances of progressing from the group stages in the World Cup. The draw to find out how the thirty-two nations were to be placed was scheduled to take place in a few months. They all hoped that Jamaica would be placed in a favourable group – one absent of international heavy weights such as Brazil, Germany and Argentina, which would make it easier to advance to the next round. Angela, the person with the least football knowledge around the table, listened contentedly as her man and parents talked like old friends. At that moment, she was feeling like the happiest person in the world.

Laura raised her head and looked at her husband through her sobs. He was so livid that he was almost unrecognizable. She had to do something to pull Lenky back from the cliff that he seemed to be teetering on. If he went over, before the dust settled, she would be a dead woman.

"Lenky! Let me explain. Please!" Laura shouted, as she jumped off the bed and hugged him tightly.

Lenky angrily pushed her from off him but he stood still and allowed her to speak. Still lying on the floor next to the love seat where she had fallen, Laura gathered her thoughts and spoke for her life.

"Baby...please just listen to what I have to say," she implored. "What I'm about to tell you is the honest to god truth."

Lenky waited for her to continue.

"I love you more than anything else in this world baby, but that night, when you accused me of cheating, hit me and raped me, it really traumatized me. I haven't been able to totally get over it yet and when I got pregnant that night...as badly as I want us to have children...I just didn't want our firstborn to come into the world bearing the mark of the worst experience I ever had with you. I'm not saying thinking about getting an abortion was the right thing, or that I shouldn't have told you...but please, if you love me, and I know you do, please try to put yourself in my shoes and understand where I'm coming from."

Lenky's anger dissipated from his body as he reflected on the things she had said. He hadn't realized or even considered that she could have been affected by what had happened in such a manner. He looked at her sobbing, disheveled, bruised form lying on the floor and his heart went out to her. Laura wasn't used to those kinds of things. She wasn't a ghetto girl like Jada who could relate to and deal with that sort of situation. Lenky got down onto the floor and hugged Laura, who cried even harder with relief when she realized that Lenky believed her.

"Its ok baby," Lenky cooed as he stroked her hair and comforted her. "Everything ah go work out alright. We will sort it out."

"Fuck!" Sara cursed as she stepped out of the car and examined the offending tyre. The left front tyre was as flat as a pancake. She wondered what the hell she had run over. She looked around. It was not a good place to be having car trouble. Though Shortwood Road was a busy enough thoroughfare, where it intersected with Grants Pen Road was a dangerous area even in broad daylight. Grants Pen was a volatile community where any thing could happen at any time. She cursed herself for having driven this route. She was contemplating her next move when three young men who had been sitting on a wall at the entrance of the community hopped down and walked over to her. Sara casually walked back around to the driver's side of her car. She didn't want them to think that she was afraid of them. She was terrified but looked squarely at the tall, lanky one who seemed to be the leader of the crew.

"Wha' 'appen?" he asked. "Tyre puncture?"

She tried not to cringe. His breath was fetid.

"Yeah...I'm not sure what caused it but the left front tyre is flat."

He looked her up and down, his eyes lingering on her long legs. "Yuh 'ave a spare?"

Sara nodded and gladly moved away to open the trunk. The guy gestured to the other two men and they stepped forward to retrieve the spare and the tools. Sara and her nameless benefactor stood by the side of the road and watched as the two men changed the tyre.

"Whe' yuh from?" he asked, giving her that long, lingering stare that made her uncomfortable. "Yuh look like ah uptown girl."

Sara gave him a tight smile, unsure of how to respond.

Unfazed, he continued, "Yuh look good an' yuh leg dem long an' nice...yuh eva get a real ghetto fuck yet?"

Sara looked at him, appalled that he would even go there with her.

He read the look and was not amused.

"Yuh t'ink yuh betta than me...but mek mi tell yuh somet'ing ...ah nuff society gal come dung ah de ghetto fi dem regular fuck," he said with a cocky smirk.

"Well I'm not one of them. Thanks, but I'll pass." She glanced at the men and saw thankfully that they were almost finished.

The short, well built one was now tightening the lugs and the other was placing the punctured tyre in the trunk. The man's eyes darkened at her answer and tone. This one deserved a lesson. He had been courteous to assist her and in return she had dissed him. *Nuh gal, whether from uptown or downtown caan diss mi an' get wey wid it. She mussi t'ink say dem call mi 'Heartless' fi nutten* he mused angrily.

"Well thank you –" Sara began but stopped in mid-sentence when the man brandished a shiny handgun and pointed it against her crotch. Sara trembled as she felt the cold steel. She couldn't believe that this was happening to her on a busy Saturday evening with cars whizzing pass, everyone oblivious to her plight - well not everyone - three girls, apparently from the community, were watching with amused expressions on their bleached out faces.

"Ms. Uptown say she want fi 'ave some fun wid we before she leave," he said to his two cronies. "Lock up de car an' come we go inna de lane."

He held Sara close to him with the gun pointed at her side and snarled that she shouldn't even think about screaming, and the foursome made the short trek into the community. Sara was shocked into silence. Her mind was still trying to come to terms with what was actually taking place. The men took her into a yard that had several small houses on the same property and ushered her into a one room dwelling at the back. They had passed several people in the yard that had greeted the men and ignored Sara. The tall one instructed the other two to wait outside and he placed the gun on top of a barrel close to the doorway and took out his erect dick. He barked for Sara to lie down on the filthy bed. Numbly, she did as she was told and he pulled her dress up around her waist.

"Yuh did ready fi mi," he remarked excitedly when he realized that she wasn't wearing any panties.

"Please...don't do this...I can give you money...please...I'm begging you..." Sara pleaded desperately, her chest heaving. She felt as if a panic attack was coming on. She hadn't experienced one for some time.

"Gal mi nuh want yuh money...when mi want money mi just go tek it...see wha' mi want yah," he growled as he roughly penetrated her.

Sara screamed in horror and pain as he raped her, her screams seeming to spur him on as he ravaged her mercilessly.

Sara closed her eyes tightly to avoid looking at his face and wondered despairingly what she had done to deserve this. Each of the three men raped her twice before releasing her two hours later. She was in so much pain that she had to be carried to her vehicle. They placed her in the driver seat and quickly made their way back to the safe haven of their community.

"Dinner was splendid mom," Angela said as they hugged goodbye. It was now 8:30 and she and Jerome were leaving. Her dad had wanted them to stay longer but Angela wanted to go home and cuddle with Jerome.

"You guys come back again real soon and Jerome, please don't forget to bring the jersey when you come back," David said. Jerome had promised to give him an autographed jersey that he had actually worn in a match.

"Dad!" Angela said, though she was very pleased that her dad genuinely liked Jerome.

They went out on to the patio as a red Honda Accord coupe drove onto the premises.

"Isn't that Sara's car?" Mrs. Charlton queried rhetorically.

The car was swerving erratically and they watched puzzled as the car came to a screeching halt. A crying Sara stumbled out of the car looking sweaty and disheveled. There was also blood on the front of her dress. She looked horrible.

Angela and Mrs. Charlton screamed as they all rushed over to her.

David lifted his daughter and rushed her inside as he bellowed for his wife to call the family doctor. She got him at home and he promised to be there in ten minutes. He lived in a condominium in the same area.

"Sshhh," David whispered as he held his estranged daughter in his arms. They were in her old bedroom and though she was lying on the bed, she refused to let go of him and kept muttering incoherently. David looked at the others worriedly as he comforted Sara. She was in bad shape. He wished Dr. Coleman would hurry the hell up. He was just happy that despite everything she had exercised good judgment and came home.

EPILOGUE

After arriving at the house, Dr. Coleman gave Sara a sedative and examined her. The attack had been brutal. He immediately told her parents that he needed to take her to the office of his private practice so that he could give her a more thorough examination and run some tests. He called his assistant, who though not thrilled at being disturbed, had quickly agreed to meet him there.

The news was good. There was no internal damage but her mental state was another story. Sara was severely traumatized and would need extensive counseling. The following day, her father went over to her apartment and retrieved some items as Sara would be staying at the family home until he was satisfied that she was ok. David tried to draw something positive from the unfortunate incident and took solace in the fact that they were a family again. All the stuff that had happened in the past no longer mattered. The only important thing now was for the family to be there for her. There was also the matter of the perpetrators. In the morning, when David had gone into her room to check on her, she had awakened and surprisingly, without any prompting, had somberly told him what happened. David had been livid. There was no way that he was going to let them get away with it but at the same time he did not want the police involved. He was a prominent businessman and he knew it would leak out that his daughter was brutally raped. He didn't want Sara's or the family's name to be dragged through the mud.

He mentioned the dilemma to Jerome who had come over with Angela to check on Sara. They were sitting on the patio while Mrs. Charlton and Angela were in Sara's room along with the therapist. Sara had insisted that they be in the room. Jerome told him not to worry. He knew someone from that world who could make the men responsible disappear quietly. He immediately called Lenky who told him to consider it done. Lenky then called the 'don' for the area and told him that he would consider it a favour as the victim was a close friend. The three rapists were dead three hours later.

Laura was pensive as she ate breakfast. Lenky had taken her to the swanky Richton Hotel for breakfast. The food was great and Lenky was being very attentive and extra nice to her but she couldn't help but worry about the second part of her problem. There was still the matter of the possibility of the baby being Jerome's. They had spoken at length after their dramatic episode in the bedroom and Lenky had told her that he would do whatever it takes to help her get over that night but that an abortion was out of the question. She had agreed to keep the baby, though in reality she knew that she didn't have a choice. The only way out was a miscarriage. It had to happen without arousing Lenky's suspicion. In the meantime, she had to pretend to be thrilled about the pregnancy. She gave Lenky a warm smile and placed his hand on her stomach. He smiled and rubbed it.

He would call Jerome later and tell him the good news. He would also ask him to be the baby's godfather. He was sure Jerome would like that. After everything that had happened over the last couple of days, Lenky was happy that things were looking up. A bright future lay ahead with his wife and unborn daughter. He was positive that it would be a girl.

"Would you love me any less if something like that was to happen to me baby?" Angela asked Jerome softly. They were at Jerome's apartment cuddling on his sofa. The lights were off and they were listening to the soothing sounds of Sade's classic first album. Sara's rape had rattled her to the core and she felt really bad about how she had treated her after the Brian episode.

"Of course not sweetheart," Jerome replied as he stroked her hair. "We're in this thing together baby. Through thick and thin."

Jerome bit her playfully on the ear.

"You know that you're my future wife right?"

Angela giggled contentedly.